KU-457-335

The Roaring of the Labyrinth

Also by Clio Gray and available from Headline

Guardians of the Key

The Roaring of the Labyrinth

Clio Gray

headline

First published in 2007 by
HEADLINE PUBLISHING GROUP

1

Cataloguing in Publication Data is available from the British Library

ISBN 978 0 7553 3106 2

Typeset in Bembo by Palimpsest Book Production Ltd,
Grangemouth, Stirlingshire

Printed and bound in Great Britain by
Clays Ltd St Ives plc

Headline's policy is to use papers that are natural, renewable and recyclable products and made from wood grown in sustainable forests. The logging and manufacturing processes are expected to conform to the environmental regulations of the country of origin.

HEADLINE PUBLISHING GROUP
An Hachette Livre UK Company
338 Euston Road
London NW1 3BH

www.headline.co.uk
www.hodderheadline.com

Contents

Part 3 Through the Labyrinth

Prologue

Uwe and His Winter Leaving – Odessa, November 1806

UWE PROCTOR DVOSHKA adjusted the bag upon his shoulder, gripped hard at the handle of his case, urged the unwilling boatman on. Their boots grumbled over freezing shingle, filling the treads with keel-worn grit, sand that melted momentarily beneath their weight. The boatman's pipe began to smoulder, the draw damped by mist and the uneven pull of breath as he fought to stay upright on the rough plank that led to the jetty, sheeted over as it was with invisible slates of ice. He could barely make out the buoy that marked the tethering of his boat, wondered why this man hadn't gone out the night before as the rest had done, wanted to be slumbering by his fire.

The boat once gained, he took up an oar, had to hammer at the icy skin that hung a shiver above the surface of the sea by the soft exhalation of salt, pushed against the hard dark seaweed that clung to the jetty base, and the snails that had frozen within their grooves. He cracked at the ice with every pull of the oars, had his passenger sit in the stern and wallop at the water with a roped stone to break their way.

Uwe Proctor knelt there a moment, the rope scouring at his skin where tiny barnacles had made their home between the fraying strands, thought he saw something shimmering out there in the mist, wondered if it was his past or his future, or if, like most things, it was nothing at all. He grimaced, could feel the ache at the back of his eyes as he strained to see through the haze: what the Russians called *tymáh*, the sound of the hollow tomb in which he felt himself to be. He had watched for the dawn from his lodging-room window, high up on the Odessan cliff, had seen it draw the haar from the land to the uncertain sea, creeping over the troubled surface, hiding the world from the sun as its edge grew at the horizon. He had made his decision to leave quite suddenly during the night, and with his decision the fold of winter had come to cover the morning. He was leaving because of what he had done, and what he hadn't. He had failed. He had cost hard-grafting people their money, given them in return words and plans that had come to nothing. The locusts had come, and eaten his grand schemes along with everything else in their way.

It was bitter, this crabbed day in November. It was always like that here, always extreme, like two halves of a pendulum that has no middle ground: when the sun shone, it baked the shirt right into your skin; when the wind blew, it raised the dust from the streets and flayed your face with grit, got into your bones and made pepper mills of your joints; and when the winter came, it stamped down so fast it crushed everything beneath it. Ice cracked about the harbour walls, grew out from the silent lagoons, froze the bitterns in their reeds, tethered the birds to their roof-stacks, kept even the terns from their otherwise constant calls, set the cranes and egrets shivering in their trees.

Further out, past the harbour walls, the water dragged cold currents from beneath, caused freezing updraughts to form the mist into pillars, shimmering like spectres over the ocean. From the shore, people saw gateposts to an unknown city, shadows of long-gone citizenry shifting with the mists and tides, weird breath-like apparitions that came and went with the slow undulation of waves they could not see. The haar moved with the will of the water, thickened and thinned, showed a few ships at anchor, the grey, whale-backed hulls seeming to breathe as they came in and out of view, sails down, wrapped within their sheets and ropes, swans adrift, asleep, with nothing to wait or wake for. All was muted as in mourning, as if the earth no longer turned, as if this cold and calm was everything and always would be.

Uwe Proctor shivered. He could feel ghosts plucking at his sleeves, felt them hovering at the bare skin of his neck. He swung the break-stone with extra force, tried to keep the heat within his blood, felt his life being stolen from him with every cold exhalation, leaving him empty as a grave-robbed tomb. And then there it was, the ship, materialising so suddenly in front of him he involuntarily put his hand to his chest, felt the break-stone slip between his fingers, managed to grasp at its end just as it began to sink beneath the sea. His fingertips touched the water, made his nails brittle with salt, shrank the capillaries below his skin.

Later, when all that had happened had happened and could

not be undone, he would find it oddly comforting, this icy calm and coldness, invasive from above and below and all around him, hiding the world from him and him from the world. He would often curse the shifting of the mists that revealed him his ship, guided him to the ladder knotted and ready for his ascent, took the weight of his belongings as he dragged them with him, hands burning on the rope. Perhaps he might then have turned back, made up his mind to stay and face the consequences of his disastrous invention. Perhaps then there would be those several people walking on this earth who now lay bloated in their boxes several feet below its surface; perhaps he would never have found his Eden and made of it a land of desolation and tears.

Ipsing and the Saint – St Weonard's, 23 February 1807

Ipsing Sansibar had just finished ferrying his goats over to the island of St Weonard's-on-the-Water. He watched as they started rootling over the old grave mounds, steering past the clumps of frozen ragwort, which had made them so sick last spring. There wasn't much grazing this time of year, but the soil of St Weonard's was rich and dark with centuries of six-deep remains, generations leaching into the loam, families crumbling and mingling with the damp earth. He tapped out his pipe, refilled it with rough tobacco mixed with the camphor-weed that helped him the better to breathe. The sun was strong and bright, cast sharp shadows over the grass where the stones still stood, bleached the red from the old brick of the church walls. He shaded his eyes from the light and the smoke, coughed a little as the camphor caught his throat, heard the goats snorting their way around the old churchyard. He remembered coming here years ago, when he was a lad, before the river flooded and made the church an island. It rose every year, that river – something to do with the new canal that was being dug two valleys up. Every winter it crept up its banks just a little more. One day, thought Ipsing, it would start to suck at the cobbled walls of the old churchyard itself, begin to make its way through all the forgotten graves, start clawing and gnawing at the base of the church. There'd be no food here for the goats by then, and no point in ferrying them over. He would have to find somewhere else to graze them through the winter.

He sighed. He liked it here. It was peaceful and quiet, still smelt to him of incense and old wood and burning tallow. Every time he came here he felt younger and lighter, glad to be alone. His nose always seemed to clear, his lungs to ease and soften a little, the whistling in his throat grew less, his back didn't ache quite so much.

He got back into his boat and began to push it off the little shingle shore, which used to be the path leading to the lych-gate. He saw the solemn flight of steps on the opposite bank, which came straight out of the water and carried on up to the church's belfry, which stood on a little hill. St Weonard's hadn't always been on the water. It had started as a woodland chapel for the charcoal burners, Weonard being their patron saint, but the wood had long since been felled and the little chapel enlarged into a proper church. The belfry had been built up on the hill so it would be better heard, and on dark nights a beacon was lit high up in its tower to guide the farmhands home from the fields.

He saw that someone was going into the tower now. That blasted boy again, thought Ipsing; he knew it by the way the boy moved. His spine was fused solid like a copper pipe and he couldn't bend properly or turn his head. It was creepy the way he moved his whole body to look at you, made him seem like an insect, especially with those big watery eyes that never seemed to blink.

Ipsing shuddered, lost his balance a little as he heaved himself into the boat, set it rocking on the shingle. Cursing, he grabbed at the oars before they fell into the water, didn't notice the man who was walking up the hill from the other side, didn't see that he had a large bundle strapped to his back, half the weight being taken by the belt he had braced around his forehead. Ipsing sat with his back to the shore and the belfry-beacon steps, pushed the boat off the bank with the back end of an oar, watched his goats champing at the hard winter grass, smiled at the falling-down ruin of the church. His oars dipped into the clear-running water just as a dark frown of cloud crossed the sun and chilled the air.

Up on the hill the man with the bundle on his back had knicked the latch up on the tower door. He eased the heavy load from his back and put it over the threshold and himself after it, then pulled the boards to and closed the door.

Down on the river Ipsing Sansibar shivered as the sun slipped and the weird pink of twilight so common in the wintertime, shifted everything into grey and shadow, felt a few hard splats of rain upon his back, sculled a little quicker, breathed a little faster, nosed the boat downstream, heading for the pond-green pier and home.

* * *

The Boy in the Tower – St Weonard's, 23 February

That blasted boy, as Ipsing called him, was playing with the hedgehog he had just bought from a pedlar for the penny he had found under a heap of muck outside the wool bleacher's. He had been looking for beetles. He liked the way they shone and glittered in their black and purple shields, the rainbows playing over their dark backs. He liked that they were stiff and unbending, just like him. He had a whole pocketful of them, and now that he had the hedgehog he was taking the beetles out of his pocket one by one, sliding his finger through the little gap between the buttonholes, holding the rest of it shut so the others couldn't get out. He put one down in front of the hedgehog and watched it hobbling quickly after the beetle, which scuttled straight for the cracks in the warped wood of the belfry floor.

The boy with his hedgehog had climbed up the steps to the platform housing the framework supporting the bell, which hung high and grey above him. It was an upside-down bell, operated by a tread-wheel, secured in an oaken hammock that moved with the bell as it swung, sent its message up and out, exaggerated and heightened by the hollow of the tower above and below. Around its framework ran a wide metal gutter that held the oil and straw to be burnt when the beacon had to be lit. Its fires could be seen for miles and miles through the wall-slits that forced the light out into slats, split it into sharp bands like a sunrise seen through dust-ridden clouds.

The boy picked up a little stick. He was going to teach his hedgehog how to jump. Had seen it done in the market the year before, thought he might earn himself a few pennies with his new show, maybe make his mother proud of him. She was dead, of course, but still he wanted that she be proud of him, knew she was looking down and what a disappointment he had been to her with his stick-straight back and his inability to be useful because of it. The hedgehog moved much faster than he had supposed, but it didn't take long to learn that if it let the boy stroke its spines, it would get a swift reward.

They both paused when they heard the latch lift on the door downstairs. The boy moved awkwardly, tried to hunch himself round to see who it might be. The hedgehog snuffled off into the stack of tinder stowed at the base of the wall. The boy could hear as the man puffed and grunted, started to heave his bundle up the stone steps. The boy could smell the sweat that was wetting the thin shirt of the man's back, his coat tied around his waist. The boy could see the man edging up backwards, step by step, hauling on the straps of canvas that held the bundle together. When the stranger got to the top step he rocked back on to the platform, sitting on his heels, groaning with the effort. He wiped his face free of the overabundant sweat, got his bundle up beside him and turned to look around. He saw the boy, said nothing, took his time to get his breath, which didn't come easy, and the boy looked on that unfamiliar face with his watery blue eyes. And the man watched the boy, his face a grime of grey. The boy blinked once, then the man moved forwards and had him by the collar, and moments later was hauling the boy down the stone steps, his shanks and ankles bruising against every rise. The boy said nothing as the man pushed him into the small downstairs room, which was once used as a dungeon for drying-out the village drunks. He clanged the door shut, turned the key in the lock.

'Stay quiet, and I'll let you out by and by,' said the man. His voice was hoarse, as if he had stooped and stoked fires all his life or worked too long in a foundry.

The boy cowered in a corner, the beetles running out from his pocket as he backed against the wall. He could hear the man going back up the steps, heard the sound of something brushing against the wooden floor above his head. Looking up, he saw splinters of movement through the floor-boards, saw the man's feet crisscrossing the little room, heard the scratch and rustle of him opening his bundle, smelt the sting of sulphur in his nose, though he didn't know that was what it was. And then came the crackle of fire as the man set the beacon burning. He had scattered the tinder heap all across the floor, had covered it with the oil-soaked straw he had dragged his long way across the valley and round the village and up the hill to the belfry and up the belfry steps.

The smoke started sinking through the floorboards, made the stiff boy in his corner start to cough. The man's heavy boots came clumping down the stone of the steps. He fiddled with the lock, took out the big iron key and threw it through the bars of the prison door.

'Wait a few minutes till you let yourself out. I'm to be well gone and I'll know if I see you coming out too soon and then I'll string you up by the neck like a sausage.'

The stranger rattled the door to scare the boy a little more, though he needn't have. The boy had already peed his pants and couldn't move, stuck to the corner of the dungeon as if its two arms would protect him, pressing his back into the moss-ridden walls, the roughness of the old brick scarring crinkles into the worn leather of his jerkin.

He heard the man leave, tried to count but didn't know how to, got down on his knees and fanned out his fingers to find the key. It was dark now the outer door was closed, but the beacon was burning on the platform above him and gave him a little comfort with its light. At last he found the big iron key and clutched it safe in his hand, started to tap the minutes away with his boots though he had never been taught his numbers and scarcely knew a minute from an hour. He was coughing a bit, his eyes stinging, but still he banged his foot against the floor to pretend the time. What neither he nor the man knew was that there was no lock on the inside of the door, and that the bars were too close together to let a man, or even a boy, thread through his hand.

The boy worried about the hedgehog in the conflagration upstairs, but then the boards over his head began to burn. The man had spread the fire right out across the belfry floor and not just in the gutters that were designed for the purpose. The treadle-rope was burning, warming the air, sending a shiver of movement up into the big bell, which began to hum with the heat.

Down in the dungeon, the boy began to wail as bits of cinder fell through burning holes and singed at his skin and his hair. The old oaken framework, which held the bell upside down, began to creak and hiss, bleeding and bullying at the long-dried resin, flames flickering up and down its length. The boy held the iron key hard in his hand and fumbled for the bars of the door, tried to put his small, stiff hands through the too-small spaces. But the key would never be put back in its lock, and the boy baked like a cockle in its shell left too long upon the hearth, the ash falling from above to smoke and smother him as the fire caught, whipped by an evening wind that gusted through the beacon slats.

The embers came down through the worm-holes of the floorboards. The bell frame broke and fell, its heavy weight bursting halfway through the boy's ceiling, sending piles of burning tinder down into the dungeon, the glimmer of light on the carapace of beetle-backs and the awful heat, the big iron key beginning to melt in the stiff boy's hand, and the blink and blink of him dying badly and alone as the bell left its mooring, sent the crack and break and brittle of his bones across the cindered floor.

Outside, the rain that had promised itself earlier to Ipsing Sansibar's jacket failed to arrive, and downriver by the pier, he was keeling up his boat when he saw the unexpected flare of the beacon on the hill. He listened for the bell, expecting alarm but did not hear it, for its brim was hard down upon the boy and his beetles and its tongue was lost in the harsh roaring of the fire.

Theft and the Moon – 25 February

It is late at night. North and cold. Ice crackles upon the path. The moon hangs like a man from the gibbet, the features contorted with cloud and sorrow and unutterable distance from the earth. The man looks up, thinks for a moment he sees his own face reflected there. He shivers, but he isn't cold, though his fingers have gone waxy from lack of blood. He is taut as a wire pulled between two points but on he goes. He reaches the iron gateway. He puts out his hand. The latch leaves frost-burns on his fingers but he doesn't feel them. The dark yew hedges crowd above him and he sees a wink of berry pink, sees through the flesh to the black heart of the yew. He almost smiles. He brushes the leaf-tips with his fingers as he passes, the cut and cold of their edges sharp-ened with ice. The boom of the church bell makes him jump, makes him hurry his step, cut across the lawn to avoid the fussy gravel of the path. The sandstone of the Hall is dark with age and night, but he finds the door without difficulty. It takes him half a minute to hit a chisel through the old rust of the lock. He knew no one would have thought to bolt this old back door. He's already oiled the hinges, and when he pushes, the door opens without a murmur, just as he knew it would. It swings its face to one side, lets the stranger slip inside the home that is surely not his own. It is not the first time he has stolen from others, and it will not be the last.

PART 1

INTRODUCTION TO ASTONISHMENT

1

Stroop's Dyeing Days

London, 26 February 1807

WHILBERT STROOP SAT in his study. He felt dispirited as he always did when his Sense Map of London had been thwarted. The day before, he had tried to gain access to the Dyers' Yard at Dockend Street, only to find out it had been turned into a timber depot for the construction of yet another warship. It wasn't that he didn't understand the need for it – of course he did. He knew more than most the possible implications of the Continental Manoeuvrings of England, France and all the rest of Europe. Look at the Lucchese affair, which had happened just over a year ago: miles and miles away in Italy, Napoleon declared himself King and found a crown big enough to fit his head, and a few months later, that decision rippled its way right here to where Whilbert Stroop's feet stood and paced the streets of London. He was lucky to still have his skin wrapped warm and untorn about his bones. There were plenty from that time who had not. He knew what was going on, he read the broadsheets, talked in the coffee houses, knew about Napoleon's rampages through Europe, and the British blockade of the French coast. But he hated that a flick of military coats could curtail his life as it sometimes did: he had spent a good deal of time buying drink for the ex-Dyers' Yard foreman, who had since disappeared mysteriously and given Stroop absolutely none of the information he had promised.

He would have to start all over again and approach yet another dyer, who seemed absurdly fond of their secrets. There was no shortage of them in the immediate vicinity. They tended to cluster on the hem-edge of towns because of the stink. The incongruity of them producing colours that would make a king weep was precisely what Stroop intended to investigate. He knew they guarded vats of urine, stock-piled dungeons filled with turds, particularly of dog, for some reason. What he didn't understand was the chemical reaction that made these waste products so integral to the production of a good dye, and when he didn't know something and knew that he didn't know it, the curiosity that drove him did not like to have too many obstacles put in its way. It was like taking a sip of something wonderful and turning the bottle round to find the label missing, like glimpsing in a window the reflection of a friend, only to turn to find him gone and lost in the crowd. It tantalised him and wouldn't let him rest.

He tried to turn his mind to something else, tapped, his teeth with his pencil, took out his Ledger of Things to Do and ran his fingers along the section tabs, flipped to another page. He saw *'Offal-Processors', 'Pyrotechnics', 'Glass-Grinders'.*

He skimmed his finger further down the list: the short note on 'Leatherworkers' caught his eye. 'Try Cloistergill' read his note. He wondered if he should take that trip today. It wasn't so very far – maybe half an hour on foot – and it intrigued him how a cloister could have ended up associated with a leatherworkers. That was enough. He glanced at the window, saw the soft line of sun rising above the river, scribbled a quick note and left it on the hook from which he took his cape. Quietly, he took the few steps down the hall and closed the front door behind him, set his steps out on to the streets of London.

His Ledger of Things to Do would lie on its table untouched for many a week. Whilbert Stroop didn't know it, but out there in the cold, dark morning, there were people and plots waiting for his intervention. Stroop would be the string that tied them altogether, the Ipsings, the Pytchleys, the Dvoshkas and Bellpennys, the Orcutts and Bittlestones and stiff boys in towers. And Stroop would be the sword that severed the knot.

Far to the north, and only moments after Stroop had left his house and closed his door, Maximillian Orcutt opened his bedroom window and studied the wedge of hill that rose up behind the race of snow-swollen river. It was the colour of bilberry bells, the slate shining pink with reflected dawn. He yawned and turned away, searching in his trunk for his trousers. Next time he turned, the hill was black again, parts of it glinting, polished by an uneven rain. He stood there looking, he could see the dark gargoyle of cliff shadowing the valley. He listened to the river and the song thrush, which was singing half-heartedly in the fractal branches of a leafless tree.

Bloody cold, he thought, searching for the bird, seeing the crinkle of ice covering the small patch of lawn. He wondered if there was somewhere he could put out some crumbs, but by the time he'd reached the little kitchen he'd forgotten all about it.

He was staying in one of the small outhouses of Sedgwick Hall. It was a strange place. Not a proper hall at all, more a scatter of odd-shaped lodges strewn randomly about the grounds that surrounded the Big House. The Big House itself had a lazy lean to it and seemed from a distance as if it were lifted on invisible stilts. Closer to, you could see that in reality it rose from a huge granite boulder and was sprawled against the cliff that formed its backdrop. It had only the thickness of a double room, but in places its height reached six storeys. Obviously, thought Orcutt, chewing at the cold pork pie that was all he had left of his travelling rations, the architect had been either absolutely barking or else a genius operating somewhere within his own world, oblivious to the norms of otherwise acceptable ideas of civil engineering. Orcutt preferred the latter option. He thought the building stunning, had no other word at this time of the morning to express what else it made him feel. No wonder people came from all over the country to see it. No wonder he had spent so long trying to get exhibition space here. And now, here he was, in one of the actual lodges, with his Theatrical Science Museum almost set up in the next-door room and ready to go. There must have been seventy or so lodges, though he hadn't yet counted them all. He knew that a good many were furnished for accommodation, the larger ones housing exhibitions and curators, the smaller for the visitors who brought their own servants and household requirements with them and paid handsomely for the privilege. The Sightseekers, as they were known to the permanent inhabitants of the hall, stayed for a week, sometimes two, occasionally an entire month. All the amenities of the estate were open to them: they could ride, go hare-coursing, shoot deer and grouse, go fishing, play croquet, take walks through the woods, climb the hills. But mostly they wandered from lodge to lodge, not those they lived in, but the ones that housed The Halliday Weeems Most Curious and Compleat Collections, and the visiting exhibitions like his own.

There were shelves and cases stuffed to the gunwales with curiosities, from exotic shells to native coracles, a collection of hair cut from every nationality and race in the world, or so the label claimed, and who wouldn't believe it when they saw another room filled with sand and giant cacti, stalked by stuffed lions and gazelles, and even a giraffe, whose head rose up through the specially heightened ceiling into a glass dome, its mouth fixed around the leaves of a real, and still growing, acacia tree. There was a room that had been lined with carved stone slabs and stalactites, all natural light excluded, lamps glowing green below the central pool of water on which you could take a row in a boat shaped like a swan. Another had been completely smothered over with mounted fish, a dolphin hanging suspended from the roof on iron chains, an orca nudging it for space. A chair below was carved from narwhal tusks, an entire table from melded amber shot through with ancient flowers and ferns, scattered with dragonflies and bees that looked the same a hundred thousand years ago as they did today.

Just when you thought you'd finished being surprised, you came upon the entirely outlandish Dog Lodge, where taxidermied animals covered every surface, including the little staircase and the balcony it led up to. They stood, they sat, they lounged, they begged, they set their teeth into a growl. They all had collars, some of patterned leather, some studded with coloured glass or spikes, others of chain-link. Each had a plaque with the canine's name and breed. There was a lion dog, a Russian bear hound, a hairless thing from Mexico, a dog that looked like a monkey – and really *did* look like one – black hair ruffed around a bare black face, large twinkling eyes, a collar saying, 'I lived until I was three, and sadly died. 1768.'

No one in the surrounding valleys called the place Sedgwick. Ever since Halliday Weeems had arrived and bought up the old estate, knocked down the existing hall and built his own replacement, it had been known as Astonishment Hall. When the canal had finally come down their valley, and Potters of Darlington began arranging trips, they'd put up their own sign. 'This Way to Astonishment', it read, a big finger pointing the way up the hill to the Hall, and in all the time that sign had been there, it had never been wrong.

2

Violena and Violation

Astonishment Hall – 26 February

LEOPOLD HUXBY STOOD where the intruder had stood, his face deeply frowned and fixed. He couldn't understand what had happened. He was standing in front of an empty table below its normal stretch of wall. Every other surface was covered with objects, paintings, engravings and diagrams; the pillar behind him still supported its great glass globe, which threw rainbow columns across the floor. In one corner, a fountain filled its pool with crystal water, the ripples rocking porcelain shells, whispering and shivering, the one into the other. This was all around him, exactly as it had been the night before, as it should be now. But there was nothing in front of Leopold Huxby except a slight rim of dust where the box had once stood. He turned as someone else entered the room, almost knocked the great glass bowl from off its stand. It moved. The oil inside it slid and slinked, split the perfect spectra, sent their colours splintering into lances across the wooden floor.

'About time.' Huxby's voice was higher than usual, warbling like the loose wire of a violin. He waved his arm in accusation at the empty table and shook his head. 'Would you just look at that?'

Finkel Hanka, Constable of the Valley and its environs, took a step past the curator and eased his head a little upon his neck.

'I can see something's missing, Mr Huxby,' said Hanka, his accent slightly clipped off from its roots. At home he spoke his mother's language while she served his food, beat the day's dust from his clothes, spat on his boots to polish them. This last always made him wince, but the little tin of wax he'd bought her had been two years drying in a kitchen drawer. She'd never even lifted the lid and he knew she never would.

'It's the box,' said Huxby, 'the Perspective Box.'

Hanka said nothing. He didn't know what a perspective box was, hadn't had time yet to visit the exhibition here at the Hall.

'Well, what's to do about it?'

The old man spoke too loudly, but Hanka could still hear the faint cracking of the old man's bones as he retracted his hand, let his ancient ankles subside in their shock. The slump of his shoulders carried him a few inches more than usual towards his shoes.

'Forty-two year I've been doing this job. Forty-two year. And never, never has anything like this happened. I don't know what I'm going to say to Mr Pytchley when he gets back. He'll . . .' Huxby stopped as the pendulum clock in the hall outside chimed the half-hour. 'He'll have left by now.'

The clock finished chiming. 'He'll be home in a few days. Maybe even tomorrow. It doesn't take so long now, what with the new canal.'

He couldn't see it, but he knew that the clock's pendulum would be swinging from side to side, that every pass was another second gone.

'What am I going to say to him? What should . . . ? I just don't know . . .'

Huxby's voice trailed and dried like straw fallen from the wain. He lowered his head, atlas bones jutting white into his collar, watched the lines of colour from the glass globe moving without sound across the floorboards, thought he saw them slipping through the cracks. Finkel Hanka put his hand on the old man's shoulder, placed the other round his elbow, led the frail bones of him gently outside into the hall.

'There's time yet,' he said as he closed the door against the violated room. He'd not have said it if he'd known how little time there was left.

Blue and green, blue and green, that's what my life's become, thought Maximillian Orcutt as he looked for the marbles that had skittered about his feet like water boatmen. His Theatrical Science Museum wasn't getting set up quite as smoothly as he'd have liked. One of the pumps for the waterfalls had got blocked, and the corals were looking sick and grey despite the blankets he'd wrapped around their tank during the journey. They didn't like this cold and neither did he. Sighing like an old leather chair, he got down on his hands and knees and started gathering up the marbles one by one, putting them in his pocket for safekeeping. He didn't hear the door open but felt the rush of February air as a shadow fell across his path.

'Mr Orcutt, I presume?'

Stern, thought Orcutt, stern and sharp, just like all the others. How was it these places were always staffed by broomstick women who'd rather splinter into bits than give him a welcome of warmth? The only exception he could think of was last year, the girl who'd had chlorosis. She'd smiled at least, but had been green and tired; sat in her chair all day long, just watching him. It unnerved him, all that indolence, all that lost impetus and youth just sitting there with nothing else to do and no energy to do it with. He picked up another marble, then levered himself up from creaking knees. He'd expected a hatchet, but the face he saw was round and softly quizzical, neatly crinkled around the eyes and mouth. Almost his height, and his age, he thought, though better worn, with fine hair wisping from the tuck of her bonnet as it lifted from her neck in the slight convection generated by his machines. She held out her hand.

'Violena Sedge at your service. Welcome to Sedgwick Hall.'

He was mildly disappointed to find the hand gloved, for this was a woman whose fingertips he knew would be warm.

'Maximillian Orcutt,' he said as he kissed the glove, wishing, not for the first time in his life, that his father hadn't named him after the 2.30 at Doncaster. She appeared not to have heard him, had left her hand in his and was gazing intently over his shoulder. He could see tiny sparks leaping in her dark grey eyes. It only took a moment for him to race the few yards across the room and put his hand into the sea where the icebergs calved, releasing the pressure valve.

Immediately the eruption of sparkling crystals that had entranced her ceased, and he saw her frown as the last of the artificial snowflakes vanished beneath the surface of the sea.

'The Singing Snows of Mongolia,' provided Orcutt, 'or it will be. The mechanism isn't fully primed. If it goes off now, the whole thing will have to be stripped down and the filters replaced.'

She made no indication that she had heard his explanation. She was looking down to where his hand had left the turquoise sea. He had sent a shiver of icebergs across the silver surface and they tapped against each other like cymbal rings.

'You're not wet,' said Violena, wrinkling her nose, narrowing her eyes. 'Why aren't you wet?'

Orcutt lifted his eyes to hers. Not everyone would have noticed something like that – in fact he couldn't think of anyone else who ever had. He'd thought she was watching the icebergs. That was what most people would have done.

'Er, no. It's not exactly water, more a sort of gel. It's all a bit complicated but basically, once it's going properly it works like a self-sustaining cycle. The bergs come off the ice-cliff, sink and dissolve, which raises the temperature of the gel, which increases the pressure and depresses the switch, and that releases the snow shower, which lowers the temperature . . . and so on.'

Her face had gone quite blank.

'Sorry,' said Orcutt, 'that was rather technical.'

She looked at him directly and smiled, the life coming back into her features. 'Technical?' she murmured. 'Actually

I was wondering if a tighter fountain might not improve the spread of the stars, or rather the snow. Or maybe we could use them as stars. Not in this piece obviously, but perhaps in another. Maybe we could improvise a fog-bow or some moon-dogs . . .'

Maximillian Orcutt stared. His skin had gone quite cold, then suddenly very warm. He watched her walking around the room, pressing herself close against the cases, her breath making patterns where his fingerprints had smudged the glass.

Moon-dogs? was all he thought, the word repeating in an imbecilic emptiness; and then he found himself standing next to Violena Sedge, pointing out the intricacy of the mechanism she was looking at, asking if she knew anything about steam-operated ice chambers. Bizarrely, it never occurred to Orcutt to feel surprised when she said she did.

3

At Home in the Valley

28 February

FINKEL HANKA SAT at his kitchen table staring at the bare wall ahead of him, as Leopold Huxby had done at the Hall only two mornings before. The roasted beetroot was unpeeled, untouched, the soured cream running in unpleasant rivulets around the plate. His mother didn't scold; she knew what had happened. Silently she removed the plate and took it out to the scullery, tipped the contents into the pig-bin. The beetroot made the meat a better colour, particularly the hams. But Finkel had seen that same colour not three hours earlier, and didn't want to see it again.

He'd had a message from Dr Thacker to get himself to the Huxby house. He'd hurried, but he'd been too late – was always going to have been too late – and Leopold Huxby had already been pronounced dead. Brain aneurysm. No doubt about it. Most likely brought on by shock.

Thacker and Hanka had stood side by side in the Huxbys' small front room. Leopold's wife and the doctor had laid him out on their best table, its two extensions both in use for the first time in years. There was hardly any room left to move. She hadn't lit the fire and the room was cold, frost fingering the insides of the windows. It wasn't a room they used often, and the plates on the dresser were slightly furred with dust. Hanka felt a deep sadness as he stood in that small, untenanted room.

He had always known Leopold Huxby. He'd been caretaker up at the Hall for as long as he knew, first for Halliday Weeems himself and now for Jeremiah Pytchley. 'Curator' was perhaps too strong a word, though that was the one Leopold always used of himself. He knew nothing about paintings or statues or those strange exhibits his masters liked so much, but he did appreciate them, recognised they had a fundamental value in a world that was mostly filled with mending door handles, fixing hinges, putting putty back in window frames, replacing tap washers, fitting new wicks into oil lamps, polishing the set of tools old Weeems himself had presented to Leopold just before he'd set off on his latest and last expedition, the one from which he had never returned.

Along with the tools had come the manual for the gas-lighting system Weeems had just had installed. It was the proudest moment Leopold Huxby had ever known. It meant that his master trusted Leopold with his house and his very life: everyone knew how dangerous that gas lighting could be. He had studied that book page by page, drawing by drawing, until he knew it by rote. And now here he was, laid out naked on his own dining-room table, pale skin wrinkled into lines like the sea leaves in sand on a windy day.

The doctor had finished his examination and replaced the sheet. It was printed with violets. It had been on the bed the first night Leopold brought his new wife to this house, though nobody in the world knew that now but her, and she was weeping quietly in the kitchen, unable to believe that after fifty years of having this man to cook and clean for, to scold and laugh with, to curl up close to on cold winter nights, he was gone, and she and this house and her ancient old bed-sheets were alone.

There was still a faint whiff of his tobacco in the air, and although it was a smell she had always abhorred, she clutched at his pipe with her hand, held it close against her face. Finkel Hanka hadn't noticed the flowered sheet, hadn't noticed the dust on the dresser or the tightness of the room. All he could see were Leopold's open eyes, dark and blank with the blood that had seeped across them and set, blinding him to everything about him, barring him from his own home, his wife, his future. Huxby's head had shrunk, his dying brain pulling the skull about it like the lid of a coffin. It was all for nothing, thought Hanka. Leopold shouldn't have died like this.

He was relieved when the doctor finally touched his arm, the interval of decency over and they could go. He'd only been in the house ten minutes, but Hanka had seen a lifetime stretched out upon that table. They moved to the doorway, stood for a moment in the hall. Millicent Huxby didn't get up, didn't see them standing there or notice the creak of the door as they went or the words that they said as they passed. They'd looked back as they went down the path and paused to close the gate. Her hair was still held fast in its bun, her neck stiffly arched inside her dress, but even from where they'd stood, they could see the slight shake of her shoulders, as though the glass were rippling gently in its pane.

If Hanka had known his own table awaited him, he would surely have run from that place and that valley, right past Astonishment, and never come back.

Inside the Dog Lodge, Violena Sedge had just finished dusting the corpses with arsenical fungicide when Finkel Hanka knocked upon the glass. She looked up and smiled. She was always glad to see Finkel Hanka, had known him since she was fourteen, that first summer she had come to Sedgwick Hall, caught him stealing pears by standing on top of the big wall surrounding the orchard.

'How'd you get up there?' she'd asked, and he'd flexed his bare toes upon the stone.

'How'd you get down there?' he'd replied, and she'd told him. Told him everything in a minute, things she had told nobody else. Told him how her dad had gone off to South Africa to find his fortune and, fortune or not, had never come back. How her mother had scrounged and scrimped and begged but finally got through the savings and then lost the house. How her mother had scoured the country for distant relatives, brought Violena up to Sedgwick, believing it to be their family name, then walked away and drowned herself in the river.

Uncle Weeems wasn't really an uncle; he wasn't related at all. The old Sedgwicks of Sedgwick Hall had been second cousins twice removed but they'd long since gone and died out. Even the Sedgwick Hall that had once been was long gone. But he'd been kind when he'd found her alone and ashamed on his doorstep, clutching her mother's letter and the ratty old baggage of her belongings. He'd given her a home and a job and the free run of his house. He was frequently absent, off on his collecting expeditions and wrote her long letters, and she wrote him back. She read every book in the library about where he'd gone and where he'd been. She'd put a little sticker on the big candle-globe in the library, which was a map of the world. There were stickers all over it now, from north to south and east to west, one even in the Arctic from where he'd brought back tiny animalcules that lived in the snow.

When she was fifteen she'd made a catalogue of every single one of her uncle's curiosities; when she was seventeen he gave her charge of her first lodge. He'd asked her to choose. She'd chosen the Lantern House, which was stuck from floor to ceiling with shelves and every shelve had a different kind of lantern. There were reed lights and storm glasses and butter lamps from Tibet. There were ships' lanterns, miners' lights, Japanese floating candles. It was the hardest room to take care of because every night, half an hour past sunset, every lamp had to be lit in the proper order, and for several wonderful minutes, flames of all sizes and colours flickered and leapt, and the whole room came alive. It was a highlight for the visitors, who crammed themselves through the doorway and lifted their eyes to the walls of flame. They didn't know how long it took to wipe all the glasses clean of smoke, replace all the spent wicks, top this or that one up with oil or rendered blubber or fat or whatever it used for fuel, feed the glow-worms, tend the little mulberry bush on which they lived. But she'd loved it, and her adopted uncle had loved her for loving it, and soon she was in charge of the whole lodge collection. And then he had gone away that final time and left only debts and a vacuum she thought no one else could fill. And then Jeremiah Pytchley had bought the place and everything in it, including her services as Head Curator. And that was why Finkel Hanka was here today.

He had seen her going into the Dog Lodge with her can of spray, had watched her for several moments before he tapped on the glass, admired the purpose she brought to every movement, the way she sprayed and combed each canine pelt and then moved on. He had asked her to marry him once, and again, and a third time. She had never said yes, she had never said no, but they both knew it wouldn't happen. She would never leave Sedgwick Hall, and if it was him or the Hall, he knew he would always lose, so he had never asked again.

She came out to meet him, and they strolled across the dew-crisp lawn, their feet leaving tracks in the melting frost. He told her about Leopold Huxby. He asked her help in compiling the details of what was missing from the Weeems Society Exhibition Room up at the Hall, which, of course, she had already done, and he told her it was time to shift the exhibits around to cover the awful space. He asked her to go and talk to Millicent, and Violena agreed, as he'd known she would.

4

Quercus and Canals

1 March

THE CORK HARVEST in Algeria had been good that year. The most valuable trees grow forty years before their first harvest and have gained the century before the cork grows at its best. The bark is stripped in May and cooked and flattened and boiled again, is scraped of its hard crust. It is trimmed and graded and loaded on to ships. Some of it lands in London, where it is used to line hats, make mats, sole shoes, and some of it, though not very much, is travelling northwards to Darlington attached to the end of Jeremiah Pytchley's left leg.

He is looking at it now, is pleased with it, even proud. It is the best artificial foot he has ever had. It is light and flexible, hardly rubs his stump at all. Where his actual foot is, he has no idea. In the belly of foreign crows is his best guess. The idea makes him smile. When he was fighting the wars in India he'd heard that in the high country the natives never buried their dead. They stripped them, washed them, chopped them up and put them on a big stone slab, waited for the skies to send for the soul of the departed. The birds dispersed the flesh across the heavens in its Last Great Travelling and Unravelling, returning to air and earth the parts from which every man is made. He doubted he could get away with it in England, but after he had lost his foot, he had made an addendum to his will, just in case, and had a big stone dolmen erected in the grounds of the Hall.

It is at Darlington that the urgent telegram from Finkel Hanka intercepts him; it is with curiosity and foreboding that he rereads it, folds it back into his pocket, watches the little paddles of the steamer take him up the valley canal to Sedgwick, running through fields and woods alongside the river, which traipses lazily in its wide, snow-bloomed banks.

Already, Major Jeremiah Pytchley could see in his mind's eye the sign to Astonishment Hall. It still thrilled him to know that he now owned the place, that he had been the one prospective purchaser who had agreed to abide by Halliday Weeems' eccentric order that the hall be taken over exactly as it was and that nothing be changed for a minimum of thirty-three years. He had marvelled at the blueprints laid out with the purchase agreement, at the first sight of the building clinging to the face of the cliff halfway up the hill. He had been staggered by the inventory of curiosities that Weeems had given house to, and that were now, as the new owner, given over to his care. He still got a shiver of delight on every return to see the edifice of Sedgwick growing like a rambling rose across the bleakness of the ancient hill. He took great pains to care for his predecessor's possessions and an awkward pride in adding some exhibits of his own.

The barge was huffing to a stop as Sedgwick station came into view. They called it a station because it was a place assigned. It was the place where every visitor alighted and took his or her first breath of this valley that Pytchley took so much pleasure now to call his own. He collected his bag from the stow-hold, the same bag he had taken to India, the same bag he had trailed from tent to tent during that awful year of war, the same bag that still carried the blood of his adjutant, who had died with his head upon it, having dragged his major back to camp, without his foot but still with his life. He put his hat on his head, took up his cane and breathed the sharp afternoon air of wet brambles and bracken that had folded and fallen through the winter months, the leaves of the lime trees around the station thick and mulched upon the ground. London was good for getting new prosthetic limbs made from the best Algerian cork, but it shrank your lungs into fists with its stink and smoke.

Pytchley stepped down the short gangplank, pleased once again at the lightness of his new limb; looked for the carriage boy. He hoped the lad had spied the barge coming upriver, that he wouldn't have to wait too long. He wanted to get home, change his clothes, open a good bottle of wine, sit with his new foot by the fire, find out more about this mysterious theft, which, though strange, was surely no cause for too much alarm. New locks, he thought, or some stronger bolts and pins from the smithy. He'd have to get old Huxby on to that, give him a few more keys to dangle ostentatiously from his belt . . .

Pytchley was surprised to see Finkel Hanka coming up the boarded bank to greet him, holding his hat in his hands, eyes screwed up against the thin veil of steam. Violena Sedge was standing behind him, looking pale and stiff. And oddly for a woman who preferred the muted autumn of green and brown, she was dressed all in black.

It was a solemn ride back to Astonishment Hall, the three of them uncomfotable in the trap. Pytchley couldn't enjoy the crispness of the air or admire the frost-sparkled fields, the bare trees etched against a deep blue sky, the shadow of the moon still visible, though it was well after noon. He'd heard what they had to say. He'd looked at the paper Violena had put into his hands, the label that was all that was left of one of his prize exhibits. He'd listened while Hanka read names out from the visitors' book, said yes, he knew them, or no, he didn't. He'd tried hard to think of anyone strange or furtive, but how would he know? Leopold Huxby was the person to ask. He'd been the man to give guests the little tour, hand over the guidebook, keep an eye on the donations box and the exhibits.

Leopold Huxby.

He thought mostly of Leopold Huxby and didn't even notice when they passed by the iron-wrought gates of Astonishment Hall until Hanka started to speak.

'There is another thing which may or may not be of interest.'

Pytchley closed his eyes, listened to the hooves of the horses on the hard-rutted track.

Hanka went on, 'There is a new lodge exhibition at the Hall, just arrived. A man named Maximillian Orcutt.'

Pytchley opened his eyes. He looked at Hanka, who was

looking at the notebook lying open on his knee. He couldn't be reading it – the ruts of the driveway were too bumpy. The notebook jumped at every pace.

'He is in the process of setting up his Theatrical Science Museum. And,' Hanka lifted his eyes but looked straight ahead, 'he is the creator of the Perspective Box that has gone missing. I believe, Major Pytchley, that he is a member of your Society.'

'Ah,' said Pytchley, 'yes. That's right.'

'Could you tell me a bit more about the Society, Major?'

Pytchley cleared his throat, brought his thoughts into focus. He still saw Huxby standing in the driveway, waving his severely worn gas-lighting manual, telling him not to worry while he was away, that Leopold Huxby would care-take as he always had and always would. He pushed the image away, answered the question.

'The Society. Very easily, yes. The Weeems Society, or the Wonderful World of Weeems, to give it the full title. I decided to form it when I took over the Hall, when I learnt a little more about Halliday Weeems. He was an extraordinary man, you know.'

He glanced at Violena, who must surely have told all this already to Finkel Hanka. He knew they were close. Still, this was an official investigation, he understood that, understood the need for repetition and organisation. If nothing else, the army had taught him that.

'In essence, it is a natural history forum to carry on the work of Halliday Weeems. We have meetings, forays, discussions, publish papers and books. We encourage all manner of interest in the natural world, particularly the application of science for its study. Many of our members have taken up various obscure pathways to that end. Your Maximillian fellow has been a contributor for quite a number of years, though I have never met him.' He scoured his memory for the contributions Orcutt had made, which were many, went on with his explanations.

'As you know, I host an annual exhibition of the most interesting research that has come to the attention of the Society in the preceding year. His last project was a perspective box, which was really quite exceptional. I believe he has improved even on the work of Samuel Von Hoogstraten, who more or less invented the genre.' He stopped abruptly, tried to visualise the box, see again inside it. The principle of all perspective boxes was the same: when you put your eye to the viewing lens, the interior perspective was so engineered you felt you were inside the scene itself. In Orcutt's case, it was a system of underground caves and had not one nor two viewing apertures, but eight, one for each of the octagonal sides, which was in itself a daring and unusual innovation. Most boxes were square, to keep the mathematics simple.

Violena Sedge spoke up. 'You approved his latest application for lodge space some time ago.' She paused, went on, 'As you know, he has applied persistently over the last four or five years. And when we saw the box . . .' Violena rustled the papers she was holding, but didn't go on.

'Ah, yes,' murmured Pytchley, remembering, 'I recall we reviewed his position. Some of the exhibit diagrams he sent me were remarkable. Even on paper they could not help but enthral.'

The trap lurched to one side as the wheel hit a pothole. Pytchley's new foot hit the side of the carriage, made him wince. He hauled his leg back up by the knee and looked at Hanka.

'But who would want to steal a perspective box at all? They are hardly things you can slip into your pocket, especially not Orcutt's. It must have been at least a foot and a half in diameter. And then again, he was available for commission, that much was obvious from the display tag, and part of the reason, Violena my dear, why I finally singled out his application, though I had not expected him until later in the spring.'

Violena coughed. 'The wicker sculptor had to cancel. A fire, apparently. Nothing left to exhibit. And Mr Orcutt was next on the list, so I contacted him. He arrived a few days ago.'

Pytchley smiled at Violena. 'Quite right, my dear. No point letting lodge space lie empty. And this way he can be directly available for consulation, and his prices are very reasonable. Far too reasonable. I don't think he is aware quite how talented he is and how exceptional is the work he has produced. I must speak to him about it.' He gazed off for a moment, creased his brow. 'But it still comes back to why anyone should go to the trouble of doing such a thing. The box has already been featured in our Proceedings – intellectually the design is Orcutt's and even if some thief managed to reproduce it and sell it on, no judge in the land would contest his absolute possession to it. I just don't understand.'

Hanka didn't understand either. It puzzled him. It frightened him. And so it should.

5

Here Lies the Valley of Eden

2 March

AFTER SEDGWICK COME Wolsingham and Weardale, and a single track passes over the Pennines below Black Fell. From the tip of the fell, the land falls away to the west and you can see the backs of the Cumberland Hills, their dark heads cowled in cloud and rain. Sometimes you can see the glint of the firth where the Solway runs into the sea. On that side of Black Fell runs the switch of green that is Eden Valley, its fields and orchards sheltered by the two great lines of hills. On this side, to the east, the streams tumble down the hills and it is said you can pan them for flakes of gold, especially after storms, and in winter, when the top tarns overflow through the dark heather, down into bracken-coloured burns before being lost in the arms of the river far below.

In a cove, under the shadow of Black Fell, a small caravan stood. It had been built from the base of a farmer's haywain, planks of wood roughly joisted and nailed, a roof covered over in canvas and makeshift thatch. Medan Skimmington Bellpenny was sitting on the lip of the cart, the dark doorway behind him, sorting over the contents of a pewter tray. A pheasant *kek-kekked* somewhere up on the hill, and another. He looked up, fingers twitching an inch above his work. He frowned. He didn't have long to finish up this last tray. The sun was dropping fast and once it went behind Black Fell he would have to stop. His fingers didn't like the cool of evening and would drain of blood, leaving the tips numb and white and without feeling, unable to pick the tiny glints of gold from the dross. He took a drink from the bottle standing open-necked beside him. It set a tingle to his teeth and for a few seconds he kept it in his mouth, let it dull the ache of his gums, swallowed.

He heard a noise like the slow drip of a tap, cocked his ear towards the sound. There it was again. Someone was coming down the track. He couldn't see them yet; they were still round the back of Brougham Crags. He swore softly. It would be one of the estate men. They knew he was sometimes here. He was supposed to hand over a tithe of any gold he found. He opened the pouch hanging from his belt, poured in the contents of the tray, unhooked it, tied it, hid it under the loose planking of the cart. Then he sat and waited. Watched the sun disappear behind the grey clouds, which would soon bring snow. He would pack up in the morning, fetch the horse from the hobbling ground, move back to his small cottage further along the ridge going towards Eden.

Up on the track, Finkel Hanka too looked up at the roll of cloud coming in from the east. He was on his way to Claverhouse, which lay just the other side of the ridge. He'd already called at Ascham and Bedlington; Claverhouse was last on his list. He was tracking down the names in the visitors' book, talking to people who had been most recently at Astonishment and lived local, asking who they had seen, what they had seen, people they might have passed on the road. He rounded the brow and saw the small caravan sited on the green in the lee of the hill, the small fire smouldering in its shadow, the billycan hanging from its wire hoop.

'Halloo,' he called as he neared the cart, hoped the occupant would offer him a cup of tea. He got off his horse, rubbed his thighs, which were stiff and cramped with cold. The fire still smouldered, steam rising from the billycan, but he could see no one.

Panners, he thought, and wondered who would spend their days sifting the freezing waters of the burns for the tiny specks of gold that were practically without worth. He looked around, called out again, got no reply. Curious, he climbed the few steps of the makeshift caravan and put his head through the canvas-covered door. It was dark inside, and smelt like a forest floor after rain. He could see a pallet on the floor, a pillow, some blankets, shivered just to think of sleeping out here with the wind and crack of frost he could already feel in the air. There was a crate lying at the far end, and on it, an octagonal outline. He moved forward, reached out his hand, pulled open the sacking, saw the polished wood below, a single lens caught by the sun as it lowered below the level of the roof, chinked through a gap in the planked sides.

'You looking for something?'

Hanka turned, saw a man standing right outside, in front

of the small fire – rounded face, slack skin, coat bundled about his shoulders as if it were too big.

'I'm so sorry,' he said, bringing out his hands, holding them up in apology, introduced himself as Constable Hanka from Sedgwick, on his way to Claverhouse to make a few enquiries.

'That so?' said the man, who didn't offer his hand or his name. 'See anything you like?'

Hanka searched the man's face, filed away the odd intonation, the slight accent of his voice, the clothes he was wearing, the size of his boots. He came down off the steps and stood next to the man. He asked if he might have a cup of tea, tried to put the man at his ease, but he knew what he had seen, and knew the man knew that he had seen it. The man waved a hand at the billycan.

'Help yerself,' he said. 'I'll fetch a mug.'

But Medan Bellpenny didn't fetch a mug; he fetched up the heavy pewter sorting tray and brought it down so hard upon Finkel Hanka's head that a dent rose up along the tray's edge. Hanka fell face down across the fire, the hoop of the billycan still in his hand. The tray came down again and again and the embers started to burn their way into Finkel Hanka's coat, the smell of damp and singeing wool setting Medan's teeth on edge. He licked his lips, then pushed the interloper with his boot, rolled him off the billycan and on to the grass.

Finkel Hanka's head was filled with blood and fireflies swirling in a deep black night. He couldn't remember who he was or where he was. He had the vague sensation that he was falling through an open door, being rolled slowly over and over as if he were caught beneath a wave.

Medan Bellpenny roughly thrust open Finkel's coat. He

found the small gilt badge that said he was Authority. He found his wallet. He scrutinised the badge without interest then dropped it into the remains of the fire. He flicked the wallet open, smiled, took out his own battered empty bill-case and hurled it into the evening air, watched it land with satisfaction in a far-off clump of heather. He tucked the new wallet into his pocket, had the strangest feeling that he was just waking up, his thoughts clear as the streams in which he sifted for gold. He went up the cart steps and reached inside. He picked up the sack that Hanka had seen from where it sat badly hidden by the crate, took it back out, laid it gently against the wheel. He took the pouch from its hiding place and tied it back on to his belt. He moved to the side of the cart and crouched down low, pulled out two large containers and removed the stoppers.

He went back to Hanka, tied a rope around his ankles and started dragging him towards the cart. He could only get the man halfway up the steps before his breath and back gave out. Still, it would do. He climbed over the unconscious Hanka and picked up one of the containers, hurled it into the cart, heard the terracotta smash, smelt the liquid seeping into the blankets and the wood, regretted for a moment that he hadn't taken out his bedding. Still, things had to be done and he had to do them. He'd been a prisoner before for thieving and he wasn't going to do it again. He picked up the second jar and took off the lid, poured the contents over Finkel Hanka, made sure he filled Finkel Hanka's empty mouth, which gaped up at him like a sink-hole. He pulled some thatch from the roof, made a trail from the cart to the fire, poured on more of the naphtha he used to light his lamps and start his fires and clean his hands and wash his precious gold. He blew on the embers till the line of thatching caught and was sure to go. A breeze had risen like breath from the cooling river, which made the job almost too easy.

Medan Skimmington Bellpenny smiled his rare smile again. He bent and picked up his sacking package and a pair of saddlebags, then set off up the hill and unhobbled his horse. He didn't ride the old mare – preferred to walk – but let the animal carry his bags. They climbed up the brow of the hill and met the sun where it had just dropped the other side.

He turned and surveyed his work, which was how he saw it. He had always been a man who worked, though precious little he'd ever got from it. Back in the clearing below Black Fell he could see the fire beginning to hold. The cart was starting to take. He could hear the crack of wood as it fractured in the growing heat, could just make out the form of the body draped upon its steps. He thought he caught a whiff of burning skin and bone but it didn't bother him. He'd done what needed to be done, and now he could move on. He had the feeling that sometime soon he would be going home, not just to his little cottage in the hills but somewhere else, more distant, somewhere he had wanted to go for a long, long time.

Down in the lee of Black Fell, in the pool of dark below the crags, Finkel Hanka's eyes gazed up at a star-filled sky. Sparks leapt and hummed about him like tiny dragonflies. The thatch burnt steadily, the flames grew, the wind blew it along from above and below. His hair began to sizzle in amongst the dried heather. The skin of his forehead blistered and burnt, drew the muscles tight across his face, boiled the blood within his veins. Hanka saw only a star-filled sky and only for a moment. Thankfully for Finkel Hanka, he had passed and gone by the time his eyeballs pricked and sputtered and the fire had moved on over his body and up the steps and through the woodwork of the cart and up the sides of the shoddy caravan, blazing like a beacon as the sun set in the west and night came on and started to scatter its snows over the desolation beneath Black Fell, which stood the wrong side of Eden.

6

Interruption of the Senses

London – Morning, 5 March

THE CLOISTERGILL LEATHERWORKS had just finished escorting Mr Whilbert Nathaniel Stroop off the premises with the threat of prosecution if he returned. He had invited himself in plainly enough, had been given a brief tour of the showroom, followed by a briefer tour of the production rooms at his insistence. Having thought at first he might be an important customer, the foreman had become suspicious when Stroop started asking all sorts of detailed questions about how the cofferer tooled the leather and fashioned it into corners for the coffrets used to carry jewels. He had also questioned the workers on how precisely they sealed the edges of a costrel so that it would not spill the liquid that it carried. When he started prodding the huge blackjacks and bombards they had made ready for Wressle Castle, the foreman called over a couple of leather-strappers and tossed Stroop out on his badly shod heels. The foreman had particularly noted the shabbiness of the visitor's footwear and this offended him almost as much as the possibility of industrial espionage.

Stroop himself was well pleased as he walked down the back of the Cloisters and on to Cobber Lane. He had stopped a moment to scribble his notes, add the cipher to indicate that particular kind of smell, the colour of the soil in the yard, the stain that lingered on the strappers' fingers.

Just then, a dray drew up. The drayman unlocked the leatherer's gate and hauled from within the sacks of off-cuts and spoilt pieces, and loaded them on to his cart. Stroop trotted down the lane after the man as he pulled the cart by a yoke he had attached to his shoulders, and asked him where he was off.

'Glue factory,' he said glumly, wrinkling his nose, having the stench of the place permanently up his nostrils.

Stroop had already caught the whiff of boiled-down heads and heels emanating from the man's clothes, and happily jotted down the directions to the glue factory, which he fully intended to make top of his itinerary the following week. His Sense Map of London was coming on, and he had dedicated the last couple of months to researching the intricate processes of various professions and jotting down the individual smells and sights that accompanied them. It wasn't the first time he'd been ejected from someone's premises for asking too many questions. Still, mused Stroop, all in all, it was worth it.

He'd reached the end of the lane and parted company with the drayman, wondered if he had time to get down to the woolleries. He was keen to find out more about how you lined a ship with wool to deaden the impact of enemy cannonballs, knew that army men padded their coats in the same manner to protect them from shot.

He was tapping his pencil against his teeth when he saw a skinny, raggedy figure coming at him from the other end of the street, waving his arms. It was Jack. He looked like he'd been catapulted through a crate of farmyard manure, with mud making his hair stick up in spikes and giving Stroop the odd sensation he was looking at him in black and white. Just like a dog does, he thought momentarily, and a bull. He was just making a note to check up on whether cats had colour vision when Jack came into shouting distance.

'Mr Stroop! Mr Stroop!' He always called him Mr Stroop, though Stroop had tried to get him to call him by his proper name. The same went for Mabel and Thomas. For a man who had no extant family and no wife, he had gathered a remarkable amount of children about him, though Mabel, at seventeen, was strictly speaking no longer a child, and Jack, no matter how old he got, would always be one. He was taller now, was Jack, though thin as a whippet despite the amount of soup and posset he managed to get down his neck at every meal. He gangled up the lane towards Stroop, still waving his arms, though Stroop had plainly seen him.

'Mr Stroop,' he was still shouting, despite the bare yard that parted them, 'you've to come quickly, back to the house.'

Stroop tucked his notebook and pencil back into his pouch and put a hand on Jack's shoulder to stop his arms, which had a tendency to carry on by themselves. 'What's so urgent?' enquired Stroop. 'You've never run all the way here,' he added, knowing that Jack probably had.

Jack was hard-pushed to let Stroop out of his sight at the

best of times, unless Thomas distracted him with some game or other, or Mabel looked at him in that way she had, which could nail any one of them to their seat. It had taken a bit of getting used to this past year to tell at least one of them where he was going, or tack a note to the door, or on a coat-peg, telling them where he could be reached. He had taken to leaving the house at dawn so he could carry on his research without being griddled brown on both sides by questions from one or other of them. Oddly, it gave him comfort to know that someone cared where he should be and when he should be back. It also gave his work a purpose. Barely a year ago, his lists and learning had ceased being scholar's dust and food for moths and contributed to saving all their lives.

'There's someone missing,' said Jack in the voice he assumed when he didn't want anyone else to hear. It never worked. Jack had never learnt to whisper, though Thomas had coached him hard, having had many a planned sneaking of apple pies or ox knuckles ruined by Jack's unconscious announcement of their presence. Thomas had grown up on the streets and pilfering was a hard habit to break, despite now having a home and a hot dinner waiting for him whenever he wanted it. And he wanted it, and never wandered far or for too long.

'Aha!' said Stroop. 'Someone Missing is what we do. And who is missing, Jack? Not Thomas again, I hope?'

'Not Thomas,' laughed Jack, whose cotton-wool head didn't know much, but what it did know, it knew with absolute certainty. 'It's this man and woman, Mr Stroop. They say their son's gone off somewhere. They're waiting for you at the house.'

Stroop was surprised. It must have taken Jack at least an hour to track him down, his directional sense being slightly awry, to say the least, and it would take them easily half that time again to get back.

'Surely they're not still waiting for me?'

But Jack was pulling at his elbow, leading him down a ginnel. He had learnt quite a lot about shortcuts since living with Mr Stroop, though he wasn't always sure where they went.

'Mabel's giving them wine and stuff,' said Jack, and Stroop smiled at the thought.

Mabel had taken over the running of his house and kitchen without a blink. She swept every floor every morning, she washed the stoop and steps, she had emptied the cupboards of mouse-droppings and twenty-year-old sacks of dried peas and mouldy millet. She spent a lot of time in the study checking his notations and marking things up on his Sense Maps in her neat, sure hand, making foldaway copies and marking long lists in his logs.

He didn't interfere. He understood this need to order the things around her. She had lost so much, seen her entire family murdered, been confronted with death and disaster and the knowledge that, indirectly, she was to blame. The old mutt she had rescued from her father's farm could hardly bend its back these days, and spent its life getting fatter and fonder in a special bed by the fire. She pulled Thomas and Jack and himself together around her and couldn't bear to be idle or alone. She never looked at blood sausage, and every piece of meat they had was wrapped in a pastry crust or cooked to the bone, which was just as well. They all of them remembered too clearly the smell of flesh not long dead and fresh-spilt blood upon stone and hearth.

Mabel had sold her father's farm and still had the trust her great-aunt had left her for her marriage. She had bought a small garden by the river opposite St Anthony's, planted a tree for every person whom she knew to have died, and altogether that made for quite a copse. They went there every week, took a little picnic, spent time pulling out the weeds, checking all the tags that hung from the saplings, planted bulbs and honeysuckle and clematis and roses. It was a quiet time for all of them, a good time, and Stanley Izod often came over from the church and helped them pail water from the river and greased the gates and set any loose stones back into the walls that guarded their little garden and all of them from the world, at least for a while.

'And you, Jack,' Stroop asked, narrowly missing a large pile of horse manure still steaming in the street, 'you've decided to dress in mud for the day?'

Jack pulled his master on but took the question seriously. 'Oh, no, Mr Stroop. I set off in my best jerkin. Mabel likes me to look my best when I come out for you. But the pigs is being gathered in at the end of Smoke Street.' He shuddered a little, as did Stroop. They both knew what happened to pigs in Smoke Street.

'And?' prompted Stroop, beginning to pant at the pace Jack was putting him to.

'And,' said Jack, 'I had a bit of greenery, see –' oh dear, thought Stroop, Thomas has been at it again – '*and*, well, I thought that the little piggies might like a bite of it while they waited.'

They both knew what the pigs were waiting for, but Jack hurled Stroop on and Stroop's elbow cracked as Jack's grip tightened.

'Just a little bit of something before, well, you know . . .' Stroop knew. 'But while I was leaning over the fence I sort of got a bit close and I slipped.'

Stroop got his elbow free at last as Jack skidded round a corner; Jack took advantage and flourished a spray of wilted kale from his jacket, 'but I kept some for dinner, see?'

It was said with triumph, but Stroop could tell that Mabel might not be too pleased at the offering, knew she would have another talk with Thomas. Thomas always took these lectures sitting at the kitchen table, legs twiddling under the planks.

'You've not to steal,' Mabel would say. 'You don't want to end up in *that place* again.'

Thomas knew precisely the place she was talking about, and really didn't want to go back to the poorhouse again, but somehow, whenever he crossed a market square, his fingers twitched into corners and under flaps of their own accord. It wasn't really stealing anyhow, it was just taking what no one else wanted, and if no one else wanted it, what harm was there in taking it? And he was right. Stroop could see that. If a cauliflower rolled under a market stall into a puddle and no one else would buy it, there really wasn't any harm in Thomas picking it up and bringing it home. And if Mabel refused to cook the thing because it was saturated in mud, what harm in Jack taking it on to feed his little piggies? None at all. Why not give them a taste of something good before the knife slit their throats?

The thought made Stroop wince, but luckily they had turned

the street to home, and not for the first time he marvelled at the way Thomas and Mabel had brought the garden back into order. Even at this time of year, he could see the brackets of broccoli and cabbage, the leeks and turnips holding their heads above the ground. It would be chickens next, he thought. And Stroop had always hated chickens, with their peck and strut and constant pick, pick, picking at the ground. It never occurred to him that it was his own pick-picking that had brought the people who now waited for him to his home. And they were still there when Stroop and Jack finally gained the gate and let themselves in through the back door.

Mabel was there, worrying at the wine she had warming on the stove.

'Thank goodness you're here, Mr Stroop,' she said as she poured the wine into the herb jug, lit a lamp to take into the next room. 'There's a Mr and Mrs Dvoshka here.' She spoke the name softly because the foreignness of it leant itself to whispers. 'They're in quite a state.' Mabel loaded her tray with glasses and saucers and a few more biscuits. She knew they didn't need the biscuits, nor want them, but it made her feel better to have them there, something solid and nourishing. She didn't want to say what she was going to say, but she also knew it was too late to stop the bad dreams that would inevitably come that night just because she had thought the word during the day. 'They think, Mr Stroop,' she swallowed hard, knew that it would take less than a biscuit topped with caraway seed to choke her, 'they think their boy has gone and killed someone.'

Whilbert Stroop didn't notice the biscuits or the tray. He didn't question or prevaricate. He picked up the jug Mabel had given him, motioned her to follow, and went through the door.

7

Lost in the Valley

Astonishment Hall – Afternoon, 5 March

JEREMIAH PYTCHLEY WAS tired. His foot ached, or at least the empty space where his foot should have been was aching. It was a strange thing, he had always told himself, that a man should feel so acutely a loss that was such a long time passed. And yet there it was: his foot ached.

He closed his eyes, rubbed his forehead with his hand, drew it down across his face. It had been a bad morning. He had been to visit Millicent Huxby to offer his condolences, and wished he hadn't. She had opened the door to him, made him a pot of tea, offered him some brandy stilled with apricots. He had seen her shoulders bow over the range, her hand staying a touch too long before she lifted the kettle, poured the water, stirred the tea into the pot. They sat in silence while it brewed to strength and when she had gone to pour, the pot had slipped from her fingers, clattered against the warming tray and fallen on to its side. She had stood up suddenly, waited the moment out, watching the brown stain creep across her best white cloth before the weeping welled within her and came out of her unbidden, softly, silently, washing down her cheeks and slowly, slowly she sank back into her seat and covered her face with her apron.

He had reached across the steaming table and taken her hand. 'I'm so sorry, Millicent.' He could hardly speak; his voice was whispered as if his words were smoke. He saw the grey bobbin of her hair gently lift and fall in the nape of her neck, thought of the small stones in the cemetery, all the children she had almost had, and how Leopold would be the last in the line she would bury, and the sadness came over him like a lone grebe gliding across a silent lake.

'The house is yours,' he had said, 'for as long as . . .' But he couldn't finish, because he knew it wouldn't be for so very long.

Back at the Hall, he had written a few instructions to his bank, made out a small pension for Leopold Huxby's wife. He put the pen back in its stand, screwed down the lid of the ink pot, took his cane and went over to the fire.

It was so cold outside and yet oddly he could hear there was rain running down the windows and not snow, and he was pleased at least for that. The pass would stay clear and the road back from Claverhouse would be the easier for Finkel Hanka when he returned.

In another dale on the dark side of the hills, in a cottage half by Eden, another man is putting down his pen. Bellpenny has scratched three full pages of notes. He too is gazing into his fire but there is no rain here where he is. The cot is built into a pocket of the mountainside, where snow hides all the winter long, growing harder with the cold than clinker does in a kiln. His house never sees the dawn and is not harmed by the weakened rays of a dying sun. He likes it here. It has been his home, the only one of many to which he has returned. There is something of this in the words he has just written, his mind moving back and forth across the page, across time, across many miles and many lands.

He coughs his throat clear of tobacco, the rough ends of the paper he has rolled it in sticking to his lips. Tries to remember all the details the boy had in his book. He always thinks of him as a boy, even though Uwe must now be in his middle twenties. He'd looked younger then, he thinks, much younger than now. He had that look you only get with youth: a gnawing for life and whatever it would bring; an eagerness to meet head-on whatever lay around the corner, if you even saw the corner; a transparency of purpose that couldn't for a minute see that other things, other people, might get in its way. And something had got in Bellpenny's way, no doubting that. He grimaced at the thought of it, of his cart-caravan and the man who had burnt upon its steps. And just as he'd thought things were getting better, just as he'd thought he might almost have enough to get out. Of course he'd been pinching things for years, and only been caught that one time. But since he'd come back, it had never once gone wrong. Not until the constable. And the boy. Put the two things together and you got a scapegoat come in from the wilderness. A chance to leave this old home and all the parts of himself that lay buried within its walls.

He'd seen at once the use to which the boy could be put, a way to leave without anyone noticing he had ever been here. And he had never really been here, no matter where he went. People had always passed him by, looked over him for another man. And this time, he'd be glad to let them do it. But first, he needed a plan, a framework, a wire horse on which to hang his clothes. Something not so simple it could been seen straight through. Something that would not let the strings be seen behind the puppet.

And then there was that one last thing he wanted done, something he had always wanted to do. That violation not forgotten nor forgiven. That one man who might remember him and where he lived, and maybe bring back the rumours of what he had done all those years ago. Maybe start new ones. Maybe set other people on his trail.

He looked down at his notes. Read them through. Saw a skein begin to form between the words. Picked up his pen. Gave a grim smile, lit another screw of paper and tobacco, poured a shot of liquor.

For Medan Skimmington Bellpenny, the day had just got better.

For Pytchley, down in the valley, it had got much worse.

Two hours past his visit to Millicent Huxby finds Finkel Hanka's mother hammering at his door. She has passed by the yew hedge without seeing it, brushed a few berries to the rain-sodden ground. She wears her bed-slippers but doesn't feel how cold and wet are her feet. She is frantic. She shouts out for help in Hungarian and doesn't hear it.

Someone has found her Finkel's horse still hobbled up on the pass. Pytchley is soon there standing by her side, his coat and boots are at the ready, he is yelling for the stableboy.

Violena Sedge comes up the path behind them; she had come down from her room to fix the exhibition table, mask the blank, but soon she too is in the stable yard and nothing they can say will stop her when Pytchley takes the road to Claverhouse with three of his men.

When they fly out along the lane, Maximillian Orcutt sees them go and whips his horse to follow. He had come to see the major, who was exhibiting his work, had been told about the theft of his box, had hoped for private words, maybe the means with which to work at its replacement. He saw Violena Sedge go like a bolt from a crossbow and followed her over Ascham, caught them up at Bedlington where they'd stopped again to enquire what yesterday had seen. Together they took the brow at Brougham Crags. Together they saw the heap of smouldering cinders left by fire and rain.

And there lay Roze Hanka's son, all charred and gone.

And there stood Violena Sedge, stiff in her saddle, thinking, if only he had asked me just one more time.

And beside her was the man who had a cork for a foot strapped into his stirrup, choking with the memories of a long-forgotten war.

And there sat Maximillian Orcutt who, though he didn't know it, had brought this misery down upon them, like the east wind in the winter always brings the snow. And like all bad winters, there was worse yet to come.

8

Glass and Bells

London – 5 March

'MY NAME IS Albrecht Dvoshka.' The man was rotund and had difficulty getting up from his chair. His stomach lodged under the rim of the table and the chair screeched like an owl as its iron-tongued feet scraped against the floor.

'Mr Dvoshka,' Stroop replied, putting the wine on the table, moving back to make room for Mabel as she set her useless victuals down beside it, 'and Mrs Dvoshka?' Stroop added with a short bow.

Elusia Dvoshka dropped her head like a pigeon but said nothing and did not move; only the curl of her fingers shifted and tightened as they lay upon her lap, the tips of one hand locked into the palm of the other, the thumbs extended like useless harbour walls.

Said Stroop, 'I believe we have a problem.'

Stroop was urbane and assured. The adventures of last year had not been much publicised but they had undoubtedly had an impact on how he had been treated by his new clients, and how he treated them. He still remembered the Italian, Castracani, who had been through so much and yet come out so much the better. For himself, Stroop could not even contemplate the destruction of his home and all that was in it, and yet Castracani, who had lost everything, always answered when asked that at least he had the respect of his peers, and for Castracani that had seemed enough. But still Stroop shuddered to even contemplate being burnt out of his home. Having his lists and maps totally and without mercy destroyed was too much to think about. He never saw the scars upon his own hands, which had intrigued so many; had tried to forget that coal shed and the wails that seemed to weep out from its walls, the vomit-wrenching odour, the soft splat of human fat upon his skin. One thing to put out his hands and seize the burning boy that had been Jack, heave him back out into life. Quite another to abandon everything you knew and valued, take another man upon your back and scratch your way through smoke-wrought stairs to the top of your fire-bitten home, and leap out into darkness, in the hope – oh, just only in the hope – that you, and maybe the man you had thrown before you, might survive. Castracani. A man to be measured against. And Stroop did not mean to be found wanting, if ever he was tried.

'He was a good boy,' said Mr Dvoshka, 'he was a right boy. Do you know what I mean, Mr Stroop?'

Stroop nodded. He had Jack, he had Thomas, he had Mabel. He had no actual children, but these three gave him a microscope onto a world he would otherwise not have had, and he did understand.

'I do,' he said simply.

'We are glass importers, Mr Stroop,' said the man, 'Czechs, three generations down the line, and we make a profitable living.'

Stroop nodded again, watched as the man's belly settled back under the table and had no doubt of this family's monetary success. He had been to a glassworks a few months back to gain information for his Craft-and-Trade Map. It had been one of the few industries to welcome him in and boast its provenance. They had special workrooms where visitors could watch men blow up glass into bowls and send colours swirling round their sides like transparent pipefish who knew where they must go and where to rest. He had leant forward to see a blowhole of bubbles fly into a paperweight from a miniature school of dolphins wreathed around its base; witnessed fêtes and shields being worked into the bowl of a narghile-pipe, marvelled to see reed beds waded through with grebe and avocet on baubles the size of an apple to hang from a curtain-cord, doorknobs fashioned into globes of the world. But these had been Italian craftsmen, of that he was sure because it had been Castracani himself who had extended the introduction to make Stroop so welcome. He was unaware of any Bohemian connection. He awaited Dvoska's enlightenment and did not have to wait long.

'Bohemian glasswork is the best in Europe and exported all over the world as it has been for centuries. Obviously, each country has its own traditions, but as soon as our work was introduced, there was always an immediate demand . . .'

'Albrecht!' Elusia Dvoshka stood up so fast she caught the edge of the table with her hands to steady herself and set the glasses in their saucers rattling like ill-fitting teeth in a bad wind. She closed her eyes, and Mabel noted that her lids flickered with small veins that pulsed as she braced herself to open them again.

But oddly it was Thomas who was by her side in a moment and who slipped his hand beneath her elbow and spoke the words she needed to hear: 'Don't worry, missus, Mr Stroop will help you. He always does,' and with that she collapsed quick as the air goes out of a punctured pig-bladder and sat back in her chair as motionless as she had been before. Thomas let his hand drop and subsided cross-legged on the floor beside her, looking at her, hoping things really would be all right.

Albrecht Dvoshka cleared his throat. 'I apologise, my dear, and Mr Stroop.'

Stroop leant forward, poured his guest another glass of wine and held it out to him.

'Perhaps you had better tell us what has happened.'

And so Albrecht Dvoshka told them all a little about his son, who was missing, had been missing for many years, but not lost. Not like he was today. Not with the letter they had received that very morning, which sent them scurrying from their home and to Missing-Persons-Finder Whilbert Stroop's door.

In his cottage under Eden, Medan Skimmington Bellpenny had no idea the effect his letter had had down in London, nor how it would be acted upon. He wouldn't have cared if he had; felt himself safe and secure in his plan. He still had things to do and Uwe Proctor Dvoshka was only a part, if the main part, of it. He looked over to where the younger man lay on the two tattered chairs they had pushed together for a bed, and scowled. He didn't like having anyone here, had never had anyone here before now. The place was damp, the walls patched over with mould, the gutters askance and askew on the outside of the building, some bent at right angles like lance-handles empty of their blades. Within, every surface had been bored by beetles and woodlice, thin furniture gribbled with holes, the wooden mantel above the fireplace beginning to disintegrate, the edges chewed and worn into dank splinters. The thatch poked through the ceiling, clinging grimly to tired beams.

He'd known as soon as he'd returned that he had stayed away too long. There was nothing left of his big adventure but the smooth scarring worn around his ankles, lungs sponged soft by dust and disease, the hardening of a heart that had already atrophied beyond repair. He hardly remembered now why he had gone, how he had fallen for the allure of foreign places where the promised rewards had turned to water and fallen unnoticed through his hands. Fifteen long years, he thought, fifteen long years of work for unfound wages, then imprisonment and forced labour and finally release. He looked around him at the wreckage of his home, thought of all those broken, barnacled seashells you found empty on a beach after a storm. Empty, he thought, except for me. And Uwe Dvoshka.

He put a dirty-necked bottle to his lips and drank, grimaced a little as it burnt the constant ache from his gums. Dvoshka stirred uncomfortably on his chairs, tried to find the space to turn over, failed. Medan put a hand across his mouth, unconsciously hiding the stink that rose from the stumps of his rotting teeth.

He looked about him, at his cottage, at the small work bench he had hidden under a torn sheet in one corner. He knew what was under there, knew every inch of every object that he had dissected there for his purpose, though not exactly why. It was a distillation of himself, of all the bits he valued, of every memory of a long-gone past, a mother and father, all the things he had never had and never would have. It was something for himself alone. Something precious. Something no one else could have. It was like holding the entire world within his hands.

No, he thought. Not empty, only waiting, just like himself.

As his parents told it, Stroop mapped out the meanderings of their son. He'd had a hard journey, had Uwe Dvoshka, taking him from London and his family home when he was twelve years old, to Bohemia and a land of which he knew nothing but its language and his family history. That he had elected the journey, encouraged it, badgered and nagged for it, would not have made it the easier. The break had come when he'd reached the age to start apprenticeship at his father's firm.

'But I want to be a bellfounder!' he had shouted in one of his rare outbursts, and though he hadn't really thought the implications through, he had been sure as tadpoles turn into toads that was what he meant to do. He knew all about his Bohemian forebear Dvoshkas, how his father had come with the baggage of the glass-importing strand, and that two older brothers had already gone before him into that practice, saw no reason they should need a third. He also knew his mother's family, the Proctors, had worked a bellfoundry by the copper mines outside Orava for many years. Like Stroop, he had been fascinated by the churches that grew up from the London streets like rattleweed. Unlike Stroop, he hadn't cared for their history or made notes on their saints and practices. He had sat and listened to their bells. Had traced their tunes with his fingers as they rose and fell, listened for the cadence and the timbre that spelt their different compositions. He'd heard that the world and all the stars rang with their own vibrations, knew he meant to find their secrets and learn the making that went into the founding of a bell.

'He was our youngest,' Albrecht Dvoshka was telling Stroop and the collective at the table, 'and we thought, why not? Let him practise his parents' mother tongue in his native land, let him learn all the things we have forgotten.'

He stopped momentarily, perhaps thinking of all those things that he would never know, had never known, let alone forgotten.

It was Elusia Dvoshka who carried on, having unhammocked her hands and laced them round a glass of wine still warm from the spirit-stove on which Mabel had placed the jug.

'He was happy there, I think. We put him to apprentice with my uncle in the east of the country. He wrote to us often, told us he was doing well, that he was travelling with his great-uncle a little, had decided to write a short history of the glass industry.'

'That made us proud, I can tell you,' interrupted Elusia's husband. 'He has always been good at his words. We sent a writing desk with him, and to find he was doing a history of our family's commerce was very satisfying indeed.' Albrecht stopped. He took a large gulp of his wine. He glanced at his wife. He continued, 'He always wrote to us, every week, though we didn't always get the letters like that. Sometimes they'd arrive four at a time depending on the boats and such. But then . . .' he trailed off.

'They stopped,' Elusia supplied and Stroop held his glass a little tighter though he hadn't sipped it for a while, could feel it going cold beneath his grip.

Albrecht Dvoshka sighed gently as though his throat had been punctured. 'They stopped for a long while.'

Silence.

'For how long?' It was Mabel who had spoken. She knew the guilt of having been taken from one life to another, from her father's farm to the ostensibly more comfortable home of her great-aunt, of having not written more often, of having apparently better things to do. And then it had all been too late. She could feel Stroop looking at her, would not turn her head, did not want to meet that sympathetic gaze she knew would absolve her. She had been wrong, had not gone back to her proper home at all, and when at last she had, there had been nothing left.

'For too long,' Elusia said, her husband still holding the wineglass to his lips as if to halt time while he thought of the right thing to say, 'for far, far too long. Months. Many months. And God curse us, we did not worry. We thought, he's young, he's found new worlds, and how could we have known anything was wrong?'

Thomas unwrapped his legs from the floor and stood up. He put his arm around the strange woman's shoulders. She didn't stop him or shrug him off. She lifted one hand to his, bent her head and let the tears roll down and irrevocably stain the expensive silk of her dress. No one said anything. There seemed nothing to say. Each of the people sitting at that table had faced misery of one kind or another and none of them was anxious to meet it again, and yet here it was.

Mabel looked at Jack, who might have been sitting halfway up a chimney, so straight was his back and crooked were his knees. He didn't understand words all that much, but he knew when piggies and people were in pain, knew his ragged bunch of muddy kale could not help. She saw Thomas standing beside Elusia Dvoshka, his arm around her shoulder, his small wiry hand gripping hers. Albrecht Dvoshka still gazed over his glass as if the day had stopped completely and was waiting for someone to wind it up. She glanced at Stroop and found him looking straight at her. She didn't know what he could do or say but hoped it would be the right thing, if there was a right thing to say at this moment. He was still looking at her when he spoke, although obviously it wasn't to her that he directed his words.

'And then?' His voice was so soft she almost didn't hear it.

But Albrecht Dvoshka did. He hardly moved, only lowered his glass to the table, took his other hand from his pocket and let fall a small square of paper to the table.

'And then,' he said, 'came this.'

9

The Hall, but No Astonishment

7 *March*

THE GLOBE OF the world was poised between two silver pins, not at top and bottom as is usual, but from side to side so it rolled freely, allowed Jeremiah Pytchley to clearly see the lands that slid beneath his fingers. It was underlit by small lamps, and the inner skin of the orb was filled with some kind of coloured mercury compound whose heated momentum kept the world slowly turning on its horizontal axis, allowed the open seas to shiver blue and green as the liquid lapped against the painted outer surface of the globe. He traced a line across its silver shores, moved from the blue of Mediterranean waters to the tip of Turkey, back to the pinprick straits that allowed the Red Sea access to the blue. The surface of the globe had been faintly coloured, and the Red Sea did indeed look its name, and the blue of the Mediterranean sang through the faint application of pigment and made it sparkle.

This was another of Maximillian Orcutt's creations, and Pytchley had spent much of the morning taking a private view around his Theatrical Science Museum. Its ingenuity delighted him; it was like being placed inside the dome of a clock and getting to see how all the individual cogs and wheels of water worked. And most of it was about water in one form or another or the consequence of its actions.

One small exhibit, barely the size of an ostrich egg – and if you lived at Astonishment Hall you knew exactly how big that was – showed the formation of a pearl. A rough-backed oyster sat in the foreground, slowly opened a raggedy shell; the sea swirled slowly through and around, a hundred tiny particles sifting with the water as it went. Then a single particle took its place inside the oyster and adhered to its walls, the water continued to filter across and through the oyster's open body and, as you watched, a small layer of what seemed like nacre began to emerge around that grain of sand, and a little more, and a little more. It wasn't a perfect circle, it wasn't the same shape each time. It was an exercise in random action, and Pytchley really, really wanted to know how it had been engineered. He had seen men blown apart at the seams and knew that bodies are but soft and fleshly mechanisms, and he knew this too had been made to act according to certain rules and behave in certain ways; that just like people, the same ingredients could bring a different result into the world each time you replayed the action. Any man who has been in a war knows about replaying action, spends much of his time wondering what would have happened if only this tiny thing or that had been different, if only one man or maybe two had been here and not there, or done this and not that. It was not so much an allocation of blame or praise, more an analysis of the action and how things might have been. Regret was useless to a solider unless it tempered his decision for the better, unless it acted as a hone-stone to sharpen his will, refine his decision-making, push home the thrust the deeper.

He had watched the permutations of the pearl several times over. Once complete, it separated from its shell and rolled with its weight into the water, eventually falling back into the sandy base and disappearing. The oyster closed back in upon itself for a few moments, and then, by some unknown means, the whole scenario began again. Pytchley wondered if he watched it for long enough whether he would see the creation of a black pearl. He had seen them in India. They were the most treasured of things, like seeing one black swan amongst a flock of white, like finding one white swan amongst a flock of black.

'Major Pytchley?'

His concentration had been so focused he hadn't noticed Violena enter; hadn't heard her come to stand behind him. He realised he was stooping, straightened himself, saw the globe continue its turn without the slight brake of his fingers, moved its spin through Tripolitania into Ouaddai and Darfur, and then down to the tip of the Cape.

'Violena, what can I do for you?' His new foot squeaked in its shoe as he moved, the cork giving a little against the torque of his turn. Violena watched the globe for a moment, the pale skin of her neck glowing in its reflection, then with difficulty she lifted her eyes to his.

'I have made a mistake in the inventory.' She had hidden her hands in her apron but brought them out now, hooked a finger from one hand into the other. 'I thought it was only the Perspective Box which had been taken, but there is something else.'

Pytchley raised his eyebrows. He had lived at Astonishment Hall for almost four years now and had never known Violena Sedge to be wrong about anything, least of all to do with the exhibits.

'There is something else missing,' she persisted. 'It wasn't in the Weeems Society Room, so maybe that's how I missed it.' Violena was uncomfortable. She hated to have to say it, but she had neglected her duty; the missing box had left such an obvious gap that she had not looked much further. She knew as well as Pytchley that it was one thing to get into the Weeems Society Exhibition Room, for it was an old parlour room tacked on to the front of the Hall with an ancient back door, unused but for the thief's entrance; she knew also it was quite another thing to get into the rest of the house, which was separated from the outside world by another door, which she herself barred every night.

'It was in the corridor adjoining the Exhibition Room to the house, near the clock.' She found she had a lump in her throat, remembered seeing Finkel Hanka taking Huxby there, saw him guiding Huxby into a chair, holding his arm, easing him down, telling him there was time yet. She had carried on down the stairs and turned to the right wing of the Hall, hadn't wanted to intrude. Maybe if she had she would've noticed sooner, but she hadn't, and every time she had passed that corridor since, all she had seen was the empty chair where Leopold Huxby had sat the last time she saw him, looking as if time had rolled upon his shoulders like a stone.

'There was a salver there, you remember?' Violena was

standing beside him now and they both watched as the world spun slowly below them. He didn't remember. She went on, 'People used to put their cards in it just before they left.' She smiled a little, held her hand out to the spinning globe, felt a faint breath of warmth on the palm of her hand as it turned. 'They always hoped you'd pick them up and read through them, ask them to visit.'

Pytchley smiled a little too. Yes, he thought, they always did. People always wanted a little more. Astonishment apparently was not enough; they wanted to meet the man who owned it, even though so very little of this Hall was his. Even before the wars in India he had not been so very sociable, and when he came back and found his place here in this quiet valley, he had wanted sociability even less. Mostly he saw only Huxby and Violena; mostly he left the running of the Hall to them and the other few employees who scurried here and there amongst its rooms. It had been Huxby's job to sift his way through the visitors' cards. Pytchley knew Huxby enjoyed brushing company with these people, telling them of the exhibits and the Hall and of the famous Major Pytchley who had fought in the Mysorean Wars and come back home without his foot. But he never cared for such company himself. It was enough that he was passing the legacy of Weeems on to other people, letting them enjoy the things that he enjoyed so much. But he never actually wanted to meet them.

'I don't remember it,' said Pytchley simply. 'Is it important?'

Violena relaxed a little, let out a breath. 'Not really. It wasn't valuable, just plated metal. But I thought you'd want to know. It means someone was in the corridor that night, had moved out of the Exhibition Room itself. Maybe he really wanted to get into the Hall, maybe the Exhibition Room was just a diversion when he found he could get no further.'

Pytchley nodded. That was logical. Violena was usually logical. He admired her for it, enjoyed her company because of it. But what about the missing box? Why would anyone take something so bulky just on a whim? It seemed to him the thief came specifically for Orcutt's Perspective Box, and got exactly what he wanted. The puzzle was why. A missing salver from the corridor hardly seemed of account in comparison. Certainly not now Huxby had gone and Finkel Hanka murdered. That was something else he just couldn't fathom, and for an awful moment the tears welled up into his eyes and he feared he would cry. It hadn't been enough that he had already seen so many men die, or that he had served his country well; it hadn't been enough to turn his back on it all and come up here to try to do something good and worthwhile and gracious with the rest of his life. It hadn't stopped more men dying.

He thought of the report he'd had that morning of the boy who'd died in the bell tower of St Weonard's, the next valley down. No one had thought to tell him sooner, not with what had happened up at the Hall. St Weonard's was on the edge of his land, hardly a part of it. And anyway, it was a beacon. Perhaps it had just caught itself on fire. But then Ipsing Sansibar had said he'd seen the boy going into the beacon tower that afternoon, and no one had been surprised. He must have set the thing burning either by design or accident and then run off, because no one had seen him since. Or at least they hadn't, not until a couple of days later when the villagers were sure the embers were cool enough to rake away and they'd gone in to see what was left of bell and tower. It was only then they had found the guardroom door half burnt off its hinges and when they'd pushed it clear and levered up the rim of the fallen bell, only then had they found what little remained of the boy. He must have shut himself in the guardroom when he realised what he'd done, probably thought he would be safe there until the fire burnt itself out. Poor lad. Pytchley vaguely recalled the boy who'd had a back stiff as a shoe-brush. He remembered those watery blue eyes that had never seemed to blink. He couldn't remember the boy's name, wondered if he'd ever known it. He'd come to the Hall occasionally to do odd jobs, sleep in the hay-barn on a cold night, that much he knew.

The boy's mother had worked in the kitchens once, long before Pytchley had come here. Then she'd died, and nobody minded that the boy sometimes appeared and then disappeared just as quickly. Another grave in the churchyard, he thought, and saw the long line of Millicent Huxby's family and all their little crosses, and all the buried hopes and wasted flesh, and Leopold Huxby beginning to de-carcass from his bones and sink back into the earth. Just like the oyster-pearl that left its shell and buried itself for ever in the sand, thought Pytchley.

And then he did something he had never done before, and took Violena Sedge by the hand. He felt her flinch slightly at the unexpected contact but she didn't draw away. They both watched as Africa was replaced by the white wastes of Antarctica on into the desolated stretch of vast Pacific Ocean, marred only here and there by islands, many so small they had yet to be named or had names that no one but the discovering mariners knew.

'I've never really thanked you for all you do here,' said Pytchley. He was uncomfortable, his missing foot began to itch and he shifted his weight away from it. He cleared his throat and carried on. 'Nor said how sorry I am.'

He felt her fingers briefly spasm against his. He had signed so many letters of condolence, written so many names, cited so many acts of bravery, invented many such acts to give a decimated family at least something to hang their grief on to. This was too immediate for him, but looking at that deep dark ocean pass before him he managed to say the name. 'For Finkel Hanka,' he said, and let her hand fall away.

Violena was stiff beside him – just like that poor boy, he thought. She moved away, stood by the door.

'There's more,' he said, and could not bear to look at her eyes, lifted them instead to the top of her forehead, noticed for the first time a few wisps of grey in amongst the curve of her hair. 'I've had a letter from the County Authorities . . . obviously I corresponded with them immediately about Hanka. And they have responded quickly. They have appointed another valley constable. But he'll not be here for five or six weeks. They say there's nothing else they can do.' Violena did not move and he felt impelled to add the brief contents of that stark letter. 'They're short of men . . . the war . . . they have no one to spare . . . can do nothing else.'

She nodded once, put her hand to the latch.

'The salver,' she said quietly and her voice was unsteady even in those two words.

'It doesn't matter,' replied Jeremiah Pytchley, and for once, as he moved a little, watched her leave, even the cork in its new boot had nothing else to say.

The room was dark when Uwe Proctor Dvoshka woke, but then this room, this house was always dark. The windows seemed perversely faced away from wherever there was light. His hands and forehead were clammy with sweat. He was thirsty. He called out but no one answered. He caught at the blanket, which had wound about him as he slept, held him tight like an outgrown carapace, caused him to thrash and pant through a broken sequence of dreams. He called out again, his voice harsh as a heron's in the grey light. He realised he didn't know if it was night or day, saw that the fire had become cold ash, the lamp burnt out beside it on the cracked tiles of the hearth. He recognised the outline of the water pail standing beside the door, saw the glimmer of its lip where the door planks had warped and broken and a little light had crept in from the outside.

He unbound the blanket, tossed it to the floor, eased himself to sitting. He cursed the pain and bundle of his foot, which made it hard for him to move, managed to reach the stick he'd been using as a crutch and made a way across the detritus of the room. The pail was empty. The floor about it was slick with ice where the last of the water had seeped from the hairline crack in its base. Small crusts of spiders and flies flecked its surface, caught up from the cracks in the flagstones where they had lain a long time dead. He pulled at the door, which scuffed its foot against the floor and only grudgingly opened.

Uwe Proctor closed his eyes a moment, felt his skin withdraw from the scour of wind and sleet that swept at his collars, tried to tug the door back into its hole as the world outside spat menacingly in his face. He moved back a little, kicked the heavy stone forward with his good foot to prop the door and gazed out.

It must be early morning, he thought, could see a great raft of rooks lifting from the woods below but couldn't hear them. The sky was scudded over with grim grey clouds, a thunderhead shifting and sifting them as it swept above them, over them, driving them on to the east and the crags of Brougham. A pair of ravens spiralled with the thunderhead as it went, caught in its downward draught, taking advantage to survey the moors as they moved below them. A sudden scritch and scratch of straw as the wind lifted the thatch made Uwe kick away the stone and put his shoulder to the door to heave it closed. He shouldn't have done that. It had made him rest his weight upon his bad foot and it throbbed worse than before. He had broken three toes and snapped a foot bone, or so the doctor up at the works had said. Nothing for it but to strap the thing up and wait for the bones to grow themselves back together.

He felt immeasurably tired. His breath rasped at the back of his throat. The small journey across the cottage floor had worn him out and he hobbled over to his bed and sat back upon it, pulled the blanket from the floor and up around him. If only he had never come here, he could not help but think – but if not here, then where? And if not with Bellpenny, then with whom else? Who would want him now after what he had done? He could feel his pulse throbbing erratically at his temple and placed a hand upon his heart, tried to calm himself. No use thinking of times past, he thought, no use thinking of what he had lost, of how he had failed, of the guilt that turned within him like the worms that crawl beneath the bark of a tree, so small at first, but leading inevitably to rot and decay. He had to get away, to sort things through, to make amends, to carry on doing what he had been doing, to finish what he had started.

He hoped Bellpenny would be back soon. His tongue felt like a rasp within his mouth, his throat as rough and raw as a new-stubbled field. He closed his eyes again, too tired to keep them open to see the nothingness around him. He listened to the wind as it passed about, above the little cottage, made it hum. Like a bell, he thought, and wished he hadn't, like a bell just cracked from its kiln of clay that sings a little to be released, and murmurs softly before it cools and becomes still. There was so much to regret and so little point in doing so.

His hand patted at his jacket hidden beneath the blanket, felt for the small bulk of book he had kept with him all this while, that he had read since childhood, that his mother had given him, that he had carried with him, that had sustained him, inspired him. He had betrayed the book as well, he thought. How could he have ever thought it was otherwise? He had tried to rationalise his actions, to make them seem a small part of a bigger whole, but he knew now this was folly, and no matter how ill he had been, no matter how convinced he had been that he was doing right, fighting the good fight, in the end there could be no excuse, no reprieve. He had caused another human being's death and that was that. There could be no going back. He would do what he had to do and prayed God that Bellpenny would see him through and do as they had decided.

Down in the valley, the rooks, defeated, sank back into the trees and retook up their roost. There was nothing to do but wait until the day lifted the wind from them and let them rise. The ravens still hung outstretched below the thunderhead, a rainbow pillar on either side, had anyone lifted their eyes to look, had anyone seen through the mist and the morning to see what was there to be seen. All Uwe Proctor saw was that skating-rink of ice and the broken pail that stood amongst it, saw himself climbing the dark hulk of the Tunisian trading ship amongst the Black Sea mists. Even in sleep, the acid in his stomach curdled and burnt its way up his throat as he felt the weight of the ship churn through the Dardanelles and plough and lurch its overladen prow between the archipelago of the Aegean. By Malta, they were taking on water, the caulking corroded, scraped and weakened by the Black Sea ice. Before Sardinia, the crew threw all the passengers' luggage overboard to lighten the load. By Gibraltar, they'd ditched the journey and had to stop for repairs.

Uwe saw himself again wandering the ports at dawn, clutching all that was left to him, begging passage on anything that would take him. He'd ended up in Liverpool, sick with the sea and the journey, the intermittent fever that would not let him go, turning his feet to the north instead of his parental home, fixing the insane idea within him that he could purge himself and start again somewhere he wasn't known. All he heard was that voice again, shouting about home and the work to be had on the canals and in the mines, and getting away from the stinking pit that called itself Odessa, the drunken boasts of the convicts recently released from their labour, their plans and their schemes, and that one word, that one place: Eden, the man had yelled, that's where I'm from and where I'm going, and the whole place had erupted with laughter, the beer dribbling down their stubbled chins at the absurdity of it all.

Standing at the open door, Medan Skimmington Bellpenny looked at Uwe Proctor Dvoshka shivering on his chair. He saw the perspiration that had soaked his hair as if he'd had a long haul through the rain. He was gripping his stomach tightly and the skin on his knuckles was partridge-leg grey. He shifted the sack from his shoulder, let it rest in his hand as he knocked the door shut with his shoulder. He moved quietly, as had always been his way, felt an anger rise within him that now he was trying to be quiet for someone else's sake. But he didn't want to wake the sleeper. He didn't want him there at all.

His fingers itched to get at his work bench, to wield the tools he knew so well, heat up the little spirit lamp and set the crucible upon it, get the moulds mounted and ready for use. He wanted to pull out the secret drawer, which was fixed like a swallow's nest to the underbelly of the wood. Wanted to bring out his treasures and run his fingers over them, lay them out on every surface of the room, sit in his chair, watch the firelight leap all around him and bring to life every last curve of his perfect creation. Why he wanted it so badly he did not know, but that he wanted it was the only thing that drove him on.

10

The Road North

8 March

STROOP AND MABEL had had about as much of travelling in carriages as they ever wanted to do. They were riding the mailcoach from London to Darlington, which was the quickest way, but the most uncomfortable. The horses flew along, the froth flying from their mouths, flicking at anyone who put their head out of the open-sided landau, the driver chapping at them with whips to speed them on, the guard sitting behind, his pistol in his belt, occasionally taking erratic shots at hare he couldn't hope to hit just to relieve the boredom. The wheels crashed in and out of holes and ruts, and though they stopped at a coaching yard every twenty miles or so, it was only to change the horses and within a few minutes they were off again. Reading was impossible, talking impracticable, and the further north they got, the worse seemed to be the roads. Their baggage lurched and jumped where it was strapped on to the roof, the rain soaking through the cracks in the old leather suitcases and carpet bags Mabel had found mouldering in one of Stroop's ancient wardrobes. They had left the last London borough two hundred miles back and it was the furthest any of them had ever been. Even Stroop, who it transpired had travelled the least far of all, despite his tramps around London compiling his lists and maps and compendiums.

It had seemed at first like a holiday when they had set off and they had talked excitedly about where they had been before and discussed all the new things they were seeing now. Mabel had been from her father's farm by Epping into London, and back again on that disastrous day, though no one talked about that, and she had never been back since, had signed all the documents pertaining to the sale of the farm and the livestock through a lawyer known to Stroop.

Thomas had wound his way through many a London street and sewer, knew every backyard and bridge and outhouse where he could sleep or pinch a little food or fuel. No one mentioned his friend Toby, who had been with him since his early days at the poorhouse and who had died so horribly during the adventure that had brought them all together.

Strangely, it was Jack who knew most about what lay beyond the scatters of hamlets and village spires and greens that hemmed the loose townships of London. He had been hop-gathering with his mother since he was a small boy, picked apples and pears and cherries in the seasons, spent time on farms looking after byred cattle and goats and sheep over the winter months. He had astounded them all when they were nearing Cambridge and Thomas had shouted out the name of a signpost as they passed: 'Who'd ever go to a place called *Ugley*!' and Jack swore absolutely blind that he had been there once himself and it was the prettiest place he had ever seen, while Thomas swore back that no, Jack hadn't and why was he saying that he had? But Jack had always known what little he had known and he'd replied stoutly, 'I've been there, I know it and wait until we go on a bit and you'll see there's a place that sells all the geese.'

Jack had never been able to read, not till he'd met Mabel, and a year's learning hadn't done him much good at all, but he knew a picture of a goose when he saw it and even Thomas had to apologise when their coach drew into a staging post and they creaked down from their seats and unbuckled their legs while the horses were being changed, and they got leave to stretch themselves for a few minutes, and over behind the inn they saw three fields all wattled up with hedges and a sign still advertising 'The Ugley Goose Fair: Last Week in October.'

The geese had gone, as had October, but the droppings were still thick and green on the sparse brown grass, and the smell was just as Jack had remembered it, only not quite so strong.

'I told you!' He was triumphant as he ran through the fields, leaping over the lapsed and leaning wattle and hay-bale hedges, Thomas tearing along behind him, pelting his back with scoops of goose dung that Mabel had later to scrub from Jack's hair and coat and Thomas's hands up to his elbows. The coach driver called over, told them they were breaking for dinner for half an hour, food to be had at the inn.

'You've never heard a racket till you've been in a field with thousands and thousands of geese,' was Jack's opinion as they got stuck into a seriously goose-centred menu that made use of plum sauce and cherry-pickle stuffing and dumplings filled with parsley butter. 'They make such a clatter people think they've left their babies under the bushes they've been eating at.' Thomas spluttered on a wing, spreading grease right across his face from ear to ear, while Jack persisted, 'It's *true*! Isn't it, Mr Stroop?'

Stroop looked at those big asking eyes and his stomach tightened to realise that Jack had really had a life before Stroop had found him. Somehow he had thought that a boy like Jack, whom everyone knew had soup for brains, would recall nothing before that night when Stroop had torn him from the burning building that had taken his mother from him. He had never even talked to Jack about it and the neglect gave him such a jolt of guilt that he pushed his plate away. Mabel, however, leant over the table and patted Jack on the shoulder.

'You're right, Jack; my dad used to tell me that too,' and she smiled as Jack's grin left gravy dabs dribbling down his chin, though no one had ever told her any such thing.

'I *told* you,' said Jack without rancour, and even Thomas nodded his head and said, 'Yes, Jack, you did.'

11

And Further . . .

10 March

IT WAS AFTER three and getting dark, and they had followed the River Swale until it turned away from them to the west and Richmond. Stroop had the letter the Dvoshkas had given him spread out on his knees, his head leaning against the side of the coach, his eyes closed, his lips moving slightly, replaying every word of its narrative yet again.

Mabel leant forward and gently took it from him, held it to the window to catch the last of the light, tightened her stomach against the travellers' sickness, strained to make out the words.

It was more than hard to read, had been crossed, as so many were these days, to save on paper and postage. It was in two hands. The first, writing in the normal manner from left to right, was from Uwe himself. The second had been overwritten from bottom to top and it was this second message that had got the Dvoshkas so worked up. The original letter, addressed to 'My Parents' and signed with a single '*U*' had apparently been written on the morning Uwe was to leave his great-uncle's business on the Black Sea and return home. He had been ill, he explained, and had done a great wrong and would beg their forgiveness once he had returned to their home and given a full account of all that had happened to him since he had left. It was a simple letter, the words faint and exhausted, with most of their vowels missing.

It was the second message, which overwrote the first, that shocked with its bleak words, undisciplined as they were, scratched out like birds clawing at tree bark, and once or twice puncturing clean through the paper. Mabel looked at the letter again, tried to separate what was above from what was below, tried to guess who would have written it and why. She saw that unknown hand lift slightly, divide itself from the gentler phrases below, saw them like broken sticks afloat on a pond. There was no getting away from it. The words were clear. 'Yor boys klled sumwun.' And that was all there was to it. Short. Stark. The catch of a blackthorn spike as you put your hand out to pick the sloe.

Mabel laid the letter back on her lap. She felt sick and dizzy. She could see nothing they didn't already know. Stroop had examined the thing inside out, been ultimately more interested in the postage marks than the words the letter contained. He had found the boy who had delivered it to the Dvoshka home from the mail stop coffee house where it had been left, as were all the other letters for merchants who conducted their business from there. He had found the mailcoach on which it had arrived, tracked down the stamp on the letter's edge, indicating the main origin of dispatch as Darlington. There were several other marks left by more local mail stops, but he would not be able to find these out until he was in the direct vicinity. At this point, he had sent to the Dvoshka household and informed them he would agree to the parental request to find their son.

Within hours, the Dvoshkas had made arrangements and booked them passage, even sent a scout ahead to check the roads and report to the staging houses, make sure the fittest horses were waiting, mark out the best route and inns at which to dock them overnight. Soon Mabel was packing frantically and Thomas was hiding up Smoke Street to drag Jack back home, and the next morning, when it was barely light enough to see the cloud of starlings blackening the shadows of the church opposite the ostler's yard, they had all piled into the waiting coach and been driven away to only Stroop knew where.

Bellpenny too had been busy with his plans, or rather, the first stage of his plans, which was to get the boy out of his house. A few miles away to the north, the heave and pull of the canal works was starting to fill the cold bleak air of the moors with shouts and swears and the girning of men as they started to load the barrows with spoil, and balance them on the planks that served as runways up the deep sides of the cutting. At the top, the horses were being led from their stockyards of spoilt straw and meagre oat-bags, and slung over with harnesses; from them led ropes that fitted through the pulleys and these were hooked to the barrows, pulling them up the greasy walkways, while men balanced them from below, fighting to keep their footing. The light curse of snow had slowed up proceedings and made the tempers of the foremen worse where they stamped their way along the banks, shouting at the workforce skivvying fifteen feet below. Everyone knew they were getting pushed for time. This open stretch of dig-and-haul needed to be done by the time the snow properly set in, and it was plain from the heave of the clouds rolling in from north and east that this would be soon. Then they would shift to the tunnel that had already been blown into the hillside up above, and shafts drilled down through the rock to provide the men below with air. A simple rail-track had been laid to remove the brick and fill, and this would occupy the men through the weeks before the thaw and the weather would allow them back out into the sun. It was the hardest job any man could do, as every last one of the workforce knew, including those shacked up in the hospital tent with broken legs and hips and hands snapped off at the wrist from the barrows slipping back on the planks, or a sudden fall from a poorly shored side of cutting, or a badly mixed batch of gunpowder and blow.

It was here that Uwe Proctor Dvoshka had gone to seek out the man he had briefly known in the mines of Odessa, and who had shouted out the name of the place where he had lived. Uwe hadn't been daunted by the din and clamour of the workings, had found the sound of it spreading over the hillsides strangely comforting: the hard clang of pickaxe and spade against stone, the muffled thuds of explosions, the scrape and scud of pulley and horse. He'd heard all this before, lived all this before, a thousand miles away, and what seemed like a hundred years ago. Bellpenny knew it all too, and for both of them it had been the barren shores of the Black Sea where scenes like this had played themselves out every time a new city was built. They had talked it between them many a time, their throats going raw from the rough starch wine Medan brewed from sourdough and corn, set outside in the snow pockets to press out the alcohol from the ice. They had listened to the wind brushing through the scratch of hedge at the back of the cottage, keening through the holes of the stonewalls that had once sheltered black-faced sheep, their curlicued horns scraping bas-reliefs into the dyke sides against which they huddled. Medan had rolled his cigarettes, watched the smoke sidle at the ceiling, gather in corners and cobwebs waiting for the loose-windowed draughts to set it free. Just like he had thought to be so many years earlier, when he'd caught news of the adverts and flyers that had been plastered across the British press from Plymouth to Carlisle.

Workers were wanted, any kind, every kind, to join the already large colony of Englishmen in Novorussia under patronage at first of Potemkin, and then, after his death, of his consort, Ekaterina the Great, in Potemkin's memory. They wanted to create a New Empire in their recently acquired and hard-won lands, to turn the Crimea into the garden of their wealth. They wanted shipbuilders to promulgate the Russian fleet along the shores of the Black Sea, and Potemkin had known that the English shipbuilders were the best. He wanted woodworkers and fabricators, architects and engineers, canal-diggers, bridge-erectors, geologists and miners. His own estates at Kirchev had been riddled with his foreign employees, and he wanted to forge out cities from Kiev all down the Dnieper, reaching right to the swamp-soaked backwaters of the Crimea. The Turks had signed the peace, and half the Black Sea was his and Ekaterina's, and they meant to keep it. And that meant ships, and cities, and trade. Even when Potemkin died, his legacy went on and the money kept pouring in and the buildings still went up and names had to be found for the new towns and cities of Novorussia. And the English set off to find their fortunes, Bellpenny being among them. Thirteen years later, Uwe Proctor Dvoshka, who was almost there anyway, went too.

12

Paths that Cross

10 March

A BODY IS not made for this, thought Stroop as the carriage set off again. It was all he could think. Everything else was gone. He might have been an apple in a cider press for all the comfort he felt. Every bone in his body felt bruised, and looking across at Mabel, he did not need any cryptic cross-written letter to know she felt the same. Their bodies were as creased and dirty as were their clothes.

Thomas and Jack, on the other hand, had had no finer adventure and got livelier by the day. They had taken to sitting up top with the driver or the guard, both of whom seemed to enjoy the company, and though looking like three-day-crumpled pie-paper, were apparently happier than pigs escaping Smoke Street.

Stroop tried to concentrate, tried to think of the Dvoshkas and the son they had not seen for so long, tried to take his mind off his discomfort by memories of his own family. He had felt some previously unencountered pang when Mabel had dragged that old carpet bag down from what had once been his sisters' room, saw his mother packing it up with his sisters' clothes, then taking them all out again one by one and putting them back in the cupboard, hanging on to a last memory, a last scent and stitch of children now lost and dead. And they were all dead: sisters, brothers, parents. But if he was honest, it was all so long ago that they were less real to him now than his ledgers and his lists.

His memories were halted suddenly as, without warning, a wheel caught and rolled itself deep into a pothole. The horses pulled and pawed against the strain but no matter how hard the driver whipped there was no pulling the coach out of it. Stroop groaned, and Mabel groaned with him. Another stop, another hold-up in a journey that had seemed never-ending.

'All down!' came the by now familiar cry, as he and Mabel creaked out of the coach and stood crook-legged in the mud of the lane. Mabel was flushed and pale all at the same time. Her hat had fallen back on to her neck, her hair birling about in the wind, her head nodding like a sunflower, six inches of clay hardening on her dress hem, making it difficult for her to move.

Stroop held out his hand and she took it and smiled, but he could see she was exhausted. I shouldn't have brought her, he thought, then remembered how much she had begged him to take her and the boys with him, though at first he had proposed to go the journey alone. It was the leaving-behind she couldn't bear, and neither could the boys, and so he'd brought them all with him anyway.

It had seemed so logical in London: chase down the

postmark, find the man who had sent the letter, for obviously it hadn't been Uwe. The words he had penned had been done at some previous time, before he had disembarked on his journey home. Someone else had got hold of his letter and scrawled the damning message that had brought the Dvoshkas to Stroop's house and hence Stroop himself on this foolhardy trip to the north and here, and these horses, and this abominable wilderness that other people still called England, though not he. He couldn't say how much he longed to be back in Eggmonde Street in his little house, by the inglenook, his books and his maps spread out comfortingly on the large table, Mabel making tea in the kitchen, singing soft songs he had never known.

His disengagement from his home had brought at first a tingle of excitement, a desire, a curiosity to see places that were not his own. It had not lasted long, that scientific examination. The further they had travelled – and he was ashamed to say it, had not said it – the more frightened he had become. And now, as he glanced outward at the bleakness of the moors that rolled away from his feet like the sea, he couldn't stand the not-knowing of where he was, that he couldn't recognise the terrain or make out one bare plant from another, that he didn't know where upon the map a pin should mark his place. There was nothing that smelt familiar. He couldn't close his eyes and say, 'I am near the fishmongers in Causington Street,' or 'I am almost certainly by the wharf where the costers do their trade.' He hated it. He hated this journey for making him hate it. He felt a shame underlying it all, as they stood there by the cart with its broken spindle or shaft or spoke or whatever the hell it was. Stroop felt it properly for the first time in his life, despite all that he had seen and been through. He was untethered. He was terrified, and ashamed of it, and he wanted to go home. And then he saw Mabel, saw her standing as unrooted as he was, felt her hand in his, asking for guidance, or maybe giving it, and together they ricocheted away from the coach and the rucks and racks of the supposed road.

'Not to worry,' Mabel said, gave his hand a quick squeeze, might have seen all that had passed through his head and slackened his heart. 'We've come this far, Mr Stroop. We might as well go on.'

She'd got that right. Stroop couldn't even contemplate the idea that they would have to do all this again just to get home. He smiled, tried to give her a little bit of the comfort she had given him, and then Jack and Thomas came wheeling round the carriage side at them, hurtling more mud on to Mabel's already ruined skirts and what was left of Stroop's smart London coat.

'Bet I can get that out!' shouted Thomas, brandishing a stout stick he must surely have pinched from the last resting house, seeing as they appeared to be surrounded by nothing but uninhabited moorland without a tree in sight, at least not one that wasn't bent over at the waist from a hundred years of battering wind.

Then Jack was running round them like a sheepdog. 'Just you see, Mr Stroop, Thomas'll fix it. He's getting taught from the driver. Says he's going to make a job of it when he's older and you see if he don't!'

Stroop sighed, still holding Mabel's hand. Her glove was so grubby it might have been used for digging up beetles.

He remembered briefly, in the graveyard garden last spring, walking past a molehill, seeing the top crown of earth shift and move, shift and move, shovelled from below by unseen claws. He had stopped and stared, knelt down, but the vibrations of his footsteps had arrested the old velvet-breeks in its work and after a few minutes Stroop had left, still looking behind him in case the mole started up again, but it hadn't, and Stroop had walked away. It had got him to wondering about all the things that scurried quietly below our feet without our knowing it, beneath the thin scab of earth that separates our own reality from theirs, the tunnels and warrens that wove themselves one around the other, going up, going down, intersecting, veering off, a loose-knit labyrinth that contained a hundred thousand different ways of living. Who knows what lies beneath? he'd thought then, and he thought it again now, about Thomas, about Jack. Then he felt Mabel's warm hand in his own, saw Thomas levering at the wheel with the coach-driver, heard Jack repeating all the words the coach-driver made, hoped he wouldn't remember a single one. My God, he thought, what did I do before I knew them all? And what would I do now without them?

It was an existential thought too far, and luckily he didn't have time to contemplate it further. A horse was pounding down the lane towards them, the rider hunkered down about the horse's neck to keep his eyes clear of the mud that drove up from hoof and track, his cape drawn tight about his body, caught by the thick band of his belt.

'Whoah up! Whoah up!' called the man as he hauled the horse short of the abandoned coach. He hardly waited until the animal had stopped before he was launching himself out of the saddle. He dropped the reins and came straight towards Stroop, splashing through the mud as if it had been a levelled road in some respectable town.

'Mr Whilbert Stroop?' he said and waited for the nod he apparently knew would come. 'If I can beg your leave, I've a message from Major Pytchley. A carriage is following on behind me, and if you would allow it, arrangements have been made to take you to Astonishment Hall.'

PART 2

VALLEYS AND CAVES

1

The Valley

10 March

'OH MY LORD!' breathed Mabel, kicking off the remnants of her wet boots, not bothering to disengage the laces that had been tangled into unfathomability by the hard travelling of days.

'Quite,' agreed Stroop, peeling off layers of wet-wool coats and capes, and a hat with earflaps that had slapped at his face and sucked in the rain that seemed to have been falling on him since leaving London.

'Where's Jack?' he asked, and Mabel merely flapped a hand that said, *who cares?* and made Stroop smile and finish off his own sentence: 'With Thomas, of course, and where will Thomas be?'

'With the horses!' they said together, and Mabel grimaced to think of the stink and stain she would have to wash off their clothes. Or maybe not. She opened her eyes a little wider as she thought that perhaps a place like this actually had people who would do that sort of thing for you. After all, she'd never had to wash her own clothes at Great-Aunt Flora's. That had been Elsa's job. She blinked. Tried not to think but the words came to her anyway. Poor Elsa. Poor Aunt Flora.

Poor Mabel, thought Stroop looking over at her, pouring a large brandy into a glass that might have held a pint of porter. 'Have a sip of this,' he said, and pushed it into her hands. His thumb brushed her fingers. How cold they are, he thought, then pushed the thought away as he poured another drink for himself. This was something he would have to get the hang of while they were here. Different glasses for different drinks. He wondered where the normal glasses might have been hidden, but not for long. At least the bottle of brandy had been obvious enough, and the lodge neatly ordered: a small comfort room as soon as you entered the door, a tiny kitchen to one side, a larger room to the other and two rooms no bigger than a bed would allow tacked on to the kitchen. Servants' rooms, he knew and was aware that this Major Pytchley had levered out one of his more important guests to make way for them. He hadn't met the major yet, but he liked him already for having done such a thing. The workings of the Hall had been explained to him as they had left the uncomfortable confines of the mailcoach for the padded carriage Major Pytchley had sent, followed by the luxury of the paddle-driven steamer that had taken them up the canal to Astonishment.

Astonishment. That had described it with no doubt at all. One minute they had been standing knee-deep in mud with only the prospect of watching Thomas's evident glee as he flourished his stolen stick and slipped in the mud puddles surrounding the stuck wheel to cheer them, the next they had been invited into a sumptuous landau with pull-up, pull-down windows, upholstered seats laden with cushions, and less than an hour later they had been escorted on board an elegant steam-paddled barge and brought to the comfort of Astonishment Hall. Their wet baggages had been taken from them and replacement clothes were even now warming for them in front of a lavish fire. Thomas and Jack had screamed off into the late afternoon, so excited they didn't care what they were wearing, and now here were Stroop and Mabel, getting ready to meet their rescuer and a good dinner whenever they saw fit to make the time.

'So who's this Major Pytchley?' Mabel asked, delighted to be snuggled into a large-armed chair, hugging her brandy, wrapped round with a warm eiderdown, which took off the chill.

Stroop took a long gulp of his own drink, thanked God for alcohol and the comfort it gave, wriggled his feet into the fleece-lined slippers that had been provided, and sat down on the other side of the fire.

'I gather he tried to engage our services while we were in London but missed us by minutes,' he supplied, quoting what he had been told by the mysterious horse-rider sent to fetch them here. 'He has a problem of his own he would like us to solve, and given the nature of both enquiries, it seems they might not be entirely unrelated.' He ran the brandy round the glass. It wasn't quite as satisfying as having it run round the bowl of a proper brandy glass, but in the circumstances he didn't care a whit. 'You mind we'd left a message with the neighbours as to our sudden leaving, and at the usual coffee house in case business came up while we were gone?'

Mabel nodded, letting the brandy burn her lips, forgetting the near-constant nausea of the past few days.

'Apparently,' continued Stroop, 'the major's messenger sent messengers. One man on horseback can travel twice as fast as a coach and, having learnt we had already left London for the north, he hied on after and got here before us. I must say,' Stroop's writing hand twitched a little as he mused, 'this mail-and-message industry is something I must pursue.'

He began to wonder about how long it had taken Uwe's letter to reach his parents, and how long the earlier letters had taken to reach London, travelling as they must have done across vast miles of land or sea, whether they had come by official mail-boats or through merchants or . . .

'Mr Stroop?' Mabel prompted. 'You were talking about Major Pytchley?'

'Ah yes,' Stroop recollected himself, but first held up his hand and put down his glass. Mabel waited as he extracted a soggy-covered notebook from his pocket, pulled up the telescopic pencil from its spine, unrolled it, licked it, made a quick note, reversed the process, replaced the book, then carried on, 'There have been strange happenings at Astonishment.'

Mabel tried to raise an eyebrow. It was a talent she didn't possess but was eager to learn.

'Firstly, there was the burglary of an unusual item, secondly came the murder of the valley constable.'

They were both a little subdued by the use of the word. Murder was something neither of them particularly wanted to be acquainted with again. Still, they were hundreds of miles away from London and a year past all that had gone, so both of them, after a simultaneous and prolonged glance at the floor, tacitly agreed to carry on.

'What happened?' Mabel asked. She hadn't been privy to the conversation between Stroop and the messenger, as they now called him, once they had alighted on the barge. She had been so incredibly relieved to be able to stand up and walk and move about, even in her wet and sluggish skirts, that she hadn't given a curse as to the reason they had been so summoned. She had leant on the rails, gazed entranced at the wonder of hills whose height she could never guess at, had never seen, the otter-slick line of the canal upon which they rode, the dark back of the river that sometimes ran beside them, sometimes not. She worried about weirs and rapids but they never came, could not fathom how the lock system worked, the gradual lifting or lowering of the waters as they waited in their wooden box, gloried in the absolute wilderness once more released. She had never seen anything like it, had never seen such a vastness of land all around her, not the fields nor the hedge-trimmed pastures she had been used to seeing at Epping, but huge and sinister moors that stretched on for ever with no shepherd or sheep nor cattle or goats. She wondered how people made a living from such a hostile land, wondered at how sparse were the houses, how blue was the smoke from their chimneys, how strange and low were the shape of their cots, how the snow seemed to lie in every shadow.

I am so far away, she had thought, from everything, and she had moved round the rails a little as the steam began to touch her face, obscure her vision. She ended up gazing back down the valley from which they had come. Another adventure, she had thought, and, oh God, I hope it's not like the last one. At that, she had tugged badly at the ribbons that tied her hat to her head. This is the wrong hat, was the last thing she had thought. I should have brought another. And then the barge had come alongside a small platform, and she had seen the big, painted hand.

'This Way to Astonishment,' it read, and, as always, it had not been wrong.

Mabel and Stroop had been brought up to the Hall. They had been taken past the yew hedges and the violated door, since mended. They hadn't been shown the Exhibition Room, nor had they seen any of the lodge sights. They had dressed themselves in the clothes that had been provided and felt uncomfortable, ill-fitted, though the clothes had been guessed at a reasonably correct size. Mabel had had to ask Stroop to tie her dress at the back, which had embarrassed them both. Back at home, Mabel had front-tied dresses, or Jack did them and nobody minded if he'd got the ties a bit wrong. But here they were in company. Good company. Mabel had forgotten almost everything her great-aunt had tried to teach her as she had been introduced to these new people. She hoped her unbalanced curtsy had gone unnoticed, had winced a little inside when the woman called Violena Sedge had practically levered her up from where she had gone down too far to the floor.

Stroop though, seemed fine, she noticed. He must be used to this by now, she thought. Since their last débâcle – she had no other word to describe it – Stroop had been highly sought after, his name much advocated amongst the merchant class, which was of course how the Dvoshkas had heard of him, and even this man who sat before them now.

'Forgive me, Mr Stroop,' Pytchley said, then turned rather abruptly towards Mabel, 'Miss Flinchurst.'

Mabel blushed. She didn't know whether to stand up or bow or what. Her Great-Aunt Flora had only prepared her for balls and this wasn't one of them. She had half-risen in her seat when she felt an arm on her own. It was the other woman, Violena Sedge.

'Please, sit down,' she had said, and Mabel had done as she had been told. Something about her, she thought, something about this woman . . . but then Pytchley began to speak.

'No doubt you are wondering why I have asked you here, practically kidnapped you.' He looked around, smiling, but as both Stroop and Mabel saw, this was not a happy smile. This was a man who had much on his shoulders and for him, smiling didn't come with ease.

Mabel took a quick look at Violena Sedge; knew immediately the clothes she was wearing were hers. Violena was taller, slimmer; Mabel knew she had never managed to adjust to her great-aunt's ideal form. She would always be Mabel: born on a farm, wears like a farm. Only the corsets had managed to force her into the image her great-aunt had wanted. And here was Violena Sedge, a woman who quite obviously never needed corsets even if she allowed them. There was no rigidity to this woman; a tight control, certainly, but also a softness beneath. Mabel had felt it first when Violena had shepherded them into the lodge. Just like her great-aunt, she had thought. Then: oh God, stop. It's gone. Stop thinking of it. Then Violena had said, 'Please, make yourself comfortable. I've put a dress out for you if you want it. It's dry, but please don't, if you don't think it will be right.' And then she had left them, had known they were too tired and wet to go through the pantomime of pleasantries and chit-chat, didn't seem the kind of woman to enjoy such things anyhow, whoever they might have been. But the dress had been sort of right, a dim colour, not bright or fussy, and Mabel had been suddenly, horribly, confused as she tried to put it on – it was a little too slim, a little too long, a little too elegant.

And the woman confused her too: she comforted her yet intimidated her, seemed to represent all that was around her; and all that was around Mabel was a huge landscape of a kind she didn't know. Its emptiness frightened yet excited her, gave her an itch to get out and explore as she had once done so long ago at Epping. She'd felt the same clammy trepidation when she'd followed her brothers when they'd gone hunting in the forest, the awful anticipation on entering the dark sigh of the unknown; then trees, now drawing rooms and people, and probable plots she felt ill-equipped to fathom or to face.

She looked up now and saw Violena gazing at her, saw the slight crinkle of the other woman's forehead, one eyebrow slightly lifted as she had never been able to do. She poured a cup of tea from the set laid out on the table in front of her, handed it to Mabel, just as her great-aunt used to do, as she herself used to do for her father. A sister, she thought, I think I would have liked one. But then someone was speaking and she held her cup and saucer tight, tried to listen, tried not to slop her tea, tried to act as she had been taught to do, knew that, above all, she did not want to embarrass herself or Mr Stroop in front of this Violena Sedge.

'We have a problem,' Pytchley laid it out before them all, 'and I have heard you are a man who solves them, Mr Stroop. It seems you are quite famous, and I have many contacts in London, mainly through Weeems people and the Society. They recommended you, I tracked you down, heard you had left and decided to intercept. It was quite a surprise to learn that you were anyway on your way north.'

Pytchley closed his eyes briefly, leant down, ran his finger around the collar of his boot as if it were too tight or the stocking had rucked. Mabel wondered for a second at the awkward angle of his foot, but he had already begun to continue. 'I know,' Pytchley went on, 'that you have your own investigation to conduct, but I can't, I won't believe, knowing what I now know of them, that these occurrences are unconnected. We have a theft, we have a murder. You have a missing man and an accusation. Judge, Mr Stroop, are the two things not one? Is this not what you do? Make connections between the obvious and the seemingly absurd? Between things which seem at first at odds and then become entangled? Is this,' he repeated, 'not what you do?'

He was right, thought Stroop, that was exactly what he did. But here? Where were his Sense Maps, his Lists? His certainty in what he was doing? He was unsure now, unsure of what he was supposed to do; but he was here, and goddamned if he was doing that journey again without having something to show for it. He made a decision.

'I think,' said Stroop, putting down his cup and saucer,

'that you are right and that you had better tell me exactly what has been going on.'

'That I will do,' nodded Pytchley, 'but first I think we had better go in to dinner.' He nodded at Violena Sedge, who stood and rang the small bell attached to a wall sash. 'And,' Pytchley continued as he took up his cane and levered himself to his feet, looked briefly at the empty-eyed window, 'there is someone else arriving whom I think you must meet.'

Soon after dark, Bellpenny led Uwe away from the cottage and out on to the moors. They held their side-shuttered lanterns close to their feet to make out their way. Uwe saw little, but followed the treads of Bellpenny's boots, the sound of him coughing every now and then like a sheep. Bellpenny had tied a rope around Uwe's waist to keep him close and on track, but though he tried to slow his impatient pace, it was still uncomfortable for Uwe, who was jarred and jabbed with pain each time he moved his injured foot. They had made a protective shoe for him by nailing a sawn-off clog on to the base of another one, so that when he put his foot to the ground, only the heel and ball made contact, and not the broken toes. From the blackthorn hedge behind the cottage, they had selected a stick shafted at right angles and made of it a crutch.

Uwe had also been numbing his body with regular doses of corn-starch wine throughout the day, so that while not incapacitated, he was at some distance removed from reality. It was a trick he had learnt from the work crews whilst he was deep down inside the Odessan catacombs, practising his acoustic experiments. Some of the prisoner gangs lived down there for weeks at a time, hacking away at the soft limestone with their pickaxes, shaping it into blocks, loading it on to trucks. Up above them, on the cliff top, the city of Odessa was rising from its hollowed-out bones, and on every wall of every new building, on every new-planned street, the imprint of long-dead seas could be seen: the rims of empty, fossilised limpets, the swirl of snail-shells, the coruscations caused by ancient flakes of nacre and the flash of fishbone catching at the light. Architects held out their plans and erected their theatres and factories and churches; their labourers built their own small shacks during the evening hours on narrow walkways – small pockets of Greeks and Armenians, Germans, English, French, Jews, Russians and Dutch. And beneath their feet, other men burrowed their way through the soft stone like wasps through damp bark, hacking out the bricks and raw materials for the freemen's city. The heat was intense and there was no ventilation to cool the sweat from their bodies as they heaved their tools through the dark, and the dust was palpable in the air, so thick at times it sometimes doused their lights. And then the labourers would lean back against their labyrinth walls and unstrap the bottles from their belts, pull out the stoppers with their teeth, and take swift relief from the rough alcohol that was their constant companion.

This was where Uwe had first met Medan Skimmington Bellpenny, though he hadn't known it. He had stumbled across the convict work-gang where they sat like moles in a nest with all their lights gone out. A fall of rock from an unguarded roof had sent the whoosh of grit and dust through the tunnels up to a hundred yards distant. The men had hunkered to the ground, held their sleeves across their mouths and noses, waited for the air to clear a little, to let them catch their breath, relight their lamps, continue their bone-breaking work.

Uwe had been in one of the small rooms that formed the joining point of several tunnels. Sometimes such rooms were deliberately hollowed back into the rock to form a chamber for the men to rest or sleep or eat in. There had even been a chute executed for a latrine, though that had now been filled in with rubble and was only detectable by the faint trace of urine and rotting excrement that lingered in the air, like seaweed left too long on a beach. The catacombs were dark and frightening places, but after Uwe's first visit, his eyes skinned, his skin clammy and scared, he knew he had found what he sought. For acoustic chambers they were perfect. And he could carry out his experiments in peace. Mould his bells, test their timbres and resonance shifts, their effects upon his chosen subjects.

He had set up his equipment in this particular chamber, having already tapped the circumference of the walls with his hammer, as he had done several others previously, determined that this was the most suitable for his purpose. He had set up his moveable kiln in one corner, and scraped the floor flat in another. The rest of the space was used for the erection of his scaffold, and to this he attached the collars that would hold his bells. The weirdest part of the set-up, should anyone have cared to look, was perhaps the crates that lined every spare inch of wall, or rather, not the crates, but what they carried on their backs in the manner of turtles carrying their young. They were littered over with jars of varying sizes, each one fitted with a sheet of muslin at its neck and topped by a cork.

In the absolute black that followed the rock-fall, Uwe experienced a darkness so abysmal the universe might have been sucked into a pebble and thrown into some bottomless well, and the only sounds to be heard were the scrabbling of tiny feet against the glass of the jars, the tippy-tappying of antennae tasting their prison, the chafing of chitin as wing-cases shuffled and rubbed, folded and unfolded in their captivity. And the quiet, gentle pittering of the dust as it settled over every surface, assuring the blinded captives in their tunnels and their jars that gravity still existed, and thus existing, so must the world.

He had crawled about on his hands and knees, trying to locate a lamp, a candle, anything which might relieve the utter dark, and found himself in one of the tunnels, not knowing which way was forward and which was back. He heard the men coughing some way forward, thrust his blind way towards them, found them sitting, swigging, swearing, laughing. When he returned a quarter-hour later to his own cave with an escort and their borrowed lamp, he found the darkness he had left to be speckled with dimly glowing points of light, faint lines of luminescence glowing green and sickly within the glass, the backs of the locusts spitting back out the light that they had hoarded with such secrecy. The unexpected wonder of it had made his eyes shine, set his heart beating a little quickly, so that he had to hold out a hand and steady himself against the lime-white walls. He felt as if it were he that pulsed and not his captives, and by it, his resolve strengthened. Not that he had ever wavered in his aims; that his experiment might fail had not occurred to Uwe, neither then nor in the following months of planning and casting and convincing the farmers of its worth, soliciting their permission and the investments needed to carry his work to its end.

Not until the time had come to erect his scaffolds and towers and bells across the plains that made up the hinterland behind the new city of Odessa did he realise the enormity of his miscalculations, the folly of his ambitions, the devastation that had followed in the wake of his hubris, as surely as gannets follow the break of herring shoals upon the surface of the sea. He had betrayed the trust that had been placed in him, had shattered it like an earthquake will do to a tessellated floor, the tiles upheaved, the meaning of its patterns and its colours for ever gone.

Uwe thought of all these things as he limped across the miles of moor, stump-footing behind the only friend he had left in the world. He thought of where he was going, where he had asked to go, where Medan had grudgingly agreed to take him.

Bellpenny had told him of the old chalk pit where the miners had once scooped out the soft rock to help line the early canal cuttings, the only chalk for hundreds of miles, the pit practically exhausted before it had begun, scoured back to the bare granite of its walls. It had seemed perfect to Uwe, who knew his history of habitations, knew that thousands of years before, men had dug holes into these lenient parts of the landscape, first for traps and storage, and sometimes to live in safety, overlooked by their enemies, who trampled the heather and crowberry overhead, until the original occupants of the land had been exterminated.

He had explored some of the ice-caves to be found near Orava, discovered by his forebears in their search for the silver and copper with which to make their bells and a hundred other useful implements. He knew of the skulls and skeletons that had been found in such ancient underground homes, not just thrown there for burial, but carefully urned in niches dug out from the walls, surrounding the fire-holes and sleeping platforms excavated for the long-term living, the heaps of animal bones and broken arrowheads set aside or dug into pits where later occupiers found them just as they had been left. He had visited the karst caves of the Carpathians, their funnel-shaped dolinas leading to shafts more than one thousand feet in length, sunk deep beneath the maize fields of Slovakia, sometimes exceeding a ten-yard depth. He could not imagine what it might have been to live with the drip-stone stalactites to form your roof, and the sintercup rivulations upon the floor sharp enough to split your heelbone in two should you step on them. He also knew that back in those times when men had really made them their abode, such geological wonders had not yet been afforded the hundreds of years of abandonment they would need to fully form, but the science of it only greatened his awe.

It was fitting then, thought Uwe, that this was where he should spend the time of his regret, in hope of his redemption. It would remind him of Orava, his mother's family's home and the place to which he went to be apprenticed; and of the Odessan mines where he had thought to change the world. And perhaps it would serve to teach him of the time that boy had spent locked in the bell tower that Uwe himself had burnt, not knowing the boy would burn with it. Bellpenny had told him all, and he could not forgive himself. Would not forgive himself. He would spend his seclusion from the world in contemplation of what he had done. He could not correct the mistakes that he had made, nor bring back the tower nor the bell, nor the boy whom he had so uselessly incinerated. But perhaps he could learn something before he gave himself back up to the world and confessed what he had done. Perhaps he could earn himself some time, complete the little book he had promised to his parents, make something worthwhile of the life that he was left.

2

Dogs and the Moon

Evening, 10 March

As they went into dinner, Mabel was surprised at how pleasantly informal the whole household appeared to be. Jack and Thomas had been sent for, and came in with a great plate of cheese and biscuits, which was put on the table alongside the several silver-domed platters that were already there. They also brought with them the predictable smell of straw and horse, at which Violena's nose twitched, but she did not mention.

'Awful fine lot of ponies,' said Thomas as he sat down at random next to Pytchley, closely followed by Jack.

'Is it soup, Mabel?' Jack had asked hopefully, just as he always did at home, seemingly unable to learn that it was always soup, already picking up his spoon in anticipation.

'I think so,' said Mabel, glancing nervously at Stroop, her cheeks a little pink, 'and then, like as not, some meat.'

She wasn't embarrassed by Jack, although he was sometimes embarrassing. He had a naïvety about him that appealed to almost everyone, and neither Stroop nor Mabel nor Thomas would ever be ashamed about that. It was the other guest that had Mabel blushing, bowing to her shortly as he was introduced, shaking hands with Stroop.

'Maximillian Orcutt,' explained Pytchley, and Mabel felt a small tingle as his dark eyes rested on her for a moment. And then she saw the look he gave Violena, and Mabel knew of a sudden that she was too young, too inexperienced, that she would never have what Violena had. And she hated herself for it.

The conversation was general at first: brief enquiries of Stroop on the latest political news from London, more detailed questions about the Lucchese affair, which had first alerted Pytchley to Stroop's existence, and his possible use up here at Astonishment. Then had followed a bizarre exchange between Orcutt and Thomas about the treadmills to be found in several London workhouses, trodden round and round by the inmates to no apparent purpose. Orcutt couldn't believe the power thus produced wasn't used for grinding corn or some other such activity, to which Thomas had replied that the flour would be filled with all the lice and fleas that fell from the men's clothing as they stomped the treadmill round. This had started Orcutt calculating the size of mesh that should be fixed between the paddles to stop such a problem, and Violena had offered the solution of a giant hairnet.

The arrival of ice cream and raspberry sauce had Jack jumping from his seat with rapture, tugging at Mabel's sleeve and begging that she make it for them back at home. It was the first time she had tasted ice cream too, but here enthusiasm was cut short when Violena explained how long it took to make, churning the creamy custard in the ice-barrel. Orcutt wondered if he could not devise a chemical coolant to do the job much more efficiently, and laughed greatly when Pytchley challenged him to make a working model.

'After I've made a moon-dog,' he had said mysteriously, and the look he cast at Violena made a sudden heat rise to Mabel's throat and she had to turn her head away.

The meal was over, and Pytchley folded his napkin into a neat oblong, laid it slowly on the table. 'The time has come for business, I think,' he said, and led the way back to his study, where he stoked up the fire, pulled the chairs a little closer to the hearth.

Outside, the wind scratched at the windows and a heavy sleet fell against the glass, ran down it in dark rivulets like miniature canals. Violena drew the heavy velvet curtains against the draughts, set the tasselled bell-pulls shimmering in the light from the fire. For Jack and Thomas, she unfolded a small table to reveal a backgammon board and after patiently explaining the rules five times over, they had embarked on an erratic game that soon descended into some weirdly three-dimensional variant of fox-and-geese, which had them laughing and shouting and utterly captivated.

The others sat around the inglenook, and Violena poured them drinks. Pytchley sat down heavily in his chair, fiddled with his foot and set it on a small stool. He then laid out to Stroop all that had been happening at the Hall, and Stroop sat with pen and paper on his knee, listened to everything and made his notes and lists, set out some rough conclusions and a rougher plan.

3

The Cave

Night, 10 March

UWE PROCTOR DIDN'T know the game of fox-and-geese. If he had done, he would have known that though the geese are many, in the hands of a skilful player it is almost always the single fox that wins.

At about the same time that Stroop was scribbling and Jack and Thomas were setting up for another game, Medan Bellpenny was unstrapping the rope from Uwe's waist and wrapping it tight about the bole of an old hawthorn, its branches sweeping down almost to the ground. In Russia they called them running-trees, the winter gales having forced them to their knees so they appeared to be always setting off for some never-ending race. They had set their lanterns steady amongst the sharp-bladed grass that grew at the lip of the chalk pit.

In summer, it was the only place for a hundred miles where the salad burnet grew and scented the air with its smell of cucumber. In sunny years, the horseshoe vetch spread its golden flowers about and fed the chalk-hill blue. Only one man had ever seen the butterfly and known it for what it was and wondered at its rarity and the improbability of finding it here where it should never have existed. Alfred Bittlestone had come back many times with his nets and little vials lined with laurel leaves, but only twice had he ever caught a specimen and popped it in his poison-jar and staked it to a strip of satin with his pins. It had earned him a fine gold pencil when he had presented it to his collector, only a couple of inches in length, but when you pulled the ring at one end, the graphite holder slid out the other. It was his finest possession, apart from the other chalk-hill blue that he kept in the glass drawer at his home, the notes of its capture written in a cryptic code known only to one man, and Alfred Bittlestone had never told another soul of his hidden glory.

There was no smell of cucumber, nor butterfly nor vetch as Medan Bellpenny struggled in the night, only the dim cloud of his breath as it caught the lamplight and the sour scent of the sweat that ran beneath his shirt as he lowered the Dvoshka boy down his hole. He'd hoped they could just let down the rope and have the lad haul his own way down, but the walk over the moors had been hard on the boy's foot and his face was white as the chalk they had come to find with the pain of it all. He had almost fainted when he first tried to push himself over the side, almost let go the rope and fallen. Medan had seen his fingers loosen their grip and just for a second considered letting the boy fall. But that wouldn't fit into his plan, not at all, and so he'd shot out his arm and grabbed at the boy's wrists, hauled him back up so he creased across the edge like a piece of broken bracken.

Uwe felt himself hanging there but couldn't move. He felt as if there were no blood left in his veins, as if his bones had melted within his skin and there was no more strength to them than in a sack of water.

Bellpenny heaved him back on to the heather, grunting with the effort, his own bones cracking at the joints with the strain. They both lay back a while, panting up at the starless sky, watching a faint grimace of moon as it leered out through the heavy clouds, then Medan set himself back on to his feet, pulled up the rope and started to tie it around Uwe Proctor's ankles.

'You'll have to go down bit by bit, take some o' the weight with yer hands. Not to worry,' he growled as Uwe began to protest, 'I've knotted plenty o' ropes about a pulley-shaft and it'll not give.'

It was with a certain amount of satisfaction that he saw Uwe Proctor crawl on his stomach towards the empty pit, spreading out his hands, feeling the bare chalk with his fingers. He'd coiled the slack about his waist and braced himself against the tree, and then Uwe was out over the edge and Medan felt the breath tugged out of him as the lines of rope tightened, every muscle taut to take the strain and stop himself from falling. And as Uwe descended, Medan slowly turned and unwound the rope from his body, and Uwe tried not to shriek with the horror of it and fought to keep his hands clutching at every hold he could not see, and the blackness kept on getting blacker as he descended, inch by inch, foot by foot, yard by yard.

'Well, Mr Stroop, what do you think?'

Stroop held up a finger and Pytchley understood, stood

by the fireplace, poked at the logs now and then but tried to make no noise, filled his pipe, smoked, waited. Orcutt and Violena had removed themselves to the backgammon board, started to show Jack and Thomas how it was really done, kept putting their fingers to their lips to keep Jack from shouting out as the dice were rolled and the counters moved their lines across the board.

Mabel was still sitting by Stroop, leaning slightly forward, watching his thin white-scarred fingers as he drew his lists, itemised everything he had been told, changed the order, rewrote his clues and questions, rescheduled his points as he tried to see the answers. It was the only way he knew how to come at situations, and Pytchley felt a certain comfort in having his own confusion ordered by someone from outside. Just like Weeems, he thought, here is a man who can observe the world and extract a catalogue from it, give one thing a link to another.

A calmness took him over as he, like Mabel, watched Stroop work; it was a little like the nights he'd spent before an impending battle. The dreadful heat of the day had passed and the night cooled the blood that had spilt all around him, hid for a few hours the butchery and stench he no longer had the stomach to endure. He could see again the moon that seemed so much larger in India than in England, the stars that seemed so much further away, the way their very indifference brought out the stark realisation of what men and their armies really were: nothing but sticks wandering over sand for a few short years, until their shadows took them over and they were no more. He'd thought he'd got over thinking such things, but they had never really left him, and now, in the dim light and hiss of the two gas-lamps that were lit and the unsteady staccato of Stroop's pen across its page, he saw the plains of India and its wars and every battle he had fought rise up to greet him. He ached with such sadness he had to sit down. Left his pipe smouldering in the tray on the mantelpiece. Closed his eyes. Tried not to smell Finkel Hanka's burnt-up body, the horror on Roze Hanka's face as she'd struggled to run along the road to meet them, slipping on the ice, the grit grazing her cheek as she wept, because already she knew the news they brought and her life had been snapped off at the stem, her apple fallen to the ground where it could only rot.

Stroop was unaware of this deep emotion, heard only faintly the *shsh* of the lamps and silenced giggles from the backgammon board, the soft sighs that escaped Mabel as she drew back in her chair, curled her feet beneath her, smoothed her borrowed dress. His list was almost done and his plan of action, although sketchy, already formed. He looked up suddenly as Violena Sedge refilled the empty glass at his side, saw her smile briefly at Pytchley, who had raised his head. Saw that the man had been sitting by the fire, one foot straight out in front of him, his forehead still marked with the imprint of the cane upon which he had rested his head.

Violena turned to look at Stroop, and Stroop, feeling obliged, tapped at the notepaper, sent a skid of ink across its surface and said, 'We may have something.'

Violena moved forward and Stroop saw Maximillian Orcutt standing awkwardly behind her. He saw the pallor of Mabel's face as she turned towards him, heard Jack and Thomas abandon their game and come scampering across the carpet to stand beside him. He wondered again if he should not have left them all in London, but it was too late now. They were here, and the problems were laid out upon his page. He'd made his lists and thought his thoughts, and now was the time to speak them, though he wasn't sure anyone would really want to hear what he had to say.

4

Vengeance, a Long Time Coming

11 March

DAWN BROKE OVER St Weonard's-on-the-Water with the first crack of frost in the many footprints left at the base of the belfry steps, where people had gathered two weeks before, clutching hopeless lines of buckets and pails and knowing that they had got there too late and there was nothing to be done.

Alfred Bittlestone glanced up at what was left of the tower as he took the path to the river. He remembered that first morning after it had happened, how he had climbed his way up the little hill. Inside the eleven-foot circle of stone that made up the base of the tower, the great oak timbers that had supported the gallery still smouldered end-on-end where they had fallen, quills of dark smoke protruding from their charcoaled lengths, puffing occasionally from the gaping doorway as something else within collapsed and died. The smell of conflagration still hung over the compound of the village on the far side of the bell-mound, settled on to the thatch of their cottages, laid the street end to end with tiny briquettes of charred wood and a fine layer of ash only gradually dispersed by the wind. The women venturing out to milk their goats for the morning's brose still felt desolate as they cast quick glances to where the beacon had once gazed across their lands and given them a sense of being watched over. But their custodian was no more use to them now than a sentry severed at the waist. There would be no more warning bell or beacon lighting them home from the fields on stormy nights. There would be no more ringing out their births and marriages and deaths. There was just the dreary black-stained thumb of hill to remind them that they had lost their church and now their tower, and who knew what would be next?

Alfred Bittlestone rubbed his hands in the still, chill air and continued on his way. He didn't care much for the tower's torso, glanced at it as usual, but had other things to do. It wasn't spring yet, but there were buds to be seen on the bare trees if you knew where to look, and he did. He was off to the great poplar hedge at the edge of the lands leading up to the place they called Astonishment Hall. He took the curve of the hill with no more than a glance, his nose dithering at the unpleasant smell but his eyes firmly fixed on the path that led upriver and away from St Weonard's and its ruined church and its newly ruined tower. He followed by the bank, remarked with satisfaction the slip and flip of fish nudging the water into short circles, the soft symphonic beat of swans' wings as they flew low over the gleaned fields, looking, he supposed, for kith or corn, the cackle and bruckle of geese crossing the horizon, unfurling and folding like ribbons in the wind. He savoured the raw scent of earth and grass as he moved away from the middens of the village and the damp-cindery smell of the tower.

He came to the crooked arm of the river, his hand cupping his chin in anticipation as he turned it by. It astounded him, as always, that great fan of hedge stretching out across the fields: a hundred and twenty-three white poplar trees, layered since sticks first planted and woven together into a peacock's tail marking the edge of the manorial land, and, close on its end, a double line of linden trees, grass cropped short and tight along the lane that led up to the Hall, inviting you as always to tread its soft green path as if you'd been invited. But it was the poplar creation he was interested in now. He hoped to be better able to pinpoint his quarry now that the buds had begun to swell, and the worst of the winter had scoured the boles of detritus, and the frost had etched the fissures of the splitting bark.

He came at it slowly, watching, examining. A few of last year's flower-plumes could still be seen caught between the woven branches of the hedge, looking like amputated lambs' tails decaying to brown and mould. He took out his knife and began to explore the cracks of the bark, his fingertips melting the frost from the small holes and furls of wizened wood. He had come in the hope of finding a specimen of seraphim, a moth that hibernated over winter and flew for only for a short time in May and only here, on this hedge, hovering at the edge of day, in that special time of spring-evening when the poplar moths flew. He wanted to scrape the chrysalis from its hole or the whole moth where it lay hidden and hibernated and his thoughts were for little else.

A damp dawn mist had risen from the cold grass across

the water meadows and a heron croaked as it woke early from the heronry in the elm copse over the bridge, just beyond the hedge. It was last year's young and tilted awkwardly as it came to land by the water's edge, its feet cracking through the eggshell of ice that was suspended above the mud. It brought to the man's mind why he had come here, which was not just for the rarity of the moth, although to discover it would have given him the greatest pleasure. As much as when he had found that chalk-hill blue. Two such rare and beautiful things, he thought, in one man's lifetime – now that would be astonishment indeed.

He spent a few more minutes scraping at the bark with his knife, moving from one trunk to the next, but the *crawk* of another heron halted him, and he knew that once more he had failed to find what he was looking for, and would have to look again tomorrow. He touched the small jar in his pocket with its carefully stoppered lid and sighed a little as he sheathed his knife. He knew there was work to be done and already he heard the pike-men moving down to their boats, getting ready to haul in their overnight lines to see what they had caught.

He ducked through the small arch in the poplar hedge that led to one of the brooks that fed the river, paused every now and then to prod at a piece of likely-looking bark in the hope of uncovering the seraphim he had sought these last long years and still never found, squeezed a few of the poplar buds just to spread the aroma of balsam they released on to his hands. He looked over to the elm copse, which housed the heronry, and adjusted the wicker basket that was slung over his back. It was roomy but light, woven from willow, specially made to hold the young herons he was about to shake down from their sleep, sending them toppling to the ground from their twig-stack nests. He withdrew the wooden cudgel from the side of the basket and slotted it into his belt. He anticipated the breakfast he would have once he had passed the main catch up to the kitchens of Astonishment Hall. It was his duty to cull the birds once a month and was allowed a bird in return. He could already taste the buttery flesh of young heron in his mouth, had saved some cream, and he'd maybe add a little chicory from the pantry or some of the wild garlic leaves he had dried, perhaps even a few of the radishes he still had left in the pantry.

He smiled as he stepped across the little wooden bridge and the smile was still on his lips when something struck him hard in the chest just below the breastbone. For a moment he saw the flight-quiver as the crossbow bolt came to rest within him and he raised a hand, but already his knees had given way beneath him and he fell backwards on to his basket, the wickerwork creaking and cracking under his weight, an overturned turtle staring straight up into the green-blue of the new sky whose night he would never see, the morning star winking at the edge of a pale moon, the line of the shaft an unshadowed gnomon in his chest.

The bars of the basket weren't built for his weight and without warning they caved in, sent him sliding down the bridge on to his side. He scrabbled at the straps, trying to release them, his body twisted with his fall, every movement making the pain wrench through him as his ribcage tore. One hand headed for the intrusive bolt, but as he touched it he felt the tip of it rip through him with such pain he couldn't breathe. So he stayed there unmoving, panting, his left foot starting that awful cramp he knew so well, which could only be cured by leaping up and stamping on it until the muscles released him. But he couldn't jump now, couldn't even move, and his eyes began to twitch with a torture he didn't understand. He thought to cry out for help, knew the pike-men were near but just to draw breath was hard enough with that strange shaft still trapped within him. The basket gave a little more and the shaft shifted and scraped across his spine and his foot spasmed wildly as his spinal cord was plucked like a harp-string. The agony was so acute his elbows tried to push himself up against it, forcing him to look in dismay at his own bright blood spilling down his chest and further through the boards of the bridge. Fright clutched him, clawed at his skin, forced sweat to prick up on his face and cold tears from his eyes, made his teeth ache, tightened his throat. He watched his blood come out of him, like a stream finding a new way down to the sea without remorse, or any thought of turning back, and all he could do was lay back his head upon the ruptured basket, eyes flicking over the dark crowns of the elm glade, drooping down over the streaks of heron detritus on their bark, further, to the leaf-dark thicket of blackberry and elder below, to the boots that were coming towards him out of the gloom. Panic pumped at his heart, which quickened then slackened as it rid itself of blood.

There was hardly anything left inside him when he heard the boots as they came across the bridge, the loose planks jumping beneath him as they stepped fastidiously astride the dark stains. His eyes had closed when the man leant over him and he didn't see the white-knuckled fist steady around the unsheathed knife that was so like his own, didn't feel the ripple of air lift the strands of hair across his head as the knife came fast towards him. He thought lastly not of his wife, nor his two sons nor the daughters who died before he had time to name them, but of the chalk-hill blue he had caught that morning by the chalk pit, and the seraphim he had sought but never found. Where did it go? The words were still echoing in his head as the knife cracked down upon his skull. It stunned him but came no further, and he didn't see the hand that held the stone, coming down on the knife one more time, and one more time again until the blade shattered a way down through the bone and parted his brain and the roof of his mouth and came to rest with its point upon his tongue. A last pink spot exuded slow as sap around the indentation of the knife-point, then a last hammer at the knife haft and the point went through, and Bittlestone's heart finally ceased its shallow beat and the little blood left in him started to thicken in his veins.

The bridge swayed slightly on uncertain groynes as his body sank and sighed upon the boards and the footsteps of his assassin faded away across the grass. They had paused only briefly before they turned away. The big hand had let the rock fall into the water, and now he moved it back slowly, held it a second or two above the other man's pallid face, shadowed it, kept it from the sky. Then the assailant saw some of what he had come for, and the hand snatched down and broke the chain and tucked the treasure away in his pocket where it belonged. Only then did he straighten and walk away.

His boots left imprints in the dew but they would be gone by the time the morning had risen and the grass would spring back against their fall and the pike-men who found Bittlestone wouldn't know which way the attacker had come or where he had gone or why he had been here and killed the man on the bridge.

Downriver by the ford, the young heron hunched its wings over the water, lined its beak up against a shiver of silver fish, didn't know the water was turning red about its feet. The world was no more to it than scale and shadow, day and night, food and sleep. The beak struck without warning through the water to spear the salmon smolt, shifting the merrybone between its shoulders as it moved. A faint creaking alarmed the heron and it lifted its neck, gazed back towards the bridge. The wind wove through the basket, loosened one half-undone strap. The man's arm hung further over the bridge, his fingertips trailing the water. Within minutes, the minnows were nibbling at his skin. They had no need for chicory or butter. They liked their morning meal just the way it came.

5

Paradise and Bittlestone

11 March

THERE WERE A lot of things that Stroop did not understand, but when he woke that morning, he at least had an agenda to follow. Everything had been discussed the night before at the Hall, and, no one having any other ideas, they had all agreed to do as he had asked. Stroop and Pytchley would go over to St Weonard's and take a look at the site of the bell tower, then they would ride out to the scene of Hanka's murder.

Having been introduced to Maximillian Orcutt the night before, Stroop had asked him to reproduce as much of his stolen Perspective Box as he could – obviously not the box itself, for that would have taken months, but some sort of visual reconstruction that would help. Stroop had studied the original plans Orcutt had brought to the dinner, but not having seen the actual object, he could make very little of the complex draughtsmanship. Orcutt, for his part, was happy to oblige, indeed was never happier than when he was fiddling about with coils and levers, fastening this bit to that bit, planing wood, grinding lenses, tweaking at nozzles and valves, prying at the internal organs of intricate parts of machinery, oiling their spleens, adjusting the lie of their tripes and kidneys, improving the efficiency of their knitted-togetherness.

For Violena and Mabel, Stroop had a more subtle task. The Dvoshka letters had given mention of a book much valued by the younger Uwe. The parents had already told Stroop that the script alluded to was *The Paradise of the Heart*, written by Jan Komensky, a native of Bohemia and taught as a parable of Christian living, a little like *The Pilgrim's Progress*. He wanted Violena to search Weeems' library for the work or any allusion to it, also any information on Orava, which Uwe Dvoshka had made his second home. He also wanted to know about Odessa, the Black Sea port where Uwe had last been known to be. Mabel was keen to help Violena, seemed to enjoy her company, was glad to participate in the research, as she had always helped Stroop back at home.

It was harder to put Jack and Thomas to anything useful – they clattered around like jays in a nut tree and were having such an exciting time of everything that nobody could help but smile to see them at it. Already they were sneaking peeks at every lodge, at every turn, at every room, at every tree that grew wild and grand in the grounds, jumping like the monkeys they had seen stuffed and mounted in Pytchley's hallway. They brought an air of unconcern and wonder to everything they saw or did, so that Stroop was not alone in feeling that maybe things weren't as bad as they had seemed the evening before.

He laughed out loud when he left to meet with Pytchley at the stables.

'Isn't it all so grand?' Jack had said, one boot on and the other trailing a snag of laces as he tried to keep up.

'It's brilliant!' added Thomas, who had just finished falling out of a huge oak tree that had been blasted by lightning and hollowed out at its nape into a dovecote, hurriedly deserted in a flurry and flap of wing as he used its roof for a stepping stone. 'I should like to live here always, shouldn't you, Mr Stroop?'

Not Stroop. He found the whole place bewildering. He wasn't used to such space or the vastness of the skies and the unfeeling roll of the never-ending land that seemed to suck the precision out of the world around him. He wanted to be back home, sitting in his map room, surrounded by his books, and the knowledge that he knew where every single one of them lay and where to find them. He wanted to see his Sense Map of London papered on his walls and all the certainty it held, to know that Mabel was safe and making soup in their little kitchen, and that Jack was up Smoke Street trying to rescue every living thing that passed its way, and that Thomas would never have to worry about sleeping under bridges ever again.

But he didn't say any of that. He could see the excitement bursting like brandy in their cheeks, had seen Mabel's rapt looks at Violena, had realised their time here would do more to make her forget what had gone before than ever he could do.

'Now, boys,' he had said, hiding the homesickness that welled within him, the trepidation at what he feared might come to them all yet again and hoped would not, 'I have a task for you.' And he had told them he needed them to mill about amongst the estate workers and the maids and stable-boys and anyone they might meet out in the fields; had said it was vital they learnt whatever they could learn, had asked them to go down to the steam house on the canal and quiz the man who took tickets from the sightseers.

'Ask him if he knows who sent this letter,' and he held up the mysterious crossed missive from Uwe, together with its accusatory scrawl. 'Ask him if this missive came from here, and if it did, if he saw the man who brought it and what he looked like, anything about him he remembers.'

He had already surmised that if the separate events they were investigating – the disappearance of Uwe Dvoshka and the happenings at the Hall – were indeed connected, then it might not be beyond the bounds of luck that Uwe's last letter had been delivered to London from this very steam stop, it being the main drop-and-post for the canal workers, as Pytchley had already informed him the night before. He also had a strong suspicion that it had not been Uwe himself who had delivered the letter, that it must have been handed over by someone else, most probably the same person who had added the overwritten accusation. He asked them to get a copy of the stamp that every mail stop used to mark the edge of any post that passed through that office; hoped it would match one of the ones on the letter. He wondered about that second letter-writer, that friend who must have delivered it. He wondered deeply about the accusation therein. He wondered how long the friend had held on to it before sending it off to London.

His deep suspicions didn't affect Jack and Thomas, who laughed and leapfrogged their way across the lawn towards the drive and the main gates. Stroop smiled a thin smile, wondered if he had ever been so young and full of life, thought that probably he never had, knew he never would be. He distracted himself by looking at his by now dry notebook and the notes he had transcribed that morning.

He stood in the stable yard waiting for Pytchley, tried to make connections between the listed events: the disappearance of Uwe from Odessa, the burning of the bell tower, the theft of Orcutt's box, the murder of Finkel Hanka, the arrival in London of Uwe's last letter and the indications of its postal marks that it had come from somewhere near here. He found the coincidence of these several events a little too neat, a set of dovetail joints too carefully cornered. And fitting together to what purpose? The missing Dvoshka boy and the incidents at Astonishment apparently grafted the one on to the other. Or perhaps each separate happening was part of a larger whole, a craft of creation he couldn't yet see.

Stroop heard Pytchley coming across the cobbles, the boy bringing the already saddled cob from its stable. He closed his notebook, replaced it in his pocket, increased the speed of his stride as he saw Pytchley raise his arm and wave him on.

He was not the only one to speed his pace.

The Creator had been on the move and was beginning to enjoy his craft.

Pytchley and Stroop had not long reached over the hill behind Astonishment Hall into the next valley, Pytchley on the short-legged horse he favoured, which moved slowly and with an ease that did not chafe the cork within his boot, Stroop keeping stride, preferring to keep on foot for the day, eager to stretch his limbs after days of enforced inaction on the way up from London. They had not taken the lime-tree drive that kept to the lowland curve of the hill, but had come up over the top of the valley, giving a view down towards St Weonard's and the whole basin of the river. Stroop looked with interest at the heronry of elm, the trees streaked white with a hundred years of bird-droppings, dotted with the darker thickets of their rough-twig nests. More impressive still was the sweep of wide green field that ran down before them, vaulted over by the audacious hedge that Weeems had planted of poplars wattled at their bases, the stronger trees a little less restricted at its centre so growing taller, giving the impression of a vast peacock's tail fanned out across the field, the stream running merrily beside and between.

They could see more. They could see someone riding helter-skelter through the fields and a bunch of men gathered about the bridge that crossed the stream and led from hedge to heronry.

What more? thought Pytchley as he saw the rider divert his course as he spotted them outlined up on the hill, his heels frantic against the sweating flanks of his pony, the cart hitches flailing behind them where they had been too hastily loosed.

Stroop peered down at the men gathered about the bridge, creased his brows, couldn't believe this was anything good, wondered if another slot had been chiselled to take another joint.

He set off fast down the hill, heard Pytchley's foot creak as he raised himself in the saddle. The man on the pony ceased his headlong race up the hill as he saw Pytchley make his way down towards him, started yelling and waving his arms, the pony snorting, stamping its feet, flecking foam on to the grass, which was still stiff with dew and frosted spider-webs. Stroop could see the swath of sun slowly inching up the valley from behind the crumbled stones of what he took to be St Weonard's church, for surely it could be no other. It slept serenely on its little island, a tumble of gravestones against its back, the dark swirl of water eating at its banks. Opposite, on the small hill that grew up from the waterside like a large burial mound, a set of stone steps had been laid into the shadow of its side. At the top he could see the truncated tower rise up like a broken tooth, all blackened with age and smoke, surrounded by a skirt of cinder and the trample of wood and splinter and charcoaled thatch that had once made up its height.

He felt Pytchley pass by him, heard him sigh as he urged his horse into an uncomfortable trot, heard the leather creaking on the saddle where he drew himself into it, tightened his knees against its sides, clutched a little harder at the reins and pommel, stood a little harder in the stirrups.

Stroop followed him down, wondering if he had a part in all this. Perhaps it was just some worker who'd had an accident, maybe an older man whose one last breath of cold morning air had been too much for age-addled lungs; perhaps those old lungs had just given up and said, 'no more'. But even as they drew closer, he knew this wasn't so, and so did Pytchley. The way the rider had hastened towards them, the slump of the fallen man on the bridge, the whispered words in Pytchley's ear as he dismounted, the suspicious glance at Stroop, the way Pytchley went as if he were trying to hurry, body pulled forward, shoulders hunched, leaning too heavily on his cane, the way the pike-men parted as Pytchley stepped on to the bridge. One of the men still had his hat on, a line of sharp, mean hooks crooked inside its band, a mess of snarled-up line clutched in his hand, a suggestion of blood on the small Judas stick strapped to his waist.

'What's happened here?' Pytchley tried to demand, but his voice was weary and there was no fight to his words, only sadness and defeat.

The man with the line in his hand tried to shove it into his pocket, which only made it worse, and it caught in the stitching and began to fall in a tangle down his leg. He brushed at it angrily, swatted it with hands calloused and segged from years of dragging in the lines set out across the banks.

Pytchley looked at him. 'Satterthwaite?' he said, and the man kicked the angry ball of yarn away, didn't watch as it fell behind him into the stream and slowly spread its twine through the rushes and reeds, snagged at the thin trail of ice that grew from the bank.

'Us found 'im like this a few minutes back,' he said, and made a vague deferential motion of hand to hat. 'We was pulling for pike down beyond the elms, like, came up from the village t'other way over lower bridge.' He gestured down towards the old church of St Weonard's, the highest of its still-standing walls just visible beyond the sparse fingers of poplar as they leant out over the burn. ''Twas only when young Davy here came up to fetch Bittlestone down for a spot of breakfast with us that we found 'im.' He moved a clay-capped boot towards Bittlestone's body, but didn't touch it, nor put his boot inside the dark-stained circle surrounding him. 'We didn't move nothing, seeing as how . . .' he sniffed, put his hand roughly to his nose, nodded down at the dead man, 'well, seeing as how . . .' he repeated, but again could find nothing else to say.

'Go on, Davy,' said another of the pike-men and a boy of seven or eight came forward and added, 'He sort of fell forward a bit when I came on the bridge. I thought he was ill or summat, but soon as I saw his face I knew he weren't.' He sounded proud of his medical knowledge but nobody noticed.

Then Satterthwaite growled impatiently and took the Judas stick from his belt, took a decisive step forward and pushed at the dead man with the stick.

Pytchley leant over and saw what they had all seen. He didn't say anything. Kept his face from movement, pulling at the muscles, clenching his tongue between his teeth, swallowed hard. The man had been driven through by a crossbow shaft, and, worse, seemingly for no purpose, a knife had been hammered through his skull until it shattered and gave. It was easy to see, where the man Bittlestone's mouth lay slack and open, that the point of the knife had pierced his tongue and gone clean through it like a stick through a snake. Pytchley bent down, coiled back with difficulty, his cork-footed boot twisting badly against its stump. He allowed the nearest man to him to help, put his weight upon his strong fish-pulling arm as he set himself straight again. He'd recognised the corpse, knew him to be the man who delivered heron and other wildfowl to the kitchens. Pytchley could see the pale green tinge to the man's skin, like the underside of an aspen leaf caught in rain. He motioned Stroop forward.

Stroop didn't want to come, was already nauseous at the smell of the black blood that had soaked through the planking, clotted between the slats, formed a small ocean around its island owner. But he went and he looked and he tried to examine the details of the wounds. His eyes flittered, not wanting to see what he was seeing, caught sight of a small scrap of white lying trapped beneath the man's elbow. He poked at it a little with his cane, dislodged it from the rigor that had held it fast, eased it out a little, tried to avoid the slick of blood that had pooled through its spine.

'What's this?' he asked nobody in particular.

It was the boy Davy who spoke up. 'He collected bits and pieces of moths and the like,' said he. 'Showed me once. Used to go poking round bits of bark looking for 'em when they was asleep through the winter. Said he could get good money for collecting the right ones. We all called him the Butterfly Man.' The boy was pleased to be able to supply information, was having an enjoyable day of it, despite the body at his feet. He seemed unaware of the slight escape of gas that the older men could smell, the vague unease it gave them, the crawling of your skin as you crossed a mire only to find the skein of it wobble beneath your feet, realised how little there was between you and oblivion. 'He kept notes of everything he found and where he found them,' Davy added, jutting his chin at the little notebook as Stroop pinched it between his fingers.

The boy noted the scarring upon his hands with curiosity but said nothing more.

The men were beginning to shuffle their feet, rubbing their hands with the cold, eager to get back to work and the warmth it gave, now that they had seen what was to be seen.

'But where's the pencil?' Stroop asked. Nobody seemed inclined to answer.

'Perhaps he kept it in his pocket,' Pytchley suggested, but Stroop had already seen the broken chain around the dead man's neck and guessed the truth before the boy Davy so helpfully supplied it.

'Oh! Oh!' he said, holding up a hand. 'I remember now! He used to have a little tubey pencil round his neck. Like a little telescope. Ever so proud of it, he was. Some old buffer give it him for something or other he'd collected.'

Pytchley straightened his back. 'We'd best get word to his wife. Arrange a stretcher. We'll need the doctor out to take a look and remove the . . . er . . . the implements.'

'We done that,' said Satterthwaite, and they all turned as they heard someone coming up the path from the village: two boys carrying a curtain slung between two poles.

Pytchley cleared his throat, moved back off the bridge. 'Take him to the beet-house,' he said, gesturing vaguely towards the communal barn the villagers used for winter fodder, though it lay out of sight at the far end of the small cobble-housed street. 'Lay him out but don't do anything else until Dr Thacker gets there. I'll come on behind.'

He went to stand by Stroop, and they both of them turned away as the men on the bridge started manoeuvring their burden into place, unstrapping what was left of the wicker basket from the man's back, loading him on to the curtain-stretcher as the boys got there, rubbing their hands vigorously in the stream when they had done.

Pytchley watched four of the men shoulder the body of Bittlestone, was thankful when it sank into the slack of the curtain, watched them take their way off across the wide green field, which was the quickest route to the village and the barn.

'Have the day at home,' Pytchley said to the men left behind, shuffling their bloodied boots, uncertain what to do, 'or go back to work – whichever you will. Mr Stroop,' he turned abruptly away from Bittlestone and the bridge and the men who were starting across the field after the others, 'will you come?'

Stroop shook his head, said he would go on to the tower as he had planned, that he would meet Pytchley later at the Hall.

'Make sure the doctor doesn't damage either the knife or the crossbow shaft,' he said to Pytchley, 'and take everything out of his pockets. Bring everything back with you.'

Pytchley nodded, then put his hand briefly on Stroop's shoulder, silently thanked God he did not have to deal with this alone. Then he struggled his way back into his stirrups, set off after the procession of pike-men and pall-bearers, thought of the valley and the home that he loved so much, hoped that Astonishment would not deteriorate into dread.

Stroop was thinking quite other things as he made his way along the bank of the small burn that emptied out at the confluence just above the island and its waterlogged church. He was wondering what the significance was of the man on the bridge, what connection, if any, it had with the tower. Bridges and towers: two quite opposite things in one way, he thought, in that bells bring people towards them and bridges take people away. He kept glancing at the burnt-out stub of the tower that could be seen in the distance, couldn't help thinking that apart from the arrival of Uwe Proctor to this bleak country, assuming he had come here and who knew when and where or for what purpose, the tower's cremation had somehow been a start to everything. Uwe had clearly been running away from something, judging by the tone of the last scribbled communication to his parents, but what had he been running towards? They were still hoping for word from Elusia's family back in Orava, though when it would arrive, and if it would hold further information, they could not be sure. Letters usually came with shipments of glass from the factory in Bohemia, or at least they had done until the son Uwe had been sent to the Black Sea, that much he knew.

He also knew why Uwe had been sent there: to capitalise on the growing influx of immigrants to Novorussia, who in turn came because of the establishment of new ports along the shores of the Black Sea. It helped that export agreements had been made between Russia and the Turks, and that the tariffs had been slackened on the ships and their cargos that left for the Bosphorus, and on uninterrupted to the seas of Marmara and the Aegean, and then to the Mediterranean. This in turn gave access to Cyprus, Syria and the African coast, to Italy and the Adriatic, on past the straits of Gibraltar to Spain and further, to Portugal and England or wherever else a ship might want to go.

He understood the enormity of the trade routes thus made possible, the amount of wealth that stood to be gained. He knew also that Napoleon's fleets were scurrying up and down the selfsame coasts, but so far had done little but skirmish with the British and bark like a stoat backed into the corner of a chicken pen. He wondered what it was that had happened to Uwe in such faraway lands. Stroop knew the names and read the papers, listened to the merchants chattering in the coffee houses, but always these things were just words and games: one country declaring war on another and winning battles, losing others, treaties being made and broken. It would take the tide of history to sort out which strands eventually ran to something and tied a knot, and those that were severed before they went anywhere, limp loose ends that would come to nothing. Wherever war and trade collided, espionage and treachery soon followed. Was it possible that Uwe Dvoshka had been caught up in something of the kind? If so, there had been no hint of it in his letters. Rather he had written of a great project he was undertaking, something that would make his family proud both in England and Bohemia. That he would soon make his fortune.

Every young man dreams of making his fortune, thought Stroop sadly, and few are content with what they have, though it might have served them well if only they had been content. And then for no explicable reason, Uwe's frequent letters had stopped . . .

He interrupted himself by stumbling as his walking cane hit a stone, set his ankle at a twist, almost making him fall. When he'd gained his balance, he saw that he was almost at the curve that brought the riverbank alongside the island of St Weonard's, saw the stumps of gravestones in its yard. He stopped abruptly, his cane still twitching in the air, turned back and looked from where he had come. He could still see the bridge below the fan of poplar trees, looked down briefly at the stone that had almost made him fall. Quickly he took out his notebook and scribbled. He paused a moment with the pencil still in his hand, looked at it, jotted another sentence below the first. There were things he would need to ask Pytchley, and the doctor, once he had been found. And there was something else he must check on his return journey, something else about the bridge on which the man Bittlestone had died.

Stroop stopped short as he rounded the bend. A goat stood there in the path, blinking at him incuriously with reptilian gold-slatted eyes, a cud of half-chewed grass sticking sidewise from its mouth. He heard a gruff voice *chuck-chucking*, and a man ascending the few steps from the riverside.

'Henrietta come,' his voice coaxed, and the goat lifted her head, set the crude wooden bell clanking at her neck, turned herself away from Stroop as the man came up beside them. 'Morning, sir,' he said, tapping at the goat's side with a switch of willow. 'Come come, Henrietta,' he continued, and the goat chewed another moment, then turned and trotted down the steps on to a flat-bottomed punt to join the rest of the crew. All goats, all belled, all staring up at Stroop with their yellow-jacketed eyes. Stroop found them faintly menacing, but returned the man's greeting.

'Hello,' he said. 'A melancholy day.'

The man looked at him, his head slightly torqued upon

his neck as by arthritis or some other disease of the damp. Stroop noted the bend in the old man's back, the outward rick of his knees, the loss of height that had come with age.

'You're the fellow staying with the major?' asked the man, tapping at a goat nose as Henrietta, or possibly another, tried to escape the punt and reascend the steps.

Stroop didn't know much about shepherding, knew even less about goats. Was surprised anyone had even heard of his arrival at the Hall.

The man chuckled, his lungs sounding heavy and full. 'We all know as you're here,' he said, 'and we all know about poor Mr Hanka. Terrible shock it was, even if he were a foreigner and a constable to boot.' The man turned, went back down the few steps to the riverside and secured a small rope across the gate-end of the barge. 'Should keep 'em in a moment,' he said, coming back up the steps. 'My name is Ipsing Sansibar,' and he offered Stroop a hand that was stained brown with years of holding a leaky pipe-bowl too tight and too close. 'Anything I can do for you?' he offered, and Stroop told Sansibar his name and yes, there was, and together they turned away from the goats and the river and went up the stone steps towards the remnants of the tower, Sansibar shaking his head all the while and saying it was a terrible thing.

He hadn't really liked the stiff boy with the strange unblinking eyes, but in the two weeks that had passed since they'd found him up there, all curled and grey like a squirrel in an ash-pot, he'd missed the lad, and had nightmares every night, and even some days, about the way the lad must have died. And he'd wondered about it too, wondered about the man he'd seen coming down the far brae a while earlier in the day, as others had seen him whilst they pulled their turnips from the ground, a man who carried a heavy load upon his back, who'd been seen before the tower went up in smoke, but not a wisp of him since. He'd wondered about it a lot, and when he'd heard about the man coming up from London, he'd spent a lot of time on what was worrying him, finally figuring something out, something he should have figured long since. So now he'd let the goats wait a little while before taking them out to the island. He'd show this man Stroop the tower, turn the puzzle over to him and let him do with it what he would.

Up beyond the bridge, beyond the heronry, past the brow of the hill and the valley and the canal workings, and over the moor for a mile or two, the new shoots of horseshoe vetch on the lip of the chalk pit had been crushed and would not grow again this year. Almost thirty feet down, where the chalk layer met the granite, a crescent of sunlight began to belly-slink across the chipped stone, the halo of its horizon increasing at one side with every hour, losing it at the other as it passed. It edged towards the rough heap of sacking that Uwe had scrabbled about himself to make his bed before passing out. The small warmth of sunlight tickled at the loosely woven sacking, placed a smooth finger on the forehead exposed by the fraying edges, lifted the dust of long-spent flour, set Uwe sneezing and waking by turns.

He had never felt so tired and stiff, so like a scarecrow felled by one too many winters. He opened his eyes, watched a patch of light slide across the high walls, might have been at the bottom of a well. He rolled on to his side, back too sore to take the weight of him as he levered himself to sitting, felt the sudden increase in his heart rate as he stared from the light to the dark that surrounded him, heard the hollow drip of water on stone, felt the cold creeping at him from the hollowed-out tunnels where the sun couldn't reach, hadn't reached for hundreds of years. Reflexively, he jerked himself backwards into the full circle of light, felt immediate relief, tried to ridicule himself for his fright, but took a long while to calm his heart.

He looked around him for his belongings, saw the familiar outline of his foldaway desk, the several packets of food and candles and bottles of lamp-oil, felt the hard outline of his little book close by his chest. He needed to get organised, explore a little of the chalk pit, find a place he could use as a latrine, a dry ledge he could perhaps lie on for a bed. He needed to count out the extent of his rations, find a small source of water to supplement what he'd brought, allocate his day's use of candles and oil. Bellpenny would be back in a few days to check on his progress, bring him more food, haul him back up if he found he could take no more of his self-imposed prison.

But first, before he did any of this, he pulled the handle of his foldaway desk towards him. It would be the first time he had opened it since he left Odessa last November. He couldn't believe he had so neglected it, made him realise how ill and upset he had really been. The desk had been his constant companion since he left England fourteen or so years before, and rarely had it left his side. Even when that boat had almost sunk, he had clung to it, kept it with him, would gladly have thrown away the last of his clothes, his food and water, jettisoned anything so long as he could still feel its handle steadfast in his hand. It had been his most guarded possession, given him by his parents when he left for Orava. It was a neat contraption, especially designed for his needs according to their specifications. The size of a suitcase, it hardly left his side and wherever he went, he would take great pleasure in setting it down, unclipping the clasps that held it closed, first folding it out into a flat surface with locked boxes aligned to the edges of one side, which gave the suitcase its depth. These held his papers, ink, seals and pens. As you locked the two splayed sides of the surface into one, a depressed catch dropped a central limb from below the base, and from this, three legs out-folded like a milkmaid's stool, which locked the second they were released until you pressed the small bolts that allowed them to be refolded, one by one, into the stem.

It had been engineered by Bockwiths of London in Bond Street, and every time he conjured his table from its wooden suitcase, he thought that one day, when he at last returned to London, he would march the length of Bond Street, hammer on the Bockwith door and demand his slice of profit from all the commissions that must have been made from the people who had admired it during his travels. He had lost count of the times he had been asked where his writing desk had first been fashioned and who could be sought to make another. He had been introduced to many people he would otherwise not have met and been invited to places he would otherwise not have been, all because of this table. If there was one thing and one thing only he could thank his parents for, it was his gift for wanting to record all he saw about him and the means with which to do it.

The hunters who roamed the Russian Steppes needed only a rifle and sled for their survival. For Uwe it was his desk. Both would have jettisoned everything and anyone to keep such possessions by their sides.

Uwe's fingers trembled as he undid the clasps. His eyes were wet with emotion as he popped the two halves of the desk open, locked them into place, ran his fingers over the small boxes, with their keys still held within their locks so cleverly had they been designed. He dropped the central stave, unfolded the tricuspid legs and set them stable upon the rock of the cave floor. He marvelled as always at its ingenuity, its compactness, then he frowned, licked his finger, leant forward to rub at a stain he had detected on the desk's surface. As he rubbed his finger over the latticed veneer, small pieces of inlay began to lift, bowed like seals basking on hidden sandbanks, gently curled from head to tail.

Horrified, he crooked his upper body closer, cursed again the broken foot that curtailed his free and certain movement. Suddenly, he could see spots of ruin everywhere, the stain of salt, the crack of lacquer that has been stressed and pressed, the warping of wood that has damped and dried. Breathing fast, he grasped at the first of the small keys and tried to turn it in its lock. For a moment it seized between his fingers, then it moved and ground past the sand and salt that had held it fast. He pulled at the small knobbed handle, but the drawer didn't slide out as if on waxed runners like it should, but shrieked, as did Uwe's heart within him as of a sudden he knew what he would find. And so he found it. Each key bent and protested as he fought to turn it, each drawer cried out to be forced from a shape no longer its own, each hidden pocket revealed inkpots cracked and broken, seals snapped into pieces, the rust and splay of useless nibs, and there would be worse. His throat ached like an overtightened fishing line, felt the hook within his throat, a deep keening begin in the depths of his stomach as he turned the final lock, hauled open the last drawer with fingers smarting from the blistered metal, the splintered wood.

And there it lay, like a corpse within its tomb, his little *History of Glass*, started but unfinished, crammed like a chest with jewels with his research and his notes, ready to be picked over and polished into something that might at least have redeemed a part of the wicked things that he had done. A thin wail escaped his lips as he lifted the book. The leather was no longer limp with the seawater that had washed over it as they passed the ports of Malta, had turned hard as tack-biscuits, scabbed and cracked by the harsh wind that met them by Gibraltar. The pages still hung by their binding threads, but they had been so deeply steeped with brine, and for so long a time, that they would no longer separate, but stuck together like concertinaed conjoined twins, and every jot of ink that they had held had left them, leached out by sea and salt, every last word he had written dissolved into the black waves.

Uwe sat beside his ruined desk and wept. The last prop from his life had gone and the tunnel collapsed. He would never finish his little *History of Glass* because now he had lost the first of it. He would never atone for what he had done because he had burnt a boy alive in a tower when all he had been trying to do was sing out his redemption to the world. Who cared that he had been fevered and sick? Who knew anyway? Only one other man.

He gazed up at the sun as it slipped its circle around him

like a noose and something inside him turned over, and for the first time since he had left Odessa he felt some strength return to his blood and he raged and boiled over with an anger that surged through him like a bore rides an estuary. He cried out and shouted, and the cave roared and echoed with his voice as he picked up the nearest stones he could find and, with one in each hand, he beat upon his desk, smashed his past, his sickness and despair into a pile of rubble. He raked his hands against the edges of the pit, he smashed his clogs into the rock, seeking footholds that weren't there. He screamed with rage at the man he had allowed himself to become. He fell back upon the wreckage of his desk and the spilt oil and spoilt food and broken candles that lay scattered all about him, and swore at the circle of sky that was out of his reach, saw a buzzard shift its lazy wings far above him. Found a mettle hardening within him and took an oath that he would claw his way back out into the world, however long it took and hard it be, and take with gladness whatever the world saw fit that he deserved. One last thing he did as the sun slid away from him across the western sky: he pooled the lamp-oil up with the edges of his scabbing hands, piled the bed of sacking upon it and the battered tinder of his desk, struck a flint and set a flame across the deep scars of its old and faithful face. Burnt away his past, sat beside the fire and warmed the pain in his hands and feet, tried to concentrate his thoughts on escaping this exile he had brought upon himself, because among the many things that had become clear to him in his self-regenerating fury: he knew that Medan Skimmington Bellpenny wasn't coming back.

6

Worms and Books

11 March

AT ASTONISHMENT, THERE had been talk of Uwe Proctor Dvoshka though no one but Bellpenny had any notion where he was. They talked about Bellpenny too, though they didn't know his name. Stroop had gone to the lodge after getting back from St Weonard's, had spent what was left of the afternoon trying to lay his thoughts out like bricks, looking for the mortar that would keep them all together. He would have liked to talk things over with Mabel, but she was nowhere to be seen, presumably being still up at the Hall with Violena. It was only when Jack came panting through the door to call him up to dinner that he realised how late it was.

Jack looked as reassuringly unkempt as ever and as Stroop closed his notebook and brushed his jacket down with his hands, he asked Jack how his day had gone. Jack could hardly breathe he had so much to say, and talked all the way back up to the Hall, his boots dropping cakes of mud off at every step. He gleefully told Stroop how Thomas had nearly fallen into the canal when he thought he saw a fish the size of an ox, and how it turned out to be an actual ox, which had tumbled in and drowned, and they'd stopped to watch two men winch the animal out with hooks and ropes and chop it up into bits right there on the bank.

'They said they was going to give it a good roasting when they got it home,' Jack continued, waving his arms, ripping the armhole of his jacket until the sleeve almost fell off as he carried on with his enthusiastic account of the day. 'They said it was a right old ox that had got out of its field that morning and gone blundering straight into the canal because it didn't know as it was there. They said it'd not been out for years on account of it being mostly blind now and that they was just keeping it there because it was a good ox to the cows.'

Stroop raised his eyebrows, glanced at Jack, who as usual hadn't understood the implications of what he had been told.

'Fancy that, Mr Stroop! Fancy not even noticing a canal being built in your back garden.'

'Did you speak to the man who looks after the mail?' Stroop enquired, trying to steer Jack back on course, noticing a faint faraway look in Jack's eyes as he did indeed try to imagine a canal being built in his back yard. 'The mail man, Jack?' Stroop asked again, and Jack finally got around to answering.

'Um, yes, we did. Well, Thomas did. I was too busy trying to read the notice they've got there. Did you know they've got a sign there like a huge hand? It points all the way up the hill. Blimey,' said Jack, as they started up the gravel path and through the yew hedges, 'imagine how big your glove would have to be if you had a hand that size. You'd have to order them special made, don't you think, Mr Stroop?' Stroop agreed. 'Or maybe they could use an old jersey . . .'

By the time Jack was calculating which of his own jerseys he would sacrifice for such a worthy cause, they had reached the hall, and Violena was already standing at the door to let them in.

'We're all in the library,' she said, and led them down the small corridor, which went past the Exhibition Room, and past the door on the right that led to Major Pytchley's study, and the one on the left that went to the dining room, and past the stuffed monkeys affixed to the beams of the roof as if they were climbing in their native canopy.

It was the first time Stroop had encountered the rest of the house and he was immediately struck by its odd design, not at all what one would expect. The staircase rose abruptly in front of them, the stairs being steep and laboured, there being no further width to the building to let them sail backwards as they would have been allowed to do in most grand houses. It wasn't obvious from the front of the hall that it only went back the depth of two full rooms, and that the rest of it was built outwards and upwards. More startling to Stroop was that parts of the back-facing wall had been scraped down to the rock, caught by wooden frames as if a picture were waiting to be hung there, climbing erratically up the vast atrium of the stairwell, which he could see rising upwards for five, maybe six floors. Tacked to each frame was a label describing the bare section of wall it housed, its composition and age, listing points of interest as indicated by arrows affixed directly to the rock: a fossilised fern, a shard of mineral, a volcanic lesion. Violena pushed on and led them down the hall to the left, and through a door into the most magnificent library Stroop had ever seen.

Jack, who had taken Stroop's hand on the walk up to the hall, dropped it and ran towards Mabel, who was sitting at one of the many desks, her chin resting on bunched fingers, reading the book laid out before her. Jack kissed her on the head and she stood up and smiled.

'You've had a good day, so Thomas tells me,' she said, and started automatically straightening Jack's jacket and smoothing his hair. She noted the great rip in his sleeve and tutted but said nothing more, only smiled.

'Mr Stroop,' she said, and Stroop saw that she was standing a little straighter than she usually did, her shoulders a little squarer, holding her clasped hands in front of her, something he had never seen her do. Something Violena was doing now. It pleased him, though he couldn't have said exactly why, gave him comfort that she was comfortable here in their new surroundings.

And what surroundings! The room was narrow and long, and had bookcases sewn the length of it like herringbones, a desk at every intersection, lit by gas-lamps at each side to eliminate the shadows cast upon whatever book might have been placed there to be read. More than that, the roof above was independent of the rest of the building, had nothing above it but sky and a dozen huge glass domes to let the sunlight pass unhindered into the room below. He turned his head upwards to gaze at them, never thought of the boy who had to scamper up there every day to brush the snow off them with his broom, rub the glass free of bird debris and wet leaves with his rags so that the room below shone with as much brightness as the day could afford.

Major Pytchley was standing, as was habitual, with his back to one of the several fireplaces, his hands neatly folded behind him, his legs outspread, his weight slightly more to the right than to the left.

'Ah, Mr Stroop,' he said, but didn't move; he knew the effect the library had on people, particularly those who had an affinity with books, and there was no doubting Stroop to be one of those. 'Welcome to the wonder that is Weeems' Bibliopoly.'

Stroop could find nothing to say. He was trying to calculate how many tomes were held within these walls: one hundred to each shelf, six hundred to each stack, twice that taking into consideration the stacks were double-backed, a minimum of ten stacks to each side . . .

'I had no idea,' he managed to say at last, and then Mabel was by his side, put her hand on his arm, moving him to a chair.

'I know,' she was saying, 'isn't it extraordinary? And every one of these books has an index card and they're all cross-referenced by author and subject. Violena did it all herself. I was thinking, when we got home . . .'

But Stroop wasn't really listening, could already feel the tips of his fingers itching to wander down the spines of these books, had quite forgotten the reason he was here at all, couldn't wait to start exploring. He might have been a mountaineer who has climbed every mountain in the world in every possible way, only suddenly to find a mountain range undiscovered, and one so vast it would take a man's whole lifetime to be explored.

Violena came forward with a tray and poured everyone a glass of wine. She had to wrap Stroop's fingers about the glass stem one by one.

'Uncle Weeems was a great man,' she was saying, 'and in so many ways. Some of these books are in languages we don't even know how to translate. They have illustrations of animals and plants that no one has ever given a name to, except in their native lands.'

'There's still a few crates of books that haven't been unpacked,' Mabel was kneeling by Stroop's chair, 'that Mr Weeems sent back from his last expedition. They've taken nearly four years to get here. Just imagine, Mr Stroop, what might be in them!'

Stroop at last managed to refocus, and he patted Mabel's hand where she had rested it on the side of his chair. 'Perhaps you could help, my dear,' he said, and as he said it, he realised with a horrid jolt that it might be true, and that perhaps Mabel would rather be here cataloguing books with Violena than at home with him. For the first time since entering the library, he looked around at the room as if it had no books at all, saw Pytchley by the fire; Jack and Thomas engaged in some game of their own devising involving firedogs and cinders; Violena, so erect and sure, handing a glass of wine to Maximillian Orcutt; Mabel with her face upturned, like the moon emerging from a cloud, eager for the sun to give it light. Perhaps she would be better here, he thought, and just as quickly: Could I bear it if she stayed? But the moment was over and Pytchley was speaking.

'So, have we learnt anything today, Mr Stroop? I am eager to hear what you have found. What with Bittlestone,' he shifted uncomfortably, pushed his shoulders out of their habitual stoop and back into it again, 'it seems perhaps things have changed.'

Stroop put his thumb and finger to his eyes and rubbed his lids a moment, brought his hand back over his mouth, down again to his lap.

'There are things I have found out today,' he said, 'as I'm sure everyone has done,' and even Jack and Thomas put down their fire-tongs and nodded, 'but I think maybe we need to start somewhere, so perhaps I should go first.'

And so he did.

The tower experience had been illuminating for Whilbert Stroop, and disturbing. It had reminded him of when he had pulled Jack out of that fire; the smell of skin ripped from burning timber, the large black blisters that bloomed upon them both like soft-skinned eggs about to hatch, the purple domes that swelled like jellyfish from which blood and serum carelessly spilt whenever they were poked or caught. He had kicked at the earth with his foot, at the charcoaled halo that lay in the lee of the tower where the wind had blown the flames, a rust-coloured rim holding it in where the iron had been leached from the soil by the heat. They had gone over the threshold, Stroop first, Sansibar behind, holding his hat in his hands.

Stroop saw the stone stairway rising in front of him, each step felted over with ash. He could make out footprints, guessed that children had found it fun to run them up and down them though the steps no longer led anywhere. Their pock-marked faces rose hopelessly into nothing above the carapace of charred stone walls. The loft was gone and lying all around them, reduced to dust so insignificant in quantity, so light, so friable, it was hard to imagine that not long before it had strength and height, and been seen from all the fields for miles around. Stroop also saw the remnants of the metal gutter. Bent in several places, fatigued by the heat, the circle could still be plainly seen. It had settled by the head of the stairwell like a hoop at a fairground stall around a broken skittle.

'What was this?' asked Stroop of Sansibar, who was standing quietly behind him, feeling this more of a graveyard than the one in which his goats so frequently fed. Stroop indicated the broken circle with his hand and Sansibar obliged.

'It's what used to hold the fuel,' said Sansibar. 'The tower was in way of being a beacon. We'd set it burning if there was something needed saying, like a storm coming, or a wedding, or . . .' he stopped. He had being going to say 'funeral', but he couldn't bring himself to utter the word, not here. Not where the stiff boy had died so alone and untended. He explained about the kindling and the fuel kept up top for the event, about the guttering that circled the upper wall to hold the fire.

'But surely,' said Stroop, 'there couldn't have been enough there, even in storage, to bring the tower down?'

This had been one of the things that Ipsing Sansibar had been wondering about and he said so.

'I think there's something else you should see,' he went on, and put his hand on Stroop's elbow, tilted him slightly to the right. 'This here was the guardroom. It wasn't much used, but the door was tough and the window in it barred.'

Stroop could see the guardroom door lying flat where the last of the hinges had been broken, the slight space around it where the debris had been pushed by the pressure of the air as it fell. Stroop stepped over it, on it. He put his hand out as if there were no light to see, though the morning made everything in the round remnant of tower visible. The bell was still there, and someone had taken the time to polish the ash from its surface, making its brightness too incongruous in these surroundings, a too-new rose on an old-dug grave.

'The boy?' asked Stroop, and Sansibar pointed. There were a few jagged indentations in the blackened earth where levers had been placed to lift the bell from what was left of the boy, the raw brown of his shadow obscene in amongst the surrounding grey.

'There's something else.' Sansibar coughed as Stroop began to scuff his feet through the inches of ash, which were all that remained of the upper loft of the bell tower, sent a drift of it up into the air, saw it shaft through with light like a sunrise lifts from the horizon and pierces the haar from off the sea.

'Where was the key?' asked Stroop, who had already noted the thinness of the gap between the bars of the guardroom door, had already guessed that something here was wrong, that the boy couldn't have set this thing alight with no help. It was possible he had ignited the tinder in the gutter by accident or design, possible even that he had added every last bit of wood from the stockpile to the gutter, but surely even that couldn't have done this much damage. He could see the small blister-marks that pitted the outside metal of the huge bell, involuntarily clenched his hands to hide from the heat he knew must once have been.

Ipsing Sansibar came up behind him, took care not to step on the guardroom door as if it were the lid of a sarcophagus. 'We found it near his hand, sir,' he told Stroop, and Stroop could see it still: the thin grey bar of metal next to the thin grey disturbance in thc dust where the boy's arm had been lifted from the guardroom floor.

'Why would a boy set fire to the tower and then shut himself into a guardroom he knew he couldn't get out of?' Stroop spoke the words that had been troubling Sansibar all week. He had seen it himself when he had come with the men of the village, when they had kicked down what was left of the guardroom door, when they had lifted the bell off the boy and seen the little heap of ash by his hand, when he had come back later and kicked a little more ash off the heap and knew it was the key to the guardroom, which was always left in the lock. He had left it where it was because he knew something was all wrong about it. About the way the tower had burnt. About the way the boy had died.

'Someone did this,' said Stroop, and Ipsing Sansibar heard his goats complaining in the punt, heard the bell the last time it had sounded when the heat was taking it down, heard the crack of timber as the bell loft gave and fell, heard the whimpering of a dog he had once had to kill because it had dug its way into the chicken net and left the feathers flying and the blood around its mouth, how the dog had cowered, his eyes wide and frightened because it didn't know that what it had done was wrong and couldn't understand the axe that came towards it but knew what it was and what it meant. He closed his eyes. Saw the nightmare of the boy again as he lay trapped beneath the bell and hoped without really hoping that the boy had died before the fire had set his skin alight and burnt him like a wick burns through a lump of tallow.

And so this is what Stroop told the people gathered in the library, told Violena Sedge as she sat so straight and trim in her chair, and Maximillian Orcutt as he leant on the back of that chair as if he already owned her, told Major Pytchley who had seen so much worse in the Mysorean Wars and yet known nothing so bad as this, told Mabel and Jack and Thomas as they sat on footstools by the hearth.

'I don't believe that boy set fire to the tower,' said Stroop. 'I believe that someone went there deliberately to burn it down. I believe it was the same man seen earlier that day carrying a heavy load upon his back. A man who came down the track from the hill behind the heronry.' He paused, watched Pytchley as he irritably tugged at the edge of his boot; went on, 'I don't believe the man who burnt the tower deliberately harmed the boy.' Mabel had her hand resting on her collarbone. He saw her fingers twitch, hoped he hadn't been too brutal. 'I believe he gave the boy the key, which we found still in the guardroom, thinking the boy would let himself out. And for this reason,' he took a sip of the wine Violena had given him previously, 'I don't believe the man came from here, or surely he would have realised the bars in the guardroom were too narrow to let a hand through to reach the lock, with a key or without.' He stopped, allowed himself a brief jealous glance at the library he would never have. 'And for this same reason, I don't think the person who set the tower alight is the same man who murdered Finkel Hanka.'

There was a brief pause, and then Pytchley moved quite violently forward, dropping his cane to the flags of the hearth. 'But then,' he spoke too loudly, 'I don't understand this. What about Bittlestone? Surely you don't mean to tell me there are two murderers or even three on the loose?'

He was too upset, Stroop saw, to evaluate things logically. He wondered why Pytchley didn't disengage himself from the foot that so obviously bothered him. Thought that in this company he wouldn't have hesitated to unclip it or unlatch it or however it was attached.

'Of course not.' Stroop tried to be soothing. 'Coincidence of that kind is just too rare. No. I don't believe that at all. I believe the person who murdered Finkel Hanka was the same person who killed Bittlestone, but I do believe it was done for quite different reasons.'

They talked that night at Astonishment Hall. They talked through all that had happened and all that they knew.

Stroop laid out before them a list of events: Uwe Proctor Dvoshka had come here, he told them, from some disaster that had befallen him on the shores of the Black Sea. This much he knew from the letters Uwe's parents had given him – not of the disaster, whatever that had been, but of some great thing that Uwe was about to do. No one knew what. The Dvoshka parents were still awaiting news from Elusia's family, with whom Uwe had worked so closely for so many years, but letters from them came with the firm's mail, and only sporadically, accompanying the latest shipment of glass from Bohemia. What they did know from the last letter Uwe himself had written to them, was that it had come from somewhere in this area.

They also knew that two weeks ago, the bell tower of St Weonard's had been set alight and burnt to the ground, the stiff boy with it, that someone must have brought fuel to it, that the fuel must have been primed with alcohol or oil.

Soon after that, Orcutt's Perspective Box had been stolen from the Astonishment Exhibition Room. Immediately after that, Leopold Huxby had died of an apoplectic stroke from the shock of it and though it was a natural death, it had probably come before its time.

Then had come Finkel Hanka's ride out to Brougham Crags to find out what he could about the theft of the Perspective Box and the people who had visited the exhibition and left their names in the visitors' book. That he had been murdered below Black Fell was not in doubt. The doctor had been most emphatic about the crushing of the skull, which must have been done to incapacitate him before the fire had taken hold.

And then there was the killing on the bridge. Pytchley had brought the instruments back with him from the village as Stroop had instructed him to do, and the crossbow shaft and knife that Dr Thacker had removed from Bittlestone's body now lay before him on the table. The shaft had been engineered for distance and speed: it was thin and the barbed spike sharply angled. Most probably it had originally been made for the use of a deer-bagger. That implied someone local. Stroop had been surprised that such weapons were so freely available – at which remark, Thomas supplied, and Pytchley agreed, that he had seen several crossbows in the stable tackroom and that they were common hereabouts for stopping deer. The knife had been a hunter's knife: heavy, horn-handled, it had impact marks on its haft as if it had been repeatedly bludgeoned with a stone. This was the thing that Stroop had thought of when he had stumbled that morning a few moments before his encounter with the goat. After visiting the tower, and thanking Ipsing Sansibar for his help, he had retraced his steps to the bridge, had searched meticulously in the grass about each side, and found the indent where a stone had long lain, and only recently been removed. He had looked under the bridge, careful to avoid the stains on the boards when he had lain down for a better look, had seen a stone the size a man's hand might encompass not one yard distant, risked his boots, got them wet and made the walk back to the Hall uncomfortable, but had ascertained that the stone also had blow-marks imprinted on to its underside.

'It came from the side of the bridge that led from the heronry,' Stroop added. 'There was a clear mark in the grass from where it had been lifted.'

He looked at Major Pytchley. 'What is there behind the heronry? I saw a track going on up the hill. Where does it go?'

Pytchley informed them it went up to the valley where the first canal works had been sited. At Stroop's prompting, he explained a little more. He told them about the planned

Carlisle-to-Darlington canal, a branch of which had already been dug through their valley, the same that had brought Stroop up from the side of the Tees. It was being constructed in stages, dependent primarily on how the fuelling rivers and reservoirs lay, and also on the subscriptions raised from local land and business owners. The initial works had been started closest to the several lakes and tarns that lay in the valley of Eden. It had necessitated the diversion of several rivers, one of which had caused the flooding of St Weonard's church and the land of the low-lying plain that fell away below Sedgwick. The track from the heronry led up to those initial works, which had started some twenty or more years ago. Stroop had surmised the same, and had found a small area just inside the heronry elms where a man had stood and stamped and leant and waited. It was from here that the crossbow had been fired, he said, and from here the assailant came to finish off the job on the bridge, picking up a stone on the way.

'It is the same direction from which a man was seen prior to the tower incident,' added Stroop, 'a man who was seen carrying some kind of heavy burden.'

'But many men are seen,' objected Pytchley. 'People come here to work on the canals because the money is reliable. They think it better than working in the cotton factories of Lancashire or wherever they have come from, but they find the work too hard. Then they scratch up their belongings and go, often coming on here for Sedgwick and the boats to take them over to Darlington.'

'But,' said Stroop, 'how many go back through St Weonard's? Wouldn't they rather go the other way? Back the way they came? Or follow the line of the canal directly down the valley to Astonishment?'

They were sitting around the largest of the library desks, which faced the main fireplace. Several trays of cold meats, pickles, cheeses and bread had been placed there. Pytchley tore at the goose on his plate but didn't answer. Didn't eat. Pushed the pale flesh back into its sauce and tried not to think of all the corpses he had seen and forgotten until he had been up to Brougham and smelt Finkel Hanka's death, tasted it in his mouth, wanted once again to retch, but covered it with a mouthful of sharp wine, wondered if he should not have served another vintage, felt ashamed that he should think of wine at such a time.

'Isn't it more likely that the man who killed Bittlestone is the same man who set the tower alight?' It was Maximillian Orcutt. He had been quiet up until now, had been content to stand and wait. Had been sick with guilt that his Perspective Box might be linked to the death of Hanka, had been looking at Violena and felt embarrassment that he could not help but be glad that this had so obliquely brought them together. Had felt jealousy at the way she looked at this Whilbert Stroop when he spoke. The man was so articulate, so compact with his words. He didn't know that Whilbert Stroop saw no one before him when he told them of his visit to the tower, only a small boy crushed beneath a bell without anyone to rescue him, and that his thoughts were moving inside his head like millipedes in a woodpile, and that he didn't see Violena Sedge at all.

'The same man?' said Stroop. 'No,' he looked at Orcutt, but without focus, the landscape of his vision still at the tower and the journey back, 'I don't think so.' He fingered the haft of the knife absently, the indents on the horn handle caused by the repeated blows of a stone that sent it cracking down through Bittlestone's skull until it drove through his tongue and into his jaw. 'I think these things are quite separate. On the one hand, we have the burning of the tower and the unfortunate but unplanned death of the boy; on the other, we have two vicious and brutal killings carried out by someone who plainly knew the area and what went on within it. Otherwise why wait for Bittlestone? How could a stranger possibly have known that he would be coming that morning to cull the herons instead of further up the river for duck or geese? The murderer might have waited weeks if he had not already been intimate with Bittlestone's routine.' He fanned his fingers over the notes that Violena and Mabel had made that day, though they were still unread.

Jack and Thomas had just sprung their news of the visit to the man at the steamer post-house. They had asked about Uwe's last letter, had held it up to the man who had been prepared to dismiss them immediately as a couple of scamps until they had mentioned Stroop's name. Everybody knew that Pytchley had hired the man to help find out who had killed Hanka, and everybody wanted that. He had thought hard, turned the letter over several times, looked for his stamp, found it, and then he had remembered the man vaguely. He'd been a canal-man, he thought, maybe fifty, thickset, well built, maybe sandy-haired. He'd not spoken that he had remembered, just shoved the letter through the grille with enough money and a bit more. Not often that happened, said the ticket man, not often at all.

So, they knew now for certain that there were two men involved: there was Uwe, who according to his parents had been a small, dark, pale-skinned boy, and there was the sandy-haired, well-built man who had delivered his letter to the post-house. Presumably this second man was the one Uwe had come to visit, and presumably it was this second man who was Uwe's accuser, having scrawled a hasty message over the letter he had been sent to post. Or perhaps he was just a man who had been given a letter and asked to take it to the post-house. They talked about it, over and over, but could find no means of deciding which of the propositions was most likely.

It was Stroop drew the conversation to a conclusion as he fingered the papers on the desk before him, recognising Mabel's neat cursive.

'There is something else going on here,' he said, 'something we cannot see. We have the tower incident and the theft of Orcutt's Perspective Box, and only later comes the violence. Possibly the constable stumbled on something he was not supposed to see, but the brutality with which this was confronted is beyond most men. And Bittlestone? What of Bittlestone? A man who by all accounts was like any other. He laboured on the estate at whatever he was needed. He collected butterflies in his spare time and once a month, during the spring, he culled the young heron at the heronry.'

'Who did he sell his butterflies to?' asked Mabel. 'Didn't you say, Mr Stroop, that the boy on the bridge mentioned a collector?'

'Ah, yes,' said Stroop, and sat up abruptly, 'the collector. And the pencil. You remember the boy mentioned a pencil?' He looked around at nobody in particular, tapped at his notebook with his finger, withdrew the small telescopic cylinder from its spine. 'Just like this one.' He held all three slender inches of it between his thumb and middle finger, then grasped its middle with his other hand, and pulled on the ring at one end. Immediately the pencil extended to treble its original length, the shaft from one end, the point from the other. 'There is something here we are not seeing, one thing hidden inside another. One thing masquerading as something else.' He closed his eyes briefly, then suddenly stood up. 'I must think about all this further, and there are certain things I must find out, and yet other things which I must ask you all to do.'

Standing just outside the library door, the cook, Ada Ribblesdale, overheard this exchange and frowned. Copious wrinkles furrowing her forehead like a new-ploughed field.

'What's he getting up to?' whispered the frizz-haired housemaid, who was digging at her back with an empty tray.

'Hush,' was all Ada answered, gesturing the girl along the hall before her, down the short flight of steps at its end that led to the pantry and the kitchen.

She hadn't discovered anything she didn't already know, except the bit about the man down at the steamer post-house. She was down there often, not to buy tickets or post letters, but because with the canal came the steamers and with the steamers came all sorts of things they would not have otherwise seen, and the station had turned, with no hurry or outward fuss, into the Valley Stores. She knew the man who ran the place, and thought she might have her own private word with him. They both of them knew everybody hereabouts, had lived here all their lives. Of course, she didn't know the men at the canal works – no one did, apart from a couple of the young girls who should have known better and soon regretted it. And she agreed with Sid down at the stores on this: the man who had come with the letter must have been a canal-worker or he'd have known him, just like she would have. Just like she knew everyone, including Bittlestone and Leopold Huxby.

She sighed a little to think of Leopold. She had stepped out with him once, years ago, when they were barely more than children. She remembered his face as it had been then, so full of the things he had wanted to be and do but, like so many of them, he had never left the valley despite his talk, and had ended up at the Hall with everybody else. She also knew that he had been happy here, as she had been, even after the turmoil of the Sedgwicks dying out and the interloper Weeems buying the place to pay the debts no one knew the old family had had; how he'd ripped down the old hall and built it all back up again so strangely, using the same stones but putting them together so differently. Still, she had a soft spot for Halliday Weeems. He had kept all the old staff on, paid their wages even though the new Hall hadn't even been built and there was nothing for them to do.

And she'd liked Major Pytchley well enough when he had come, admired him even, being an old war veteran and all, and having no left foot to speak of. He had treated them well when he had taken over the Hall. And Miss Sedge. Everyone knew how decent he'd been to her, and they all appreciated it. Ada thought of Violena, and of Finkel Hanka dying the way he did. Everyone knew they ought to have been married but somehow never did. And now here was this man Stroop, with his strange little entourage. Quite obviously they weren't family, though they treated one another as such. The children were his wards, Major Pytchley had said, but how did one man come to acquire so many? The girl plainly wasn't related to either of the boys, and neither they to each other. They looked too different, sounded too different. Brothers and sisters moved the same, said the same things, had similarities of profile or the way their hair grew or had the same set to the chin or mouth or eyes. And then there were the scars on the older boy, and on the stranger Stroop's hands. Like everybody about the place – the three housemaids, the stableboys and the carriage-driver, not to mention all the estate workers – they'd talked about nothing else but the bizarre goings-on and the man who had come up from London to sort it all out.

Ada dreaded meeting Roze Hanka in the lane. She'd been friends with the woman ever since she'd arrived here, her and her boy, brought back as straggle-whips from one of Weeems' expeditions. That they'd come from Hungary was most of what she knew, though she didn't know where Hungary was. Apparently the woman had helped Weeems out when he'd got into a scrape with some Prussian soldiers and he'd brought her back here by way of thanks. Ada had been a kitchen maid back then and Weeems had asked her to make the foreigners welcome. The boy had only been a toddler and she'd liked to play with him, enjoyed the way he'd made games out of everything he touched, out of every piece of stick or blackbird feather.

Ada felt the lump grow in her throat and the tears begin to push at the back of her eyes. She hated the way everything had changed. She wanted the last few weeks to wipe themselves off the calendar and start again. She wanted to see Leopold fussing in his Exhibition Room or fiddling with the taps in the kitchen, pretending to stop the drips that never stopped, while she slapped bread from one side of the kneading-trough to the other, the two of them gossiping about the latest lodge guests, boasting about their titles, laughing at their silly hats and impracticable clothes. She wanted to be able to go over to Roze's after she'd finished for the night, take a little tipple with her, play a game of cards, laugh a little at the way Roze still pronounced her words even after so many years here at Astonishment. Instead, she let a few wet tears slip down her cheeks as she took off her apron.

She looked out into the darkness of the evening, saw her own face reflected in the window like an overgrown apple, saw the dark clouds behind the hill rolling off the moor. She took off her house-slippers, put on her clogs, stepped out and closed the door behind her. She looked to her right, saw the soft glow coming from the library roof domes. The yew hedges were moving slightly, as if pulled by an unseen tide and she caught the smell of open-roasted ox coming from the farm down by the river. She glanced back once at the door, crossed herself, thought of the stranger Stroop. Prayed God that he had come to set things right, because she knew the major couldn't, and the authorities wouldn't, and that someone had to.

She saw Roze's little house, paused for a moment with her hand on the gate, but then the dim light she thought she had glimpsed through the window was extinguished, and she lifted away her hand and turned for home.

7

Bellpenny and the Field of Dogs

11 March

LIFE HAD BEEN hard and bleak for Medan Skimmington Bellpenny, but no harder and bleaker than for anyone else. He knew this, but still he felt cheated. He had been given a name, but no idea where it came from or what it meant or where most of his family had been, or where they had gone. He sat on the outside step of his cot door, didn't feel the cold, which was the same inside as it was without. He looked up at the sky, saw the clouds move for a moment and reveal an indescribable density of stars. He tried to picture the battles they represented, the old legends he had been taught about the Norse gods they depicted and their dogs and their beasts, and the disagreements that were supposedly frozen in the heavens for ever to remind the men below of what had gone before. He spat out of one side of his mouth. Sharing his disgust, the clouds pulled their curtains closed across the astral theatre, shielded him from the petty plays of the gods. They looked different here, he thought, those stars.

They changed as you rounded the world and made nonsense of those tales he had once been told. He preferred the words he had learnt from the Siberians indentured into labour as he had been, of the Great Raven who had sharpened his knife against the millstone of the sky, made stars of the sparks, and men of the dust that had fallen to the earth. How the Creator had spread his immense black wings over the world, darkened it with the snow that fell from them until he could no longer see what he had made. He rolled another spill of tobacco, lit it, watched a few shreds shrivel and die as they fell into the frost at his feet. So many things done and gone, he thought, just like that. One brief wink, then out. That was what he would be, what everyone would be. He thought of the sacrificial grounds the Siberians had told him of, where they killed their dogs and hooked their lower jaws on to sticks and left them hanging there for the ravens to gather into their gullets and take them home. A forest of pole-poked familiars swept away in the snow-storm of their gods.

The futility of the universe overwhelmed him as the snow began again to fall, screened him and his house from the moors and the hills and the valleys and the rest of the world that he had travelled and not cared for until he had come home. He dropped the cigarette from his mouth, crushed it into the soft drift that had accumulated already by his boots.

He went inside, scraped the door into the untidy warp of its frame, looked for a moment at the rusty bolt but didn't try to draw it. He stamped to free his feet from snow, was pleased the boy was gone and the place his own again. He moved across the darkness of the room, drew the sheet back from his work-bench, lit the spirit lamp, thought of the Great Raven tenting the sky with its wings, could almost hear the wind fluting amongst its feathers as the snow slowly fell away from them and blinded the world to its god. He slid his hand underneath the desk, released the movement, drew out the drawer. He picked out every one of his creations and placed them carefully about the room, stood for a moment as the lamplight caught at them, then moved to run his fingers over their smoothness and curves, gently possessed them one by one with his fingers, saw them shine on every surface.

A sudden snatch of song shone inside his head. A woman's voice. A strange voice. Those words he had not heard for years and years and years. From his homeland. His real homeland. The homeland of his mother. And then he recognised the words for what they were: the lullaby that first had eased his sleeping, and later his loneliness. That hard wrench that took him from what should truly have been his and brought him to a land that was not his own. 'I have, in the evening, playmates . . .' He could remember every last word and almost laughed to growl it out as he glanced his eyes about the shoddiness of the room, the small pockets of perfection he had placed here and there, the absolute power they gave him, the breaking-down and building-up. The taking. The possession. Just as his mother had once told him in those songs, in that old poem he had tucked into the wallet his father had once given him.

He was his own Great Raven and everything else outside of his own skin was nothing but a sacrificial field of dogs.

So be it, he thought, and knew the implications, laughed at them, rejoiced in them. Until the Alltsaman. So be it. And once again, he growled out the old, old song, which no one but himself would ever hear.

8

Entering the Labyrinth

Morning, 12 March

IT WAS THE shiniest morning Jack had ever known. He woke early, before Stroop and Mabel and even Thomas, had needed to get up to have a pee but didn't like to use the pot so had crept out of the bed, leaving Thomas and the bedsheets he had pulled up over his head to hide the cold. Had gone out through their room into the little kitchen and opened the door. The ice had caught at his lungs as he eased it open and he saw the vastness of the landscape stretched out before him like new-scraped vellum swept clean by the snow. It still fell soft and sparse, blown here and there by the breath that exuded from the land as it began to wake – from the marshes and the rivers and the warmth of cattle and sheep and goats still byred in their pens. He saw the clouds settled on their hills glow pink as the sun began to break somewhere far beneath, heard an owl call its way home to the big oak just beyond the lodge where the dovecote lay, where Thomas had scattered and flappered the pigeons far and wide with his climbing and falling the day before.

Right up towards the Hall he saw, heard the slight high pitch of pipistrelles flitting around the bole of an old elm, the faint movement of hooves in their stables as the horses began to wake as he was waking, felt a part of everything and everything a part of him and, without thinking, he ran out from the door and began cart-wheeling inexpertly across the tide of snow, never caring for his hands freezing and his nose going blue and his long johns skittering up his legs where the elastic was too loose.

Mabel woke suddenly, lifted from her light sleep by the sounds she was hearing. She shivered. She drew her counterpane around her shoulders, still unnerved by noises she didn't understand, like that noise now, like snow sloofing from an overburdened roof. She sat up, moved to the window, cautiously drew back the one shutter that had blown closed during the night. She didn't put her face too close to the glass for fear of what might be on the other side, but she could see the blue of morning light spreading across the valley, the last few scuds of snow lifting in a gentle breeze from the drifts that had gathered on the underside of tree-limbs and hedges. And she saw Jack, circling through the wide blank white beyond, arms outspread, face lifted, catching a few last flakes with his tongue, eyes closed, a look of such ecstatic happiness on his face that she had to step back a pace and catch her breath, and the tears started falling down her face before she could stop them and she wanted to be out there with him and be a part of what she knew that he must feel but also knew that for her it was a long time past. So she withdrew the counterpane from her shoulders, straightened her underclothes, climbed back into the dress that Violena Sedge had laid out for her the day before, never wondered why she didn't assume the dried-out dress that was her own.

She wasn't the only one who saw Jack that morning. Jeremiah Pytchley so often did not sleep, and particularly not these last few nights, and had spent the dark hours once again in his study, had drawn back the thick velvet curtains so that he could gaze on the blackness of night as it hemmed its way so effortlessly about him and his hall. He had felt such despair after the meeting with Stroop in the library that he had not bothered to climb the stairs to his bed, but had started rereading the journals he had kept all through his Indian campaign; regretted doing it now, regretted each person lost, each letter of commiseration and commendation he had had to write. And now he looked down on the lawn that was his own, past the yew hedges and the gravel paths, the blank glass of the Exhibition Room that lay accusing him to his right, gazed past it all and saw a small dark figure playing handstands in the dawn and the snow, felt his heart give a sudden jolt as if some stone had rolled away from it and opened it up a little, let in a little light, and thought for the first time in what seemed a lifetime that perhaps, only just perhaps, things might yet see themselves right. That this Whilbert Stroop might be able to help him after all. That Astonishment and all it held might yet be preserved and not for ever sullied by what it and he had seen.

Stroop was in good order when he finally awoke. He could not remember ever sleeping so deeply. He put it down to country air and the exertion of the past few days. His mind was clear as ice. He could smell bacon frying and toast toasting and could hear Jack and Thomas laughing and arguing.

'That was never you!' shouted Thomas, a boy who was always awake the second he opened his eyes, though the longer he had been at Stroop's, the longer he took to open them. 'That was Big Woolly Foot. He's all huge and hairy like a wolf with red eyes big as saucers and eats children for breakfast.'

He could hear Jack bouncing on his chair, and Mabel telling them to be still or they'd upset the porridge pot and she'd have to start it all again twice at thick.

'Yuk!' said Thomas. 'Who wants porridge anyway?' though Stroop knew quite well that Thomas loved the porridge Mabel made, dribbled with honey and cream and so unlike the gruel they'd called porridge in the poorhouses Thomas had once had to endure.

'It was me! It was me!' Jack was yelling, 'I'd've seen old Silly Foot if he'd been out there, honest I would. Wouldn't I, Mabel?'

'That you would,' said Mabel, and Stroop heard the sizzle of egg hitting hot bacon fat, shoved his feet through his breeks and his arms through his jacket, came into the small kitchen to join them. They were hard pushed for space, the table being barely bigger than two boards' width, but already Mabel had made griddle scones and drizzled them with butter and some jam she'd found in the cupboards, and a big pot of tea and a couple of kippers fried in bacon butter.

'Mornin', Mr Stroop,' shouted Jack happily as Mabel spooned him out some porridge. 'I've been up for *hours*! I've made lots of pretty patterns in the snow. You should see, shouldn't he, Mabel?'

Mabel poured hot water into the tea kettle, put milk into a pot, laid some cups out on the table. 'I've seen them, Jack. And very good they are too.'

She smiled at Stroop and he vaguely remembered all those breakfasts he used to have, when not even Jack was with him, when he'd come down of a morning and set last night's coffee on the range only to find it cold and dead. Drunk the old coffee dregs anyway, straight out of the pot, felt the bitterness of it in his throat, never wanted to taste that bitterness again.

They set off soon after breakfast, each according to the task Stroop had assigned them: Mabel to the Hall to work with Violena; Jack, Thomas and Stroop to Brougham Crags.

Mabel and Stroop had talked over the notes she had taken from the day's work in the library the day before. As Stroop had asked, they had tried to find out as much as possible about the little devotional book that Uwe had mentioned so often in his early letters. They didn't have much to go on, just a name, Jan Amos Komensky, and it wasn't until Violena stumbled across the Latinised spelling that they got anywhere. Once they had Comenius in their grasp, Violena's system worked swift and smooth as a sled across snow, and they soon had several salient facts collected.

Komensky/Comenius had been born in 1592 in Uhersky Brod, a trading town in the White Carpathians, become a bishop of the Moravian Brotherhood, travelled, taught theology, even came to England by parliamentary invitation, and would have built his radical College of All the Sciences there if the Civil War had not intervened. He'd ended up, via Sweden, back in Sarospatak on the Latorica River, a stone's throw from the borders of his native land. So far, so dry, Mabel had thought, and though she had been diligent in her note-taking and enjoyed burrowing through the book-stacks like a mole explores its castle below the earth, she hadn't found out anything she thought might actually help.

It was then that Violena stopped running her fingers through a tray of catalogue cards, plucked one out, stared hard at it a moment, then sent her chair screeching across the floor like bats pouring from a belfry.

'Come on,' she'd said to Mabel, sweeping past her and through a thickly curtained arch, which led to an adjunct of the library Mabel hadn't even realised was there.

If there could be any room more breathtaking than the library, here it was. The place was decked about like a ship: smooth-planked floors bare of rugs and carpets, the wood continuing up the walls for about five feet, every yard of it pierced by a porthole, the glass painted over with a fine yellow paint that made the light soft as honey as it flowed through the windows over the wood and on to the glass cases that stood in rows across the length of the room. And there was more. Where the panelling stopped, the mirrors began, and ran the whole wall up and across the ceiling so the light danced everywhere and shadows were eliminated entirely.

'This way,' Violena had said, gently taking hold of Mabel's arm and propelling her across the floor as if she were on wheels. She gazed at each case as she passed and saw within them the outspread arms of a hundred books, some branded across with bold, wide letters, other swimming with colour, rimmed with gold, yet more of huge size, holding plated-etchings or woodcuts, or the actual blocks from which the prints had been made.

'Some of these are very old,' Violena said. 'They are our incunabula, the cradle of the books and broadsheets we are so familiar with today. But what I want to show you is . . .' She tapped her fingers one by one against her thumb, counting off her catalogue in her head, coming to rest just past the middle of the room. 'Here it is,' she said, and Mabel could see Violena's reflection cascading away into infinity where the mirror met the glass and each looked into the other. 'The *Orbis Sensualiam Pictus*, the whole world collected in one book and its knowledge described in pictures. Not an original from 1658, but very close. Some say it was the first encyclopaedia ever made. This was published in Germany in 1667. It is Comenius' *magnum opus*, a whole new way of teaching people by illustration. And . . .' She put her hand below the base of the case, found the hidden lever, released the catch. There was an almost imperceptible noise, like a snake gliding through dry grass or zigzagging over sand, and she slid the top of the glass case, the one side over the other, and Comenius' world view was revealed, the simple woodcut and its accompanying text showing the terrestrial sphere and all the known lands of the world, the paper slightly raised at the edge of the ink as if it somehow expected more. Violena leant over the glass and carefully picked up the book, blew on it, though not a single speck of dust rose from her breath. Then she flicked gently through the pages from the world's creation to its end.

'I thought so,' she said, and held the book out and open

so that Mabel could see, translated the Latin script as she pointed out the second tiny book hidden within the hollowed-out cover at the back of the other like a sleeping child. '*The Labyrinth of the World and the Paradise of the Heart*,' she breathed. 'As your Mr Stroop wanted, so have we found.'

It seemed they all found out something that day, including Jack and Thomas. They had gone up to Ascham and on through Bedlington, over the crags and down the brae towards the panning grounds below Black Fell. They could see the place Pytchley had described, a circle of flat ground between track and river, innocence restored by the bright blank snow sparkling beneath the bowl of blue that was the sky. A large group of birds had congregated at the far end, and Stroop could hear them arguing and pulling at something beneath the snow. As they neared, the rooks and crows scattered themselves like twists of black paper, flapped and worried above the dozen buzzards, who for the moment had stayed put, feet splayed across the snow, yellow beaks tearing at the raggled heaps they held between their claws. Stroop felt sick, wondered if they had found a part of Finkel Hanka somehow left behind, didn't share Pytchley's views of people being buried in the sky. He saw the dull red splashes in the snow, the dirty skins of rabbits turned inside out, patches of fur and vein adhering to the membranes separating skin from flesh. And then he made out the untidy line of traps, simple strands of wire tied to a stick at one end, a sliding noose at the other. The sort that a man would set at night and empty in the morning. The sort a man might use if he were staying here panning for a few days. But no one had been here to check them and the animals had strangled as they struggled, left little pools of bitter urine to turn orange in the snow, had frozen and thawed, frozen and thawed, and now, ten days after Finkel Hanka's death, the congress of carrion-eaters watched Stroop's arrival with mistrustful eyes, reluctantly beat their speckled wings against the snow and departed, carrying what they could between their talons, leaving sigils of spoilt green guts and little clumps of bloody fur to drift across the virgin snow.

Thomas and Jack, being on foot, were a few steps behind when Stroop pulled his horse to a stop, crumpled off it without grace, watched the swirl of rook settle and craw in a nearby copse. Avoiding the squiggles and scrawls of entrails, he squeaked his way across the snowy circle, saw the humped shoulder where the remnants of the cart still lay, pushed a little at the snow around it, could see the dark scorch of earth beneath, but that was all. They followed a stream as it departed from the river, enjoyed the sound of the water as it went beneath the singing-gallery of ice that had overgrown the bank from side to side. A small hill led them to a flattened plateau, and they could see the indents of a track leading away on to the moors. Stroop gave Jack and Thomas the spyglass he'd brought with him and sent them off up the track a way to see what they could see from the other sides of the crags. He told them to make a quick sketch of any cottages or hamlets, ripped a page from his notebook for them, gave them a spare pencil. Then he started kicking away at the snow, pushing it to one side with his boot, brushing it back with a piece of heather he had twisted from the bank. And underneath he could see quite clearly where someone else's horse had stood and worried at the grass and pawed at the hard earth.

Jack and Thomas came back with a scrawl of a map showing one or two cots and the round walls of sheep pens over in the valley, a further scatter down towards the river, one tumble-down shed tucked into the side of the north end of the range of crags as they grew a little before falling away steeply into the river and the hidden valley of Eden below. They also pointed back a little along the way they'd come, and over in the distance they could make out the scrumpled edges of the canal works, the necks of cranes and pulleys scratching at the sky. Now they'd seen it, they could also hear it: faint clangs and the persistent, though arrhythmic, ring of metal on stone, an underlying rumble of wheels upon boards, barrows along tracks.

'Off to the canal works, boys,' said Stroop, brushing the snow from his knees, the small pieces of heather from his hands. Jack and Thomas couldn't wait to get going. This was what they'd come along to see, so they pitched themselves head first back down the hill, rolling and tumbling like human toboggans, flinging handfuls of snow at each other and shoving it down each other's backs.

And then Jack had called out, 'Hie! What's this?'

And Thomas had called out, 'Mr Stroop! Mr Stroop! Come and see what Jack's found!'

Stroop had started sliding down the hill in his own haste, could make out the square of leather Jack held upwards in his hand, wondered what it could be, doubted it could be an accident that had sent this thing into his hand. Didn't know it was the ancient wallet Medan Skimmington Bellpenny had tossed to the wind as he waited and watched for Finkel Hanka to burn.

9

Another Cave, Another Country

12 March

HE HAD CROSSED the River Bečva at dawn, using the small roped footbridge that swayed from side to side with every step, made him feel suspended in the mist that rose from the soft-flowing water, so that for a few moments he could neither see the way forward nor the way back, and all there was above him was the lazy slink of sunlight on cloud, and all there was below was the sound of water running slowly over stones, the planks beneath his feet moving quietly in their slings, the rough edges of the guiding ropes in his hands. He didn't move, didn't breathe, felt the dampness on his skin, the serenity of solitude so extreme his heart began to slow within his chest. And then the mist cleared a little, and he could see the path leading away from the bank, the dull green of the grass, the thrift flowers bleached of colour, daisies and asters drooped and closed, the sharp smell of the turpentine trees that clutched at the sparse soil, resin beaded on their branches.

Beneath the ground where he walked lay caves so old they had collapsed. He approached the only part of them that still reached the outside world, a single chimney-hole chasm dropping through three hundred and twenty-seven feet of precipice leading down to a small lake. One side of the rock-face had slumped and subsided, come to rest at a lean angle that was only barely descendable. Already his feet had begun to slide down the scree, his hands gripping the hard spiked grass, seeing the billow of green far below where a scroggle of small, snowy-mustil trees had seeded, grown up through the spill of soil that had covered the rocks over the years.

He reached the trees, the sweat cold on his back, white petals sticking to his shirt where he brushed against them, the mist sinking after him into the hole; he leant against a stub of trunk for a few moments, catching his breath, freeing his toes from the tips of his boots into which they had been crushed by the constant downward pull of the descent. And then he was through the trees and as far down the rock as he could go and all there was below him was the small lake that filled the cave, coming up from the inside of the earth like a nose-bleed, grown over with weed that sucked at its warmth. He dragged his shirt over his head, kicked off his boots and trousers, threw himself into the green-blanketed water, felt the heat of it against his skin, the duckweed moving and closing about him as he swam across its surface. He lay on his back, arms moving in languid circles, gazed up at the hundreds of feet of rock separating him from the sky, the fluster of jackdaws beginning to settle again into their crevices, at ease now he had desisted his clumsy interruptions, beginning again the twig and weave of their nests.

Uwe lay on his back at the bottom of the chalk pit, opened his eyes to the different lumb of rock that surrounded him, a different circle of sulky sky far above. He closed his eyes, tried to think himself back to Bečva, to another place, another time, but he knew that when he opened his eyes again all he would see would be the dull white of walls scraped back to the bone, the dark empty arms of mine-shafts leading away from him, the menace of the cold breath that had groaned from them throughout the night, the creak and give of pit-shafts echoing in distant tunnels, complaining at the weight they had carried too long upon their backs.

He pushed himself up, ran his broken nails through the fine dust that had gathered over him during the night. He saw the damp cinders of his desk, a brief scrap of unburnt paper, a few metallic nibs. He sat up too quickly, felt dizzy and nauseous, rested his back against the rock, waited for his foot to relax itself in the clog that encased it, the ungiving wood clamped against his swollen toes like a scold's bridle holds still its tongue. He laid his head back against the rock, looked up, saw a shiver of chalk dust descend through the lacklustre light, tried to concentrate his thoughts. He had plans, things he must do. First was to face the dark eye of the tunnel he had chosen the night before.

He had sat as close as his fear would allow him to each of the seven outlets leading away from the hollow of the cave. He had listened for the drip of water, or the movement of bats, had tried to taste and test the air that came from each of them, tried to tell if it was damp and corrupt or dry and fresh. One of these tunnels might lead to another opening, another way out. But that wasn't his first priority. His first decision had been for fire and light and heat. He had to take down some of the beam joists, drag out any that had fallen. He would need several stout bits of wood for levers, some rocks he could heft as hammers. He needed to allocate one of them for his bed, and another for a latrine, still didn't feel brave enough to go more than six feet into any of them, his hands shakily outstretched against the hostile walls, his eyes straining through the shadows until the shadows ceased and he could see nothing at all, though his eyes still stared and sought the light as drowning lungs will suck and struggle for a last mouthful of air.

10

Canals, and Moving Through Them

Afternoon, 12 March

THE GROWL OF the canal works underlay the heather on the moors, fed through every hoof and foot that trod its paths, groaned like trees splitting from bough and bark. The wind caught up scrimmages of brick dust and grit, greyed the green of new-shot crowberry and low-slung juniper bushes that had pushed out from the snow in morning warmth, crushed the wrinkle of berries, gave the tint of gin and just-dug graves to the air.

Stroop shielded his eyes against the strong sporadic gusts that came at them from the west, whipped up the loose dust and snow from the boulders that were scattered about the moor like deserted chesspieces. He had massively underestimated the enormity of the building works, the noise it would generate, the mess and spill of huts and shacks that fell away from the central nerve of the construction site, where a deep trench had been excavated for a full two miles, the truncated end of which they had just reached. It had been shored up with beams and the sides bricked between them to a depth of almost twenty feet. Beside the canal, which still waited for its water, for its beginning and its end, great mounds of spoil heaped over the heather, roughly caked into banks, being sieved and sifted by the wind, lifting what was loose, compacting the rest as its weight collapsed and settled. Already he could see that rosebay and bracken were pushing up through the rubble, birch and hawthorn taking a hold, the six-inch stands already bent to the angle at which they would grow if they survived. He estimated the first of the man-made hills to be a minimum of two years in their abandonment, wondered how long it would take to dig right through to Astonishment Valley, which lay another five or so miles further east, wondered how the engineers would cope with the shift and contour of the landscape, the drop in height, realised now why the canal bed had been blown to such a depth. At intervals he saw the twisted remnants of rabbit fur, the long leg bones of hare, a couple of sheep skulls, a more recent carcass of deer. All had tipped over the edge in the snow maybe, where they had not known the drop, had not the claws or the energy to take the steep banks, had died of starvation and broken legs, dragging themselves up and down the rut looking for escape, the snow now scoured from them by the constant wind.

He turned his head away. Shouted suddenly at Jack as he ran close up to the edge and peered down, his boot tips sticking an inch over the edge. Jack didn't hear, but didn't fall, just ran on, throwing stones into the abyss, playing some game with Thomas, trying to count how many times each stone bounced, maybe aiming at something Stroop couldn't see. He could make out the forms of men now, rising and falling like pistons as they hammered and shored, horses kicking at the top of the banks as they dragged barrows up gangways of planks, the shrieks of damp rope in rusting pulley-eyes, the groan of wood taking the weight as hundreds of tons of earth and peat and rock were sheared from their beds and hauled into yet more spoil-heaps of shifting slag and rubble for the wind to pick at as it would. It reminded him of a hornets' nest he had once disturbed, the angry grumble of workers emerging and patrolling their grounds, crawling over the large globe of their nest, tips and stings rising and falling with their threats. And then, without warning, the rumble of an underground explosion tore from the earth and sent his horse shying and bucking, and all he could do was cling on and watch as the animal's head came up in a panicked rear, the rims of its eyes bloodshot with grit and dust and fear, and Stroop felt it pulling to his left and towards the sharp edges of the ravine. He hauled on the reins till his arm muscles felt they had been torn in two but it was Jack who came running and grabbed at the animal, held it still and steady, put his hand on its neck, defied the hoof as it pounded in panic at the earth. Stroop put his hand over his heart as Jack brought the horse to a standstill and the last rumble of the explosion dissipated and died away, felt dizzy with the blood that had rushed to his head, his hands shaking, his legs trembling against the horse's sweating flanks, flicked by the froth from its mouth and nose.

''S all right, 's all right now,' whispered Jack, as much to Stroop, perhaps, as to the animal.

Stroop slid from the stirrups, his knees almost buckling

beneath him. 'Blasting,' he said shakily, and Jack grinned up at him like an oyster that's just spat out its pearl.

'It's so exciting, isn't it, Mr Stroop? Whoever'd've thought it?'

Stroop couldn't get anything else out, and he walked the last half-mile on foot, Jack and Thomas taking turns to lead the horse on, patting it and pacifying it till they could have walked it through a volley of cannon and it wouldn't have turned a hair.

No one challenged their coming, if they'd even seen them arrive. The track they approached on joined another and another and widened into a channel of mud and slush beneath their feet, and the first few shacks they came upon became a city of winding streets of no foreseeable direction, braziers burning and casting out great plumes of black smoke, black-smiths hammering unknown implements on their anvils, brick-workers piling hods in and out of kilns, men stripped to the waist, fighting the bark off of trees, felling them over pits to be sawn by the men beneath and above with six feet of two-handled saws.

Stroop eventually found his way to an uneven track that ran the length of the present digging works. Roughly erected cranes stood like bristles along its way, with blinkered, tump-lined horses heaving at the yokes slung around their forequarters, men shouting and gesticulating at others down below, communicating, God knew how. Stroop struggled through the morass of potholes and dark-oiled slicks of lique-fied peat, his boots getting heavier with every step he took, his trousers and stockings sucking up the mud like thirsty camels. He had told Jack and Thomas to stay with the horse, keep to the edge of things where he could find them, told them he would be as quick as he could be. Not that they cared. They were as fired up as the brick-kilns and he could only hope that somehow he would be able to find them after he had done what he came to do, though now he was here, he feared it would be a fruitless task.

He spied a man in clothes less bedraggled than most of the workers he had seen, ploughed his way towards him and caught at the man's sleeve after failing to get his attention politely.

'I'm trying to find someone . . .' he shouted, but just then he heard the low sound of a foghorn and a few seconds later another explosion belted through the air and a blast of grit and sand had him pulling his coat-front across his face. He screwed up his eyes and turned his back to the blast, could feel the ground shaking beneath his feet, wondered how on God's earth anyone could stand to take more than a few minutes of this awful tumult, felt a huge pang run through him for the silence of his study and his lines of library, wanted nothing more than to have never come here at all.

He went to move away, but the man whose sleeve he had grabbed had turned and taken him by the elbow, and as the explosion died away and the ringing in his ears subsided, he could hear the man shouting, 'Snap time!' and of a sudden the immediate noise about him abated as the workers down in the canal base put down their pickaxes and shovels and lowered the barrels back down the planks and took out a smoke and a drink and a piece and settled for a ten-minute break.

'Owt I can help you with, lad?' asked the man, peeling Stroop's grip from his arm. 'A'm guessing you'm not from 'ere,' he continued, leading Stroop across the mud, which passed for a track, and into a canvas shelter strung from poles on the other side. Stroop found himself being pushed on to an empty crate, which had the luxury of a straw bale for a back.

'My name is Stroop,' he said, gathering the shreds of what was left of him, 'and I'm looking for a man you might have working for you – twenty-six, dark-haired, has maybe been here only a few months, name of Uwe Proctor Dvoshka.'

The other man had seated himself on another crate, poured himself a cup of beer from one of the several barrels lined up on a trestle by his side.

'One man?' he said, squinting at Stroop. 'You know how many of 'em as we have working here?' Stroop shook his head. 'Near on three thousand any one working day. I've sixty in my gang, all hammerers and draggers. Then there's scaffies and diggers and bombers and horsemen and sawyers as well as all the rest. Can't find one name on all of them.' He started excavating tobacco out of a poke-tin on the crate in front of him.

'A pay register?' asked Stroop, without much hope. He had already realised how futile was his task. The place was an anthill of men, and no doubt they moved and changed and left and came with every passing day. The man lit his pipe, drew at it. It was a modicum quieter in the confines of the tent and he eyed Stroop with some interest.

'You the law?' he asked, and Stroop shook his head.

'You've heard of the murder of the constable over Brougham way?' he said, and the man nodded.

'Not much we don't hear. Guessing you're the man Pytchley's gone and brought up from London.' Stroop did not have the energy to be surprised. 'Old Pytchley's paying for much of this muck we're doing,' said the man, 'Bradley Oldmixon, that's me, by the by. I lived over the valley yonder.' He pointed somewhere unknown with his pipe. 'Known all the Sedgwicks and the Weeemses and the Pytchleys of this world. Think they've got the rest of us in their pocket, they do. But not with this.' He waved his pipe again, presumably encompassing the entire canal works with its stem. 'It'll all change once this is finished.' He puffed with satisfaction, coughed, uncorked a bottle and took a drag, offered it to Stroop, who took the neck of it and swallowed. Anything would have been welcome after the dust and grind he had come through, wanted never to be near again.

'Anywise,' said Stroop's benefactor, the foreman Oldmixon, 'you've as much hope of catching a flea in a forest as you have of finding a man here.' Stroop smiled thinly as Oldmixon continued, 'I've sixty to my gang, but there's fifty others like me and each with about the same in their gang. We pay by the week, if we're given it out, otherwise it's the month, and who knows who's come and gone since then. Best bet is the Surgeon's Hole.' He puffed a little more at his pipe, took a watch out of his pocket and shook it. 'We're slaves, same as the next man,' he said without rancour. 'No idea who's working next door doing their bit, not that much idea of our own, they change that much.' He leant over, took the beer back from Stroop and slugged the rest of it down as if his throat expected it. 'Best bet's the doctor,' Oldmixon re-iterated as he checked his watch again, stood up. 'Not many of any crew don't end up his tent now and again. Fights and that.' He sucked hard at his pipe then struck it out, stood up, poked his head back out the tent and yelled 'Time!' Immediately the noise fired up again and Stroop heard the pickaxes start to go and the men shovelling the mullocks into their buckets, and the horses start to drag them back up the planks.

'Where?' shouted Stroop as he followed the man back out the tent, and Oldmixon pointed with the stem of his spent pipe up the wayward higgledy-pig of self-adjusting streets.

'Up the jitty, 'tween the shocks,' he said, presumably meaning the small lane that ran between two massive heaps of slag, which were constantly being enlarged as the men worked on.

Stroop thanked the man and started out, wondered if the slag heaps ever slipped and buried the men who worked beneath; pinched his nose, tried to clear it of sand.

He could smell the Surgeon's Hole long before he reached it, the stink of stale blood soaking into sawdusted floors, the rot of bandages discarded in piles, picked at by rats until someone thought to drop a bucket of slag over it. The hospital seemed to have been constructed from old pit-props and ship sails and was by far the largest building in the makeshift city. He could hear the steady pull and push of a saw, and was so relieved to see a boy off to his left dragging its ragged teeth through a plank of wood that a gasp escaped him involuntarily and dispelled the visions of legs being hacked off at their knees, or arms being disconnected from their shoulder sockets.

A man emerged from the darkened opening with his elbow

tied almost to his throat in a sturdy sling, his belongings already strapped to his back.

'That's me bloody jiggered,' he muttered as he passed Stroop by. 'A'm bloody jiggered now all right, bloody fimmered, nowt but badly's gonna come o' this . . .' He looked up as a great roll of clarty yellow cloud pushed between himself and the sun, let go a sudden fling of hailstones, followed it up by more and more until the ground was covered with small hard balls of ice. The man pulled his cap down, made his ears stick out like jug-handles. 'Frigging bloody jiggering jiggered . . .' was the last Stroop heard of the man as he strode off and was lost in the deluge that had dropped like a curtain, separating Stroop from the rest of the world.

He dashed for the corner of the hospital tent from where the man in the sling had emerged, and pushed himself through the rough flap. The sound of hailstones on canvas hid out the many sounds of the men who lay on the hard pallets of straw and horsehair, or sat on barrels or on the few rickety chairs that had been pulled around the central brazier, which seemed to be a converted water cistern with a hammered metal funnel inverted on its heavenward end. The warmth was immediate and welcome, but also leant strength to the stench of raw spirits, iodine, and camphor, which lingered over, but could not quite disguise, the underlying undercurrent of blood and pus.

Stroop put his handkerchief over his mouth and took a few steps inside, picked his way through the litters to the chairs surrounding the brazier, where the men seemed to have coagulated in a fug of smoke and whisky. He asked for the doctor, and was headed in the general direction given when he made the man out. He was distinguishable by the spectacles he wore, two more pairs of which were strung around his scrawny neck. Bare-armed, he was busy stitching up a great gash that had been struck across a man's thigh by a mis-swung axe, and the man clenched and ground his teeth while the doctor worked with his needle and gut, and an assistant poured some sterilising acid over the wound to sear and seal the stitching into place. He watched with horrid fascination as the doctor's blue-stained fingers worked the large needle in and out, saw the pull of skin, the prickle of blood, a shiny white glimpse of sinew or bone, the zigzag that closed it over, the clotting on the catgut already growing black and hard, the constant disturbance of tiny flies that had managed to survive and breed and hatch in the warm confines of the Surgeon's Hole.

Stroop gagged and couldn't stop the half-digested breakfast of kippers and toast spilling out over his already filthy boots, the steam and smell of it making it worse, making him retch until there was nothing left but the sourness of bile in his throat, a thin yellow rivulet of it drying upon his chin.

'You're not the first, and you won't be the last.' The doctor had been cheery, introduced himself, given Stroop a damp cloth to tidy himself up with, a glass of sharp, strong brandy flavoured with aniseed to take away the taste and smell of sickness and open wounds. And more than that, he had been happy at the interruption, delighted to sit down and get out his ledgers and lists of patients, had explained to Stroop the system with which he worked, how he had one book for names, the other for the diseases, wounds and treatments the men had received. Stroop remembered his own nosological tome, could not but help admire the man's system. The enthusiasm he evidently still held despite the despicable reality of his surroundings.

'I'm compiling a paper on the incidence of accidents in the industrial workplace,' the doctor confided to Stroop. 'I've already made several contributions to the *Philosophical Transactions of the Medical Society*. I did an essay on the mechanics of bone-crushing, and another on a new splinting technique I've devised to cope with some of the larger fractures we get on site.' He was proud of his researches, obviously enjoyed his work and took great pleasure in seeing the interest on Stroop's face at his activities. 'One of the most interesting things I've developed since I came here is the application of the thorn apple, *Datura stramonium*. Grows wild around here and is, as everyone knows, extremely poisonous. But,' he opened one of a stack of cupboards and tapped a large glass bottle of some murky, sediment-ridden liquid, 'I've developed a way of extracting some of the active ingredient; makes a very good anaesthetic when mixed with wine, and is an excellent poultice for pain relief. Much cheaper than the opiates we're so short of.'

Stroop had to suffer a demonstration of the Patented Criddle Compound on a man whose thumb needed amputating before he managed to ask Dr Arthur Criddle his questions. Criddle at once obliged and skimmed his fingers through his patient ledger.

'Ah yes, here we are. Not often one gets a name like Dvoshka.' He swapped one pair of spectacles for another, leant closer to the page to read his minuscule notes. 'February the twenty-sixth, three toes crushed below a barrow and a possible fracture of the foot-bone?' He looked up at Stroop. 'I remember the fellow now. He was extremely agitated, hadn't been here all that long, I don't think.' He looked back down at the book and tapped the page with his finger. 'Seemed to be suffering from some form of recurrent fever, possibly malaria. We had a few cases last summer – very hot, it was, and of course the conditions here are ideal for all sorts of diseases. I rather think though that he'd caught his elsewhere.' He took off his glasses and sucked the end of one of its metal legs, replaced them with another pair. 'Kept chattering away in some foreign language no one understood. Also, he was asking for a friend of his, can't quite recall the name now. Bob!' he shouted for his assistant who looked up from the table where he had been rolling pills. 'Hi, Bob, mind that foreign fellow a few weeks back? Kept asking for his friend? Do you mind the man's name?'

The pill-roller thought for a moment, bunched and unbunched his shoulders. 'Bellpenny,' he said. 'Didn't know him myself but one or two of the other lads recognised the name. Said he worked up with the tunnel crews. We sent on a message but I don't know if he came. We needed the bed space and we had to send the patient back to his own tent. Can't mind when exactly.' The boy, for he couldn't have been more than fourteen, stretched his neck from side to side several times to indicate that was all he knew, shrugged a little and got back to rolling his pills.

'Any help?' Criddle asked, but Stroop made no reply, for at that moment the tent flap was suddenly invaded by six men running in with a seventh man screaming on a board.

''E's bust 'is knee,' said one of the stretcher-bearers, and Stroop could see the lower half of the man's leg drenched and dark with blood. The surgeon Criddle had already started to move towards his latest patient, shifted a few things off a table and scattered it with sawdust. Stroop shouted his thanks at the doctor, who merely raised a hand behind his back as Stroop retreated, wound his way back out into the afternoon light.

The air was sharp and clear after the shift in the weather. Only a few hailstones could still be seen, collected in ruts, turning the rusty colour of mud. The clouds had pushed away down the valley, and left the sun weak and watery but still shining a little in a gull-grey sky. Stroop didn't mind, didn't notice. He'd been given facts, and he latched on to them like a tick to a dog. A time, a place, and a name. He stopped short in the middle of the muddy path, took out his notebook and pencil, was already calculating, thinking, deducing. '26th February,' he wrote, 'broken toes'. He wrote another word and underlined it, something he rarely did. 'Bellpenny,' he looked at the name, spoke it out loud, felt that at last he could start to fit together some of the ripped-up pieces of the Dvoshka boy's past, and that by so doing, he might be able to figure out exactly where he had been and, more importantly, where he was going and what he would do next, if a man could do anything with three broken toes, but wait for his friend to help him.

Stroop wasn't the only person to make a list that afternoon. Medan Bellpenny's consisted of two columns connected by a cat's cradle of lines, several of which had been rubbed out crudely with the ball of his thumb and redrawn. He was now engaged in copying the whole thing out more legibly so that the corresponding abbreviations stood apart as carefully spaced, symmetrical pillars.

CF/QW	AH/VS
KM	JP
GC	C
CH	?
LdC	MO
LgC	B
F/M	B

He chewed the end of his pencil for a moment, then put small neat ticks besides the Bs and the C, was troubled by the question mark, didn't like the imperfection it implied.

It was an odd trait in a man who had lived the way he did and done the things he had done. He had no sense of the underlying order of the world and actively despised the authority that had tried to press him into its mould. He had no deep-rooted belief in belonging to either one place or another, though he liked it here fine enough, up on the moors with no one to bother him, his little pinch of earth hidden from paths and tracks and prying eyes. Its decrepitude didn't irk him in any way; he felt comfortable within the abandonment of its walls, enjoyed the kinship of desertion and exile, knew that the two of them existed only as afterthoughts in other people's lives, shadows seen from the corners of their eyes, if they were seen at all. He swallowed convulsively, felt the corners of his mouth drag upwards and the slight squint he developed when he was amused.

He thought briefly of the father who had brought him here to the moors all those years ago with a few keepsakes in an old fish sack, a few promises spoken and broken before they even passed his lips. He remembered the man's short, round head spiked with angry ginger hair, a greying beard stained yellow with tobacco around his mouth. Even then, he hadn't thought it strange or unkind, the way the man so easily shifted the son from his shoulders, untrammelled himself of a burden he couldn't bear, chose for himself a different path. He would have done the same himself. He knew it then, and he knew it now, and it pleased him that in such a way he was his father's son. They were like the boulders that so inexplicably moved across the desert sands with no apparent intervention by wind or rain or another man's hand. They rigged their own sails, set their own agendas, steered their own course.

His father had joined the whalers in the Arctic Seas. Medan knew this because his aunt had told him so, and because once, and once only, the man had sent him a message and a gift, for what reason he hadn't known, though later he had wondered if his father hadn't been about to die. He never knew for sure, but he had kept it with him always. Or almost always. He'd no need of it now, had no need of anything, had set his own sails and made his own agenda.

He looked again at the question mark, then took his scribbet in his hand and wrote two new letters right through it. Regretted only that he might not have the time to tick every name on his list and make the trail he was leaving more complete.

11

Languages Unlocked

Evening, 12 March

THE SKY HAD thickened and darkened as Stroop, Jack and Thomas made their way back to the Hall, Thomas atop the horse behind him, Stroop clinging grimly at the reins, Jack leading them on through Bedlington and Ascham, laughing as the snow began to twitch around them, to hide the holes and ruts in the tracks, making them slip and stumble. They arrived like human snowballs, Jack shouting that he was Big Woolly Foot as they fought their way into the stable yard while Stroop shivered in his coat and wondered about the men working up on the moors, what they would do when the snow began to blow into the blindness of their tunnels, began to fill again the trenches so hard won.

He didn't think such things for long, had found Violena Sedge already waiting with towels and blankets and dry clothes warming before the stove that served the stables, heating great kettles of water to soak the sugar beet ready for the horses' evening feed. She took them through a covered portico that led directly from stable to Hall, thick box hedges keeping them from the wind, which had risen like a ghost as the sunlight fell away behind the hills, began to howl like a boggard with no place to go.

She took them to the library, the large desk laid out in front of the fire with hot coffee and brandy and pieces of toast dripping over with melted cheese, chestnuts splitting from their shells on a pan above the low flames. The roof domes glowed as the snow began to heap itself upon them, gave back the orange light of the lamps and candles liberally lit, made the whole library cosy and alive, a city below the surface of the outside world.

Everyone had a lot to tell, but it was Pytchley who first took the floor.

'I want you to look at this.' He nodded to Stroop, but included everyone else gathered around the table. 'Mr Orcutt?' He motioned to Maximillian Orcutt, who had been busy fiddling with something on a further desk and had participated so far with nothing more than a distracted hello.

'It's not exactly as it should be,' he said as he advanced with the contraption he had been working on, supported by a large metal tray. 'Obviously it's more of a working model. A three-to-one scale. And only two viewing holes,' he added apologetically.

Pytchley couldn't help smiling. He had of course seen the original, and been absolutely staggered at what Orcutt had achieved in only a couple of days. When he'd asked him for a representation of the stolen Perspective Box, he had expected nothing like this, had assumed the man would just copy out a set of blueprints that would explain a little of what the original creation had been like. He had called in on Orcutt earlier that afternoon, had taken it upon himself to show the few remaining guests several of the lodge exhibitions. Most of the others, having heard of Hanka's murder and the vicious attack on the man on the bridge, had already made their apologies and left, for which Pytchley could only be thankful; had made arrangements for their return at a later date if they so wished. He had found Orcutt bent like a hairpin over his work, had been astounded to see what he had constructed in so short a time.

'I've managed to knock this up,' he had said. 'I've used some of the resin I normally reserve for icebergs. A little addition of nitrous acid has allowed me to mould them and get them to set a little quicker.'

He had moved to one side and Pytchley had seen a small square box with its lid removed, the grey-brown resin worked into a maze of winding walls. Perhaps his amazement hadn't shown sufficiently on his face, for Orcutt had bustled around to the other side of the table and started mixing up some pigment in a jar.

'It doesn't look much now,' he'd said hurriedly, 'but I've still to paint it with phosphorous, and once the lenses are in place . . . well, they're not very good. I've had to use ready-made ones and haven't had time to grind them properly as I'd've liked, but once it's all dried properly—'

Pytchley had cut him short. 'But this is marvellous! How on earth have you managed it?'

Orcutt might have blushed if he hadn't already been thinking about the next stage of the operation. 'I always have some bits and pieces lying around,' he had answered vaguely, his eyes straying to the small crank-arm still waiting to be attached. 'There's always something to be made or mended,' and off his mind wandered to the little boxes of pins and cogs he'd yet to sort through to find a working match.

'Well, well,' said Pytchley with the same admiration he used to feel when he'd seen the engineers at work on the battlefield, the way they improvised and improved what anyone else would have thought to have been shot to bits and fit only for throwing on a pyre, 'I'll leave you to it then.' And he had allowed himself a rare chuckle as he left, Maximillian Orcutt being bent back down over his desk before Pytchley had even closed the door.

Stroop was less impressed. He saw a stout wooden box on the desk where Orcutt had placed it, sealed on every side, the edges only roughly sanded free of splinters, held together not by carefully tailored joints but by round-headed tacks. Orcutt must have seen the faint lift of doubt in Stroop's eyebrows for he grimaced slightly as though he were in pain.

'It's hardly in a finished state, I know,' he explained, unable to keep his fingers from rubbing at a stain of glue marring the surface of the lid, which had been hurriedly hinged and hooked into place less than an hour before, 'but Major Pytchley thought it might be valuable for you to have an idea of the other box, and if you'll just take a look through the eyepiece . . .'

Stroop looked dubiously at the box, saw the small port-hole the other man had indicated and obediently sat down on the chair that Orcutt had hurriedly aligned, pushed the box across the surface of the table a few inches to make it easier for Stroop to reach. Stroop leant forward, unsure what to expect and at first, as he placed his eye to the small dark hole, he could see nothing. He shifted slightly in his seat, adjusted his position and slowly, slowly, he saw that something was beginning to take form before his gaze. Orcutt sat on the other side of the desk and was now turning the small crank-handle at the back of the box, and as he did so, small patches of luminescence started to take shape. Stroop gasped as he found himself within the interior of a cave, the walls lit by an apparent sheen of ice, sheets of stalactites and stalagmites taking on the eerie blues and pinks of sand-worn shells. And then he heard a strange whine and wondered if the wind hadn't found its way into the library through some misclosed pane of glass or door: the sort of sound a horse might make if it could whistle, wet and loose; of raindrops winding their way down windows; of the sea maybe, as it ran a slow ebb tide across shingle. And then the colours on those internal rock-walls subtly changed their tone and turned the opalescent yellow of well-worn pearls, shimmered with the kind of light that fish give out when spawning beneath a moon-filled sea.

'I line the boxes with metallic foil,' Orcutt was saying as Stroop sat back, let Mabel have her turn whilst Thomas and Jack fought each other for the second spyhole on another side of the box, but couldn't reach it across the table. 'When the crank turns, the friction builds up a static charge, which warms the various pigments, changes their inherent reflectivity, and of course the thickness of the resin alters the resulting wavelength . . .'

Mabel wasn't listening. Not to Orcutt, nor to Thomas and Jack squabbling, nor to Pytchley and Stroop as they talked quietly behind her. She was within the world within the box and only wanted to step the whole of herself inside it, shut everything else out. But she didn't have much time to enjoy it. There was too much else to discuss, and Mabel soon had to drag herself away as she heard Violena join Stroop and Pytchley to tell them what she and Mabel had found out during their own day's work.

'We've discovered the little book your Dvoshka talked about in his letters,' Violena was saying, 'and something about the man who wrote it. His name was Comenius, or rather, Jan or Johann Amos Komensky. Comenius is the Latinised version of his name, and much of his work was printed in Latin, as well as in German and Czech.'

They cleared one end of the table and she laid out her little sheaf of notes, Mabel taking the seat beside her, Stroop and Pytchley sitting inquisitorially at the other side.

'He was a great educator,' Violena continued, 'and wrote a great many influential works including the *Janua Linguarum Reserata – The Gate of Languages Unlocked* – "A seed-plot of all the arts and tongues, containing a ready way to learn the Latin and English tongues".' Violena had been reading from her notes, correctly translating the long subtitle from its Latin roots. 'He was extremely influential in his day, and even now is well held amongst scholars. Portions of his teachings were used in the constitution of the English Freemasons around 1721.' Violena stopped for breath and Mabel found herself tapping her feet impatiently on the floor beneath her chair. She was about to interrupt, but Violena smiled suddenly and said, 'But it was Mabel who found the most important thing. Mabel?'

Mabel flushed hotly, and flustered through the pile of notes Violena pushed towards her.

'Um, yes, oh yes!' She found the page she was looking for. 'Something else he wrote was mostly published in Czech, and not often seen anywhere else. It's like a *Pilgrim's Progress*, only written years before.' She looked up, saw Stroop had sat back, his eyes closed, knew he must be really listening hard. She tried to concentrate, to say everything concisely and to the point as she knew he would expect. 'It's about a man who wants to find his proper profession. He travels through the world guided by two companions, Searchall and Delusion, and every profession he comes across he finds self-serving and worthless.' Mabel's hands were shaking slightly as she shifted to another page; she wasn't used to giving lectures, and knew she sounded as unsure as she felt. She could feel Major Pytchley watching her intently, and Maximillian Orcutt standing just behind her shoulder, leaning down a little, perhaps trying to read her notes. She didn't want to let Stroop down. Nor Violena. She rubbed her hands together and held them in her lap. 'But most importantly, they travel to a great city, which contains all the circles and professions of mankind, but just before they enter . . . Wait a moment.' Mabel unlaced her hands again, picked up a piece of paper, wanted to get it right, read out the quote she had written so laboriously as Violena translated from the Latin, '"I found myself upon an exceedingly high tower, so high that I seemed to touch the clouds. Looking down from this tower, I saw a city spread out before me of such beauty it seemed to shine, and beyond its walls there was a moat which formed an abyss. And beyond the walls, there was only darkness."'

'A tower,' breathed Stroop.

'A tower,' agreed Mabel.

'And so at last we have a start.' Stroop opened his eyes and smiled. There was much more to tell and talk about, about the name he had discovered at the canal works of the man Dvoshka had presumably come to find, though whether he had actually found him, they didn't yet know; about the object Thomas and Jack had fumbled from the snow.

'He obviously found someone,' Mabel said after listening to Stroop's story, 'because someone posted that letter, and it couldn't have been Uwe, not if he had broken his foot. He couldn't possibly have walked all that way even if we could be certain he had left the hospital by then.'

'Quite,' said Pytchley, his own toes itching uncomfortably even though he knew quite well they had been replaced by cork. He saw Violena cast a sympathetic look at him, wished he hadn't spoken, despised the pity he knew he always evoked in others.

'Quite right, Mabel.' Stroop carried on as if Pytchley hadn't spoken. 'And there was something else. Now what was it?' He looked all around the room, studiously ignoring Jack, who was jumping up and down with his hand in the air.

'Mr Stroop!' Jack pleaded, 'I know, Mr Stroop!'

Stroop half hid a laugh as it rose in his throat and shoulders. 'Ah yes!' He held his finger to the air, then put his hand into his jacket pocket, produced the soggy wallet. 'We had a most important discovery – or rather, Jack did.'

'Well done, Jack.' Mabel smiled warmly, and Jack sat back down, though even then he was jigging a little in his seat with the excitement.

'What is it?' asked Maximillian Orcutt. 'It looks like an old wallet.'

Stroop placed the object on the table, looked at it closely for the first time. 'Yes,' he said, 'I think it is.' He put his head down further, didn't want to see anyone's face as he spoke. 'We found it up by Brougham Crags, below Black Fell. In the snow. Some distance from the . . . well, from the disturbance.'

He didn't need to say more. Pytchley looked at Violena and she looked at him. Then both turned their heads quickly away and stared instead at the object on the table.

It must be his, thought Pytchley, and stood up, reached his hand out to the mantelpiece for a spill though he had no need of it. His cigar had long gone out.

It's Hanka's, thought Violena, and wanted desperately to take it in her own two hands, hold it against her, protect it from everyone else's prying eyes, wondered if it still smelt of him, of his clothes, of his life.

Stroop avoided all this emotion by gently using his pencil to flip it open. It didn't take much. The catch that had held it closed was unclipped, just like Finkel Hanka's own mortality had been loosed from its moorings and lost. Stroop looked closer, pried his pencil into each opening, not knowing what he expected to find: money notes maybe, the badge of his authority as valley constable, some keepsake perhaps. There was nothing. And he could hardly bear to say it, so he kept on a little longer, aware how still the room had gone around him, Violena's lips pulled tight as the rope across a plough, Pytchley leaning against the mantelpiece as if it held up the world, Orcutt distracted momentarily from the short-fallings of his box, standing beside Violena, his arm held slightly away from his body as if ready to curl around her waist should she fall. Even Jack and Thomas had ceased squirming in their seats. And then, and then, Stroop moved his head even closer, twitched his little pencil from side to side. There was something. The stitching was crude where the lining had been fixed to the back of the wallet and had been loosened, by age perhaps, or the soak of snow and rain. He pushed the point of his pencil in, held back the lining a fraction of an inch, and there it was. A line of white. A piece of folded paper, perhaps.

'Violena,' he said slowly, still prodding at the opening like Arthur Criddle might have probed a man's insides through his open wound, 'can you get some tweezers?'

She could, and she did. Within moments she was back, not with one pair but with two. Putting them down beside him, Stroop lifted his head, nodded at her, noticed her properly for the first time since they had been here: her round, open face, the slight but constant look of worry occasioned by the lines across her forehead, the wrinkles at her eyes' ends caused by curiosity or amusement or maybe both. Who would have thought to bring two pairs? he thought, much as Maximillian Orcutt had thought at their first meeting when she had mentioned moon-dogs. But Stroop was too engrossed in his task to think further. He picked up the tweezers, used them like crab pincers, one holding open the slight fissure between lining and leather, the other teasing the hidden secret out. The paper was weak and wet, threatened to tear several times in several places, but at last Stroop managed to extract it whole and relatively unscathed. It was certainly a piece of paper, and one that had been folded several times over to make it fit into the hidden place.

'Could this be Hanka's?' Stroop spoke out loud though he hadn't meant to; thought this could not be his. How could it be? So blank and empty. Surely his murderer hadn't gone to the trouble of emptying the wallet out and then throwing it away. Or then again, he thought, why not? Perhaps after all, this was nothing – an old love letter. Perhaps from Violena. The thought embarrassed him. He was saved from having to say anything else by Maximillian Orcutt.

'If you can hold on a few minutes, I've just the thing.' He didn't expand further but left the library, and they could hear his fast footsteps running down the hall.

He was back within a few minutes carrying something he had evidently brought from the workroom at his exhibition lodge. It was a glass-topped box about a foot cubed, and appeared to be lined with metallic foil, several tubes running its width attached to two more substantial tubes on either side.

'Let me,' he said, and very carefully he took up the tweezers, placed the piece of paper at one corner of the box and began to unfold it, section by section. It had been folded three times, and at each unfolding everyone expected the soggy mess to rip, but Orcutt was deft, and had also brought with him several pieces of card with which he supported each out-turning of the missive until eventually it was laid out on the glass of the box.

Everyone looked. And everyone was disappointed. Violena sighed like a tree that has let go its last leaf. Pytchley, who had forsaken his mantelpiece and leant over with everyone else, moved back, turned his head away, watched the last few chestnuts on the fire-pan blacken and shrivel in their charcoaled shells.

'Just a second,' said Orcutt, apparently unfazed, and he pulled out a small drawer from the back of the cabinet, poured something into it from a vial he'd produced from his pocket, slipped the drawer back in along its runners. 'It won't last long,' he said as he began to turn a key below the drawer, 'but it might give us something.'

And so it did. Whatever catalyst he had released, and he explained it in great detail as the contraption began to work and the key began to wind the coil and the gas began to glow in the tubes, nobody heard a word he said, for a light began to glow beneath the glass and shine up through the paper, and Stroop saw. They all saw. Lines of writing appeared as if by some conjuror's trick upon the paper.

'It's to do with the salt,' Maximillian Orcutt was explaining, 'every flake of snow has impurities and some inks react in certain ways . . .'

Nobody listened. Except Violena. She lifted her face from the glass as it glowed, looked at Orcutt, at the dark cut of his cheeks, the rough red skin where he habitually mis-shaved with a razor a little blunter than it might have been, and she clenched her jaw and her eyes against the tears she knew were filling them. But it's too soon, she thought, and swallowed several times. I shouldn't be feeling this; it's too soon. She heard Mabel speaking, she heard Stroop answering. She forced herself to look back down at the lighted box.

'It looks like a poem,' said Mabel.

'It looks like two poems,' answered Stroop.

'Or maybe one poem, two languages,' added Maximillian Orcutt. Violena stared at the paper. It had blurred slightly and she had to blink her eyes a few times to clear her sight. She'd expected it to be Hungarian, thought it must be something Finkel Hanka had kept from the old country all these years. Had an awful premonitory vision of having to go to Roze Hanka's with the wallet wrapped up in a handkerchief and confess that they had read whatever it was that he had chosen to keep hidden, maybe even from his mother. And there was no doubting it had been there years. The delicate nature of the paper made that clear, and the invasive crease of the folds.

'What is that language?' Stroop asked. 'I can't make it out.'

Violena took a deep breath, turned her mind from Finkel Hanka and his mother, and from Orcutt and her awful fear that somehow she had betrayed the man she knew she must have loved but had been too proud to say the words. She bent a little further over, caught a faint smell of clove oil, couldn't stop herself from wondering if Orcutt used it on his skin to ease the razor-nicks, wanted suddenly to touch them for herself, rub in the oil that would lessen their sting. She removed her hand from the table, felt a sharp pain in her back as it took the pressure, was glad of it, of the way it shifted her concentration and once again she was able to look at the paper on the lighted box with some clarity. She furrowed her brows, knew that she knew something, dragged an old remnant up from somewhere.

'I think,' she said, and could not have surprised the others more than she surprised herself, 'I'm not entirely sure, but I think it's Icelandic.'

★ ★ ★

'So,' said Pytchley, as he and Stroop stood with their backs against the fire, watched the boys playing with the proto-Perspective Box, taking turns to wind the crank, Mabel scolding Jack because he was going at the thing like it was made of iron and would last a thousand years, Violena having disappeared into the book stacks to try to find the rudimentary dictionary of Icelandic she knew Weeems had once posted her when he was doing his Arctic survey, hiding herself from the feelings she didn't want to have. Orcutt had remained at the glass, staring down at the thin scrawls of handwriting, transcribing every little dip and dot he could see on to fresh paper, mouth forming several of the words even though one half of it was in a language he had scarcely heard of, let alone knew how to pronounce.

'So. What do we have here?' said Stroop, already knowing what he would say, but allowing Pytchley the opportunity of going first.

'We have a missing boy,' said Pytchley. He had moved to an armchair, his calf resting on a stool, the unnatural dip of his foot disturbing, unless you knew the reason why. He poked at the fire. Went on. 'We also have a curious letter sent from here to London. We have theft, we have murder.'

Stroop saw how tired the man was, wanted to cheer him, to give him something. Stroop wasn't at all sure where this accumulation of events was going but knew with certainty they were going somewhere. Curiosity had begun to pulse within him, the beginnings of a pattern, or maybe several, starting to weft in his mind. It was like being on the underside of a rug, he thought: you could see all the strands and threads of colours but until you saw the over-side, you didn't yet know what the picture would be, unless of course, you'd made it. He carried on where Pytchley had left off.

'We have more. We have the name of a possible accomplice. We have a Czech devotional book. We have a wasted wallet. We have a poem in Icelandic.'

Pytchley sighed so deeply Stroop was momentarily disconcerted. He didn't know the man who sat before him by the fire had wandered back to India, was thinking as he always did when he was tired beyond measure, of all the other men he had lost for what seemed like no reason at all, that he had seen Jack that morning in the snow and clung on to a hope that now seemed so illusory it might never have been, that he wanted, before all else, for this to go away and that he be left in peace.

Stroop waited a moment. Then he said, 'We do have something else.' He saw Pytchley tip the wasted chestnuts back into the fire, lift the tray with the fire-tongs, set it slowly on to the wide, tiled hearth. 'Two labyrinths,' said Stroop, 'we have two labyrinths. Komensky's book and Orcutt's box.'

Pytchley waited a second, watched the chestnuts disappear amongst the coals and wood. 'I wish you could have seen the real thing,' he said. 'Imagine it. Octagonal, a different view from all eight sides, easily three times the size of the model you have seen this afternoon.'

Stroop tried, failed. Wanted badly to see it, wondered if he ever would, wondered where it was now and who had stolen it, wondered if Uwe Dvoshka was looking at it at this moment, wherever he was.

'I understand at least why Orcutt called it what he did,' said Stroop.

'*Mugitus labyrinthi*,' supplied Pytchley, his voice soft, so soft he doubted Stroop ever heard it. He did, and the same thought crossed both their minds: it does, and my God, how it roars.

PART 3

THROUGH THE LABYRINTH

1

The Plague of Guilt

13 March

THE MOSS WAS vile, gritty with stone dust, tasted of earth and chalk, but at least it was damp and presumably green. Uwe couldn't tell exactly, had been assiduously scraping it from a tunnel wall with the sharp edge of a rock, collecting it in his other hand to keep in the moisture. His gut felt bad. Everything he passed, which wasn't much, felt filled with stones. His food was gone. He'd woken to the skittery sound of mice, found two of them twitching whiskers and long tails, devouring the last few crumbs of bread he'd left out for his breakfast, hadn't thought to find another living creature down here in his hole. He hadn't moved, hadn't tried to scare them away. They were welcome; he found them comforting, knew that a few breadcrumbs were not going to make a difference to him one way or another.

He had watched them disappear back down one of the tunnels when they were done, wondered if maybe he shouldn't follow them. Perhaps he could find their little cache, the magazine of food they must have built up for the winter, maybe find a bolus of grass seed, or even windblown grain. But he knew that he could never find it, not without a light to let him look, and he hardly had that. The fire still murmured weakly, as did he. He looked at the diminished pile of wood he had laboured to excavate from the tunnel walls the day before, wondered how long he could keep up his fight for life. Not long, he thought, not with this pain in my foot, this hunger in my belly.

His anger at Bellpenny and the world was the only strong thing left about him, and when he really thought about it, it wasn't Bellpenny he was angry at, but himself. He had put himself in this position, all Bellpenny had done was to do what he'd asked. He hoped the mice would soon come back, wondered what else they lived on down here, how they'd had got here in the first place, how many of them there were, if the tunnels weren't filled with mice families breeding, interbreeding, knew it could not be that way, that lack of food would of necessity limit the population. He thought of the mice they used to use in the catacomb mines beneath the Odessan cliffs. They were kept in small wood-and-wire cages set on ledges while the gangs of convicts and labourers worked, seemed unaffected by the noise and constant irritation of dust, but died the moment a bad pocket of gas was released, which was rare, the mine tunnels not being so deep.

He thought of his own experience exploring the Zbrašov Caves, lowered down by a rope into the warm depths so unlike the usual cold and clamminess of caves, the smell made acrid by sulphurous fumes, the shimmering curtains of crystals hanging like veils, vast caverns shining with icicles made of stone. Of how he had been told to hang a candle before him from a chain, watch as it grew fainter and weaker, and when finally it was extinguished, he was the closest he should ever go to the vast lakes of gas that lay like unseen leviathans in a place no man could venture, at least not if he wanted to reclaim his life and emerge back upon the surface of the earth.

He had gone too far that time, had felt the cribbling in his nose, the creeping of his skin as if it were being overtaken by tiny centipedes, or worse, by the earwigs he had always loathed, their little pincers, the way they arched like scorpions, their inability to be killed by having something heavy stamped upon them. An immense tiredness had come upon him, made the sweat prickle from every pore, a sour taste making his tongue cringe and cling to the roof of his mouth. It had been only the zealous jagging of his guide upon the rope that had saved him from faint and suffocation. Not for nothing had it been called the cave of death, its depths filled with lakes, not of water, but of gas, seeping up from the stomach of the earth men believed in their ignorance was extinct. Not dead though, only sleeping. And waiting. Just as Uwe felt himself now to be.

A sudden rush of starlings brushed the circle of the chalk pit overhead and Uwe saw them curl around the sky above, heard the chatter of rearranging wings, the renewed swirl of them above him.

And there it was.

The thing he had hidden from for so long, the fear and guilt that had brought him the long way from the Russian hinterlands to here. He felt again the huge surge of excitement when he was at last called upon to put his plan into action, when the government-paid Politsky Saranōa came hurtling down from the pillar-nests they sat in all day long during the alarm season, sending out runners to warn the neighbouring estates about what was to come, the big letters crudely inked upon their shirt-backs: 'Полиейский СаранYа', so no one would interfere with them on their way.

The Locust Police had arrived just after Uwe had had his midday meal. He'd only been visiting to see how the construction works had gone, had been taking detailed notes to send back to his uncle in Orava, speculating how much money this would earn them once it had been proved they would work, when the plan had finally been proven to operate effectively in the field. How excited he had been! His big plan about to be tried and tested! The farmers had set their faces towards the direction the swarms would come from, looked for the thin black line on the horizon, watched it grow a little bigger, a little darker the closer it came. Before the building of the towers, the men had done all they could do, had hauled the spiked iron griddles across their land in spring in an effort to destroy the eggs, had driven any emerging wingless nymphs into pits and had them buried so they could never swarm and fly, had spattered their crops with a mixture of molasses and manure fixed through with arsenic. But nothing had ever really worked and everyone knew that if the locusts came, they came, and that was that. All that was left was to pray the insects would not settle their voracious jaws upon your fields, upon your crops, upon your livelihood, and take away everything you had in less time than it took to put on your boots. The farmers and all their families had stood at their boundaries with their sticks and metal lids and kettles and pans, ready to run through the swarm, beating and hammering out their futile tattoos.

But this time it was different. This time a bell-maker from Bohemia had come along and sold them all his big idea, sunk their money into his scheme. They couldn't help but hope that one day it would save them, that his boasting would prove rightly placed. And now that day had come. They had built the towers he had designed, which now strode across the hinterland of the Black Sea like sentries, each one armed with a low-cast bell and a fire-gutter. Every bell had been pitched and timbred and tested, and they would ring out their resonant vibrations and send the enemy hurtling on in their flight, and the bright-burning fires would blind them with their smoke, disorient and divide them, and they would pass on above the farms and the lands that gave these families their living, without harm. It would be like lobbing a beehive into the stronghold of one's foe, watching them scatter and disperse like ineffectual chaff.

All those months spent in the acoustically perfect labyrinths of Odessa, the refinements he had made, the permutations and relative input of copper and iron and silver to his miniature bells, the meticulous observation of their effects on those insects captive in their jars; the second long period of scaling up all those experiments into workable models. The final casting. The building of the towers. The hanging of the bells. Uwe had not dared believe he would actually be there when the locust lookouts finally came running with the news and everyone ditched what they were doing and ran out with their hands already shielding their eyes, straining to see across the vast blue tent of sky, searching for the thin dark line that grew like a tornado from the distant horizon. Uwe's heart was pounding like a pestle in a mortar as he watched the black cloud weave and dip, shift without seeming purpose to left and right, suddenly expand and then as suddenly collapse. He saw it rise and fall and rise again, and he tried to drive it closer with his thoughts, repeated quietly the words he would come to curse, under his breath: come on, come on, we're right here, we're waiting for you. Come on!

And then they came.

Within minutes the swarm of locusts was upon them and the men scarpered over the tilth, crashed their way through the almost-ripened corn and reached the towers. They set their fires burning, piled on the dried gorse and broom to make them smoke, choked in the confines of the towers as they caught up the ropes of the bells and rang and rang and rang them until their muscles turned to knots, while down in the fields, their families screamed and clattered on their kettles until the itch of the swarm was too much, and in their hair and clothes and mouths and eyes, and they groped a blind way to the ground and held their hands over their heads and felt the insects settle and leave, settle and leave, upon their backs.

But nothing had stopped those locusts. They had hied up, relentless as thunderclouds from the east, poured across the grain-fields like ants over sugar, filled the air with the chafing of their wings, and the ground with the constant hunger of their jaws, and when they had gone, the locusts had left nothing behind but empty husks and stalks, and starvation. And Uwe, sweating in his shirt sleeves, still ringing his useless bells, shouting out with frustration and failure, weeping as he stepped out of his tower and saw the destruction he had not halted for one single moment, the resignation in the eyes of those who had followed him, had believed in him, had entrusted him with the meagre savings they could no longer spare.

Uwe watched the starlings unfurl and dissipate like a cloud of smoke. Saw the chalk walls of the tower that imprisoned him, his useless toes growing black within their wooden splint. He dragged his sleeve across his eyes, the spit of useless tears the memories had provoked, and said those words again: come on, come on, you bastards, come on. Then he took up his sharpened stone and crawled his way back down the tunnel, began again his rhythmic scraping at the rock, filled again his hand and pockets with the sludge of moss, swore for the thousandth time that he was not done, that he would yet find a way to continue his life and make his reparation. Make those bastard bloody locusts pay. The sound of their dry wings chitting, whirling, thick as snow, advancing like a dust storm across the fields of wheat, which already swayed with the wind from their thousand million moving bodies – he saw them, heard them, felt them fill the air about him, and scrape, scrape, scrape went his stone and their dry wings, and he spoke his oaths quietly into that hard, moss-encrusted rock, said the worst words he could muster, felt the sting of them make his blood flow a little faster, give him a little warmth, a little more of his life. With every strike of stone, another insect fell away and his head grew a little quieter, his body a little lighter, his anger a little harder.

* * *

Three miles to the south, Medan Skimmington Bellpenny was not troubled by his conscience at all. It was debatable whether he ever had one. He had thought about it occasionally, particularly around the time when he was maybe twelve years old. He wasn't exactly sure of his age, thought he'd probably been about five the time he'd been dumped on the moors with his father's felt-making sister. And years later, on a right windy night, she'd forced the boy to come sit with her and help her separate the wool, and fluff it a little, ready for next day's work.

'You been happy here, Medan?' she'd asked.

They never spoke much, just coexisted. He'd milk the sheep and make the butter, do the cheese, pull the potatoes, sort the hay and silage when he was able to lift the scythe. She looked after her sheep, combed their wool, made her hats and slippers and that was about that. But that night she'd asked him if he'd been happy. It had thrown him a bit, never really thought about it before, supposed he had been content in some way or another. He'd shrugged his shoulders.

'I never left,' he'd said, and she'd nodded.

'You're just like him,' she'd gone on, then thrown him a small package. 'Got this when I went down to deliver my last load of stuff,' she'd said, and he'd looked at the string and tar-paper parcel, saw his name scrawled on the front in a heavy hand, the name of the valley and his aunt underneath. It was his dad's wallet. He'd known it straight away he'd peeled off the damp packaging. The smell of it, of salt and old fish and strong tobacco, just like he'd remembered. And he'd opened the wallet up and it had been empty, except for a piece of folded paper and some scribbling. Only words.

Nothing but words. From your father to his son, and a few words from your mother. He snorted at the thought of it. Remembered folding that piece of paper again and again between his fingers, trying to make it into the nothing thing that it was, shoving it back into a tear between the leather and the lining. His dad couldn't even send him something proper. Only something he had already used. Just like him. Folded up and put away so no one else could see him.

And the next day, the very next day it was when the aunt got sick quite sudden and she'd took to her bed all shivers and shakes, and Medan, well, Medan had done nothing. Nothing at all. He'd carried on as if things were quite normal, went out to do his jobs, came back at night and ate the mutton stew she'd always made to last them the week. Only this time it lasted a bit longer because she never ate any of it, not after she'd thrown the first lot straight back up. Well, he'd thought, what was he supposed to do? That was what he'd thought then. What he still thought. She went the colour of the last sheep-wool she'd gathered, left too long in the pail and the rain, already skinned from the stew meat he was eating, left for the dehipilification process, the algae growing over it, slow and green as she was. Until both of them had finally rotted down and died, divested themselves of further use, left him to his own. He had buried her at least, planted her out in the ditch by the sheepfold, before breaking the gate down into splinters and burning it on the fire, letting the sheep wander where they would. They'd hung about for a time, expectant of the food and care she had given them as he never did, but eventually even sheep realise when something's not going to happen and they grumbled off, took their chances on the moors. Whenever he came across a carcass, its stomach and intestines gone, the bare white ribs scattered through the small heaps of grey wool, the skull collapsed and usually some way distant, he'd prod at it a little with his boot, see if he could find an ear, look for the notches his aunt had used to make to mark her own, mildly curious as to how far they might have strayed.

Medan had surprised himself. He didn't think he had thought of these things once in the many years since they had happened, yet now he found his eyes wandering to the window, to the mound of moss-tumbled stones that covered the last remnants of the woman who had put up with him for no particular reason for six, maybe seven years. It hadn't occurred to him until this moment why she had agreed to take him in. He supposed, looking back on it, that his father must have sent money – else why would she have tolerated him at all?

Then, of a sudden, the hailstones began to hurtle at the window and he rubbed his hands together, held them up in front of the fire, gave his thoughts to the porridge thickening in its fire-pan. Regretted briefly that there was no mutton to add to it, poured instead a slug of his corn liqueur to thin it down, warm it up, give it a bit of bite. The morning had grown colder as it had passed, no doubting that. The already paupered sunlight was weakened further by the fling of hail. He could see the icicles grown down through the gap at the top of the door since last night, dragging with them bits of ancient thatch, the frost-flowers on the ailing windows, which gave the remaining light an opalescent quality that seemed to lift the dim whites from the walls, made the place somehow brighter, more spacious. He liked it, didn't mind that he had to hack out some ice from a bucket to make a brew from the boiled-up coffee beans that had already been boiled three times over. He'd need to get some more, liked his thick bitter coffee of a morning: one thing the Russians had taught him, one thing they knew how to do. He rubbed the stubble on his chin, appreciated the sound and scrub of it, the roughness of the bristles upon the calluses of his fingers.

He got out his list while he waited for the porridge to cool, the coffee to heat, ran his eyes down the two columns. He'd time yet to do a little more, point another finger, and the blame, at the boy a little more, but knew that someone, someday might come looking, thought perhaps he'd better quicken things up a little. He'd not been back to the canal since the boy had come looking for him, shouting out his name like he was the only person left in the world. Wondered now if it hadn't been foolish to take the boy off just to shut him up, to send that letter of his, even though the boy had begged him. Thought briefly back over the timing: Uwe burning the tower, as he himself had confessed in his fever, Medan's pinching of the precious box at almost the same time, Uwe having gone back to the canal works with his fever, and a few days later having broken his foot, gone as usual into the Surgeon's Hole and started bawling out for Bellpenny, and Bellpenny having taken him away. Only after this had Bellpenny left his cottage for a bit of panning to get himself away from the blasted intrusion to his cottage, been stupid enough to leave the box in his caravan because he couldn't risk leaving it at his home, had done the constable to death because the constable had without doubt seen the box. And then he'd sent the letter that Uwe had been begging him to send all along. But by then, they'd both known about the boy in the tower, so his scrawled-over message had anyway been true. How clever he'd thought he'd been to add his mark, maybe shift the load a little after the incident with the constable. Wondered a little now why he had done that to a man he hadn't even known, but knew anyway. He'd been caught thieving once before and look where that had got him: ten years of shackles and hard labour. Wasn't going to let anyone do that to him again. Knew also that maybe someone, sometime would come looking, though he couldn't imagine why or whom or how they could ever connect the things he and the boy had put into motion. Especially not now Bittlestone was gone. He wondered briefly if the boy wasn't too well hidden, thought perhaps a little haste might be in order, get things properly sorted, leave a more major pointer away from himself in case someone looked closer than he might have liked. Wondered whether he would have done any of this at all if the boy hadn't turned up with his broken toes and fever and that silly little book he always kept 'close to his heart'.

Bellpenny remembered the phrase with mild disgust, felt his mouth and shoulders lift a little to wonder what the boy would have made of what Bellpenny had made of it. Remembered the time he'd been busy breaking stones for the shifters to shift up at the canal, the man who'd come and said, 'There's a lad up yonder looking for you, Bellpenny. Says he knows you from way back. Keeps on about Eden and loads of foreign shit. Won't shut up. Foreman says you've to come.'

And he had. Straight away. He'd no notion who the stranger might be, but even then he'd recognised a way out when he saw it, and he'd taken it. Spotted the man to take the blame for anything he had done and might do and judged it right. Just like his dad might've seen a whale and thrown a harpoon and dragged it in with its blood and its blubber and stripped it down for every last penny it was worth.

The hail stopped. The silence was so abrupt Medan looked up from his list, realised his coffee had started to boil away in its pan, went to pour the liquid off into his cup, soak the grains again with water for one last squeeze. And then he heard it. A faint and far-off sound, took it for swans beating overhead for a moment, but it was too slow, too ordered. Swans might fly in threes or fives or hundreds, but it was never for long their wings took the same rhythm, shared the same sound. And he knew this sound. It was horses coming up the track on the bare side of the hill where the wind scoured the snow away from the rocks and the heather, sent it to drift as the hill fell away, sometimes ten foot deep, enough to smother a fold of sheep as had once happened, his aunt had told him, many years ago. A strange sensation overtook him. No one passed this way but him. No one even knew where he stayed. No one coming along this track could be coming anywhere but here.

He didn't wait; he didn't take the coffee pan from the fire, didn't stop for anything; knew from the Russian camps that getting out was more important than taking things with you. Not that he had ever got out, not before he'd been released, and most of the ones who took their opportunities and ran, most of them had been back within a twenty-four-hour span. But the few who did get away got away because they took nothing with them except their lives and the boots on their feet and the shirts on their backs. He stepped quickly across the room, heaved at the door, sent the icicles shivering to the floor, stamped on them as his boots went over the threshold, left the wood still shaking from the impact, and disappeared beyond the ruined sheepfold, holding only the sacking bag he'd had ready but never thought he'd actually have to use. Thought strangely of the turtles who'd once beached themselves up on the Black Sea shores from who knew where, been cracked open like overboiled eggs by men who sang as they hacked off the limbs and slit through the tough skin while the loggerheads wailed and cried like children as they were butchered alive. Medan Bellpenny didn't know what had happened, why someone was coming along the track to his cot, or what they might want. But he knew fine well he wasn't going to be there when they came a-knocking; thought it was most likely tinks or travellers, knew they'd steal what they could and get out, and that he'd be waiting for them to take back what was his. He stayed a few minutes behind the tumbled stone wall, squinting across the snow, waiting for the horses to clear the brow and come down behind the big broken-down sheepfold on this side of the hill. He heard them clearly now, the horses snorting their way up the last steep incline, stumbling slightly on the ice-packed scree, a brief conversation between two men.

'Should be just over this ridge, I think,' said one.

'I hope so,' said the other, obviously tired and saddle-sore. 'Long way to come if it's nothing.'

And then the men were over the hill and Bellpenny got

a look at them as they jogged uncomfortably down the over-grown, snow-blown track. He recognised one man straight away, and the shock of it set his teeth grinding, his heart hammering. He narrowed his eyes against the shine of snow, blinked several times, but he knew he was not mistaken, not with that foot sitting like it did in its stirrup. This was Major Pytchley from the Hall, and Bellpenny could only curse beneath his breath and duck down further behind the wall. He knew they'd find the coffee and the porridge warm. Knew it wouldn't take them long to search his house, to find what they would find, know that he was close at hand. They'd horses; he'd not be able to get his from the byre till later, not without crossing the track and being seen. Only one thing to do now, he thought, and only one way to go.

He dipped his back and body behind the old stone dyke, his big hand throttling the neck of his sack, took the hard way down the hill keeping out of sight of the house, knees buckling over the clumps of heather and ricocheting against unseen stones. He took the crown of the ridge and held his hand above his eyes to cut out the sun, looked for the flat lines where the snow had settled over the old droving road, smoothed it flatter than the rest of the moor, couldn't have made it out if he hadn't known where to look. Saw it. Set to stepping its length to Ascham and only then realised what he had been too quick to leave behind. Knew it was too late to go back, too late to ever go back. Thought of how it would be to start over. Thought of Uwe Proctor in his hole. Thought of his list. Thought of that silly little poem he'd kept so uselessly for so long, thought that at last maybe he understood what it had to say. Couldn't regret leaving, only regretted leaving what he had inadvertently left behind and there was an anger in him that made his skin burn inside his wind-flayed jacket, knew the snow would be up in a few short hours to hide his tracks. Just one more time, he thought, give me one more time, and then maybe, if it was the hour of Alltsaman, he'd be ready.

Pytchley and Stroop came badly over the brow of the ridge, Pytchley's horse stumbling, making him thrust his legs involuntarily forward. He felt the skin of his stump grind against the cork. It had swollen almost imperceptibly in the damp that had come with the snow, but it was enough to cause a ratcheting-up of discomfort. He would have to dry the foot out tonight, brush it over with the sealant he'd been given to prevent just such a problem. Wished he had thought to do it sooner as he'd been advised. Felt damp, dispirited and depressed.

His first sight of the cottage didn't help. It was exactly what he had expected to see. Dilapidation and ruin. How else could it be after all these years? Just like Ada Ribblesdale had told them it would be.

She'd come in that morning with the kedgeree, put it down on the sideboard, headed for the door. But she'd stopped, hesitated, turned her face a little to the side. Pytchley had looked up, saw the cook standing there, the rosehip-coloured hands fiddling with her apron, the slight wobble of her chin and cheeks.

'Ada?' he'd asked, wondered if she was going to apologise for the fish being cold or the eggs being hard, although neither had been true. It surprised him she was there at all, always sent a maid up with the food, stuck to the old Sedgwick way of doing things. It had amused him, her way of never approaching him directly, always sending first a painstakingly written-out note or waylaying Violena as she did her rounds. Ada bobbed slightly as she turned towards him.

'Excuse me, sir,' she'd said, 'but there's been a bit of talk about the place, about what's been going on.' Pytchley nodded encouragingly and there was a slight silence around the table apart from Jack scraping his marmalade enthusiastically across his toast, oblivious. 'I overheard you mentioning a name last night when I was clearing away the supper things. Not that I was listening, you understand, just that I was walking past the library and heard you mention them. The Bellpenny family.'

Violena dropped her fork and interrupted. 'Do you know them, Ada? For God's sake, if you do, you have to tell us.'

Ada Ribblesdale looked at Violena Sedge, thought of Roze Hanka crying in her empty house, and of Millicent Huxby, whom she'd never liked; thought of Leopold, whom she had.

'I used to know of 'em,' she'd said, 'though it's a long while since. Thirty years, maybe more. They had a place up back of Brougham. The old folks ran sheep and such, used to bring them over the moor and down through the valley to market at Darlington.' She shook her head, trying to remember. 'He went off to sea eventually. Took the youngest boy. Left the last girl and the mother back home. They used to felt for the milliners, had a bit of a name until the old woman died. The daughter kept it on, though I can't rightly say as I recall her name.' She saw Violena frowning at her, willing her to say more, to say something that would help them. Everyone knew what had been going on, wanted nothing more than for it all to go away. Wanted to help if she could.

'Is there anything else, Ada?' Violena pleaded, and old Ada Ribblesdale had to swallow a small lump in her throat. She had to look away, stared off through the window, saw the river running below the slope of the garden, the old deer fields now dotted with all those peculiar lodges, saw the hills rise up behind them, thought of Finkel Hanka and the way he had died.

'She'd come down to the valley once in a while,' said Ada, still looking out of the window, not wanting to meet anyone's eyes, disrupt the few clear memories she had, 'dropped her packages off to go to Darlington on the barge we used to have running on the river.' She remembered briefly how cut off the valley had been before the canal had come. Remembered everyone grumbling about the works and the noise and the disruption it had brought, though now, only a few years later, it was hard to recall, they'd got so used to it and its boats and its constant traffic and the connection it gave them to the outside world. 'And she usually had something or other to pick up.' Ada coughed, cleared her throat, tried to go back to that time when she and Leopold had courted, about what had gone on. 'There was a bit of talk one time about the brother dropping off a boy. Everyone saw them coming through the valley, going on up to Brougham. But no one heard from them for years after that, and she just stopped coming. I think the boy was still there, though, at least for a bit. He outworked on me dad's farm a bit, during harvest and spud-pulling.' She vaguely remembered the boy when she took the pieces out mid-afternoon. Sort of gingery and quiet was as much as she could get. She turned back to her audience, could see they expected more, but she had nothing more to give them.

There was a pause and then the stranger Stroop had asked her, 'Can you tell us where this family lived?'

Ada pluffed out her cheeks. 'Well, aye, sort of. Up behind the crags on the road to Claverhouse, somewhere over by Eden.'

And then the Stroop fellow had dug excitedly through his pockets, brought out the map he'd had the boys sketch when they'd been up to Brougham.

'Can you point to it on here?' he'd asked, and stood up, brought it over to her, and she'd looked at it, tried to mind the last time she'd been up Brougham Crags, which had been so long ago, back when Bert Ribblesdale had taken her on those picnics after Leopold had thrown her over, taking her off in the cart he'd trained his dogs to pull. Putting his arms round her and telling her to never mind, that Leo would never be going anywhere despite his grand ideas. How he, Bert Ribblesdale would. How he never had.

Her face had puckered like a puffball wet with the weather, and looked hard at the stranger's map. Run her finger up the track that ran behind Brougham and over Black Fell, and went nowhere except along the ridge where it had once met the drovers' trail, before the canal had come. 'Up here somewhere,' she'd pointed, 'along the ridge a bit and down back. Can't say where exactly, but that was the place everyone knew they bided.'

And that was enough for Pytchley. He'd thanked her, and

Ada had gone back along to her kitchens, sat a while staring at the square white basin filled with dishes to be washed, put the kettles on, sent the frizz-haired maid off to see to the beds. Done something she had never done before. Took the keg of cooking brandy down from the dresser and poured herself a glass.

I'll go see Roze this afternoon, she told herself, make her some of that potted-apricot crumble she used to like so much, some of that dandelion wine. We'll have a talk – God knows the poor woman needs it.

And Ada Ribblesdale had crossed herself, poured out another brandy while the kettle boiled, got up not quite as steady as she was used to and started scrubbing at the pans, looking all the while down the valley and over the river up to Brougham Crags, saw them as if she had never seen them before, like gargoyles hunched against the morning sky. And her tears fell into the dirty water while her hands desisted their scrubbing and didn't reach for the kettle. She cried for Leopold Huxby and even Millicent, and what might have been and never was and wondered why life was so cruel to people who never deserved what finally they were given.

The rest of the breakfast consisted of Jack and Thomas shoving as much as possible down their necks as had been left, neither of them yet being able to understand waste. They might feel sick, but at least they were full and wouldn't have to worry about where their next meal was coming from. It was an old habit, and one they'd neither of them been able to break, and who's to say they weren't wrong? Certainly Mabel never stopped them, though at home she'd always been careful to leave no more on everyone's plates than she thought they could reasonably stomach. She watched them run off with their fat bellies, hoped they wouldn't be sick, thought of Stroop and Pytchley riding out over the moor on Ada Ribblesdale's say-so, hoped it wasn't all going to be a waste.

She had gone with Violena to the library to start work on the note they'd found in the wallet the night before. Had tried to use the glass box but found it to have gone dull overnight and that there was no more to be seen, the paper looking as indecipherable as it had when they'd first retrieved it. Violena sent Mabel to go ask Maximillian Orcutt for some more of the crystals he had used the night before to make the glow-box work. Mabel had been surprised, had thought Violena would want to go herself, had thought maybe he would be waiting for Violena to come and ask. Mabel did what she was told though, went out across the frost-gripped grass, knew that she would be pleased to see him again, knew that he would be more pleased to see Violena.

'Ah!' Orcutt had said as soon as Mabel had knocked and come in, and he'd realised she wasn't one of the few guests at the lodge who still remained. 'I've done it!' He was excited, came up to her, patted her hand briefly as she held it out, as she'd seen Violena do. 'She wanted moon-dogs, and moon-dogs she shall have. Come and see.'

He stood Mabel in front of a large, thin, glass case, which appeared to be empty apart from a dark blue board, which covered the whole of the back. Orcutt held up his finger as Mabel looked questioningly at him.

'Just watch, and make sure you don't move. It only works from that spot.' He ducked down to one side of the case and threw a couple of levers, fiddled with something out of sight, and Mabel began to hear a low humming and then a circle of light appeared on the dark screen and she saw a moon rising through its still, blue sky. It ceased moving at the zenith of the arc, took on the colour of honey fresh-pressed from the comb, began to darken in places with the familiar shadows of an old man's face. Then from the left, a thin wisp of yellow cloud blew in, drew across the surface of the moon and as Mabel watched, two circles began to glow on either side of the moon at nine and three o'clock, and a thin red rainbow ran out from them and over the original moon, a second arc intersecting the first, joining the false moons in an upside-down parabola. It lasted only a few moments before the cloud drifted off again, but while it was there, it bound its spectator steady to her spot.

'Moon-dogs,' came Orcutt's muffled voice. 'What do you think? Needed some clever mirror work, and the gas ratio was hard to proportion, let alone direct, but I think I've almost got it.' Orcutt came back out. 'What do you think? It's hard to tell from down here. As I say, it all depends on the angle of viewpoint.'

'It was wonderful,' said Mabel, and meant it, wished he had made it for her and not someone else.

'Hmm,' replied Orcutt, looking at her critically. Mabel hoped she wasn't blushing again, knew that he wasn't actually looking at her, but only some formula she represented in his head. 'Of course you're quite a bit shorter than Violena, maybe three inches. I'll just get a stool. Do you mind?'

Mabel minded, but wasn't about to say anything, tried not to let it hurt her any more than it already did. She'd been through worse, she told herself – God knew, she'd seen so many other things. But still, it was hard to be treated like a fly in a fruit jar by someone she . . . She couldn't even say it in her head. But he was dashing, and exciting, and he made her blush just by looking at her. She despised herself for it, knew that she was just another part of his experiment, one designed to impress one person and one person only. She sighed. Couldn't think badly either of Orcutt or Violena, had already seen how well they went together, even wished they'd just get on with it and get it done. This wasn't where she or Stroop or the boys belonged and they would soon be gone. It had been pleasant to think of them here together at Astonishment Hall, inventing weird illusions, discovering strange books in the library stacks, mystifying guests with their alien speak of moon-dogs and fogbows and singing sands. But she knew it was something that would never be. Certainly not herself and Maximillian Orcutt.

Mabel excused herself when Orcutt arrived with a stool, got supplies ready for the glow-box, wasn't surprised when Orcutt didn't offer to accompany her back, could see he was keen to get back to his display, which he planned to show Violena later that night. Mabel left him to it, stepped outside and closed the door, watched him working a few moments through the glass, saw only a pair of shoes sticking out from underneath the glass case. She smiled grimly, turned away, went back to the Hall.

They both saw it as the wind rose over the ridge behind them, sent their coat-tails slapping at their backs, put the horses snorting, blew across the chimney, drew out an almost horizontal line of blue smoke. Jeremiah Pytchley could hardly believe it, hadn't really expected Ada Ribblesdale's ancient memories to pan out in any demonstrable way, had too often sent out scouts and vanguards and got nothing in return.

Stroop had been more sanguine, had thought, well, if this Bellpenny really had met Uwe Dvoshka on the other side of Europe and had now come back, where else would he go but what was left of his home? And since he had no reason to suspect what Stroop suspected him of, why would he not stay in the place he knew best? All the same, Stroop had been surprised, thought this was just a little too easy, a little too convenient. How would it be if Bellpenny and Dvoshka were here together and there was nothing to say that they were thieves or murderers or burners-down of bell towers? If they really were just a couple of old friends catching up together, the one with his broken foot, the other making broth and chatting about whenever it was they'd met and whatever it was they had done together. But then, what of the letter? It had to have meant something. It would almost be better if the pair had tried for escape, thus declaring their guilt, then Pytchley could round up his men and send them after the culprits. All would be finished within days, and Stroop could take Mabel and the boys back to London. But nothing about the situation sat right with Stroop. He knew things to be more complicated than they had first appeared, had begun to piece a puzzle together in his mind. At least, he thought he had. A rare moment of self-doubt struck him, but he brushed it away as quickly as it had come. The only way forward was an examination of the facts and that meant the cottage and anyone who was in it.

It was a mean dwelling, squat and long, built down into the hollow, old sheep byres behind, before it and beyond. It was punctured by small windows badly spaced, the latter two on this side roughly boarded over, and Stroop could have sworn he saw something through the last, something sparkle strongly as the sun released its upper edge for a moment, tore itself from the thick clouds that had rolled up behind them from the east. He looked again, saw nothing, but felt his shoulder blades prickle, was sure he had seen something he should not have been able to see in that ramshackle building cleaving to its little rectangle of moor, held fast only by the roots of the heather and crowberry that crowded about its sides.

They reached the cot door. They dismounted. They knocked on the splintered planks but got no answer. Stroop waited only a moment before pushing his hand against the door, had to push harder as the wood scraped and caught on the stone floor, tightened by the ice that had grown down from the thatch, warped by years of storm and rain. Stroop went in, almost skidded on the patch of frozen water that had run out from a broken pail, put his hand out to the crumbling wall to stop himself from falling, jarred his spine as he gained his feet. But it was not the near fall that shocked him as he looked about that dingy room, the stink of burning coffee on the smouldering fire, the dank stench of rot and fungus running unchecked across lime-plastered walls, the dark yawn of smoke-stain, which rose like a spider-funnel up to the eaves. He saw all this, but he saw what must have caught his eye before as they came down from the ridge. He saw a mantelpiece cracked and splintered, furred with years of dust and the detritus of long-gone fires. He saw the objects carefully nested there in miniature mounds of fallen, fire-worn plaster, protected by small, hand-formed heaps of ash: five small golden eggs looking like they had just been born, as out of place and alien as if five blue moons had suddenly risen from the remnants of a setting sun.

'My God,' murmured Pytchley, coming up behind him, and Stroop heard the slight creak of damp cork in Pytchley's boot, a sigh from the fire as the wind gusted again, drew a few last cinders back to life and made them dance in the otherwise empty shell of the chimney-place, a shower of sparks cascading briefly from the fire until they died upon the blackened tiles.

'We've got something,' said Mabel as she bowed herself over the glow-box. The paper had dried overnight and the heat of Orcutt's gas cylinders shone through it, warmed the inks, began to release the letters trapped within its fibres for so long. 'Violena, we've got something!'

Violena came out of the library stacks clutching a couple of books in her hand, her face pale as she rushed to join Mabel, who was already scribbling words down on the pad beside her.

'See here?' Mabel pointed, and Violena saw.

Three separate sets of handwriting had revealed themselves, three slightly different shades of ink, three messages laid out before them. The clearest was probably the oldest, being set the closest to the left-hand side of the page, and Violena was now sure she was right about the language, recognised the strange set of letters, the odd-shaped ds with the scoring on their stems, the peculiar ps she knew to represent the sound of a 'th'. To its right, another set of words had been carefully printed out and she could see the faint pencil marks that had ruled the tops and bottoms of the lines, the words corresponding with the length and spacing of the original. And below both of them, a more deeply indented scrawl, most legible by the imprint it had made upon the paper, words revealed by shadows given them by the light below.

Mabel ran her finger lightly over the bottom section, though without actually touching the paper, and began a halting decryption of the words.

'"From your . . . father to . . . his son.This was . . . this was . . ." she peered closer, took up the magnifying glass she had been using earlier, ". . . once your mother's." I think that's what it says.'

Violena gazed intently, following Mabel's finger. '"From your father to his son.This was once your mother's,"' Violena murmured, felt the cold crawl of sweat upon her scalp, knew with insurmountable certainty that this had not belonged to Finkel Hanka, that someone had taken his wallet and discarded this one, which was their own. Felt sick with the knowledge of it, of someone searching through Hanka's pockets before they did to him what they had done. Her stomach might have turned inside out and she had to put her hand across her mouth, tried to stop the curdle of acid rising in her throat. She dropped the books she had been holding and would have fallen if Mabel had not quickly stood and put her arms around Violena's elbows, twisted her on to her own abandoned chair. Violena could not take her eyes from the thin slip of paper that seemed so cruel, with its innocent accusations, and the tears would not be stopped from gathering at the corners of her wide grey eyes and started their silent fall.

Mabel was horrified at Violena's sudden collapse, didn't

know whether to stroke her hair or rush for a cup of tea, wondered what good a cup of tea would do, searched instead for the brandy decanter, couldn't find it. Then she felt Violena's cold hand patting her own where she had rested it on Violena's shoulders, felt the older woman straighten in the chair, her voice steady and calm.

'I'm all right, thank you Mabel.' She took a couple of deep breaths, took out a handkerchief and put it quickly to her eyes, caught the small wet pools that had come to rest below her cheeks. 'Come along, I'm fine, and we have work to do.' Then she had stood up again, pulled another chair closer to the first, picked up her dictionaries. 'Let's make a start.'

And they had. The Icelandic verse had gained considerable definition with the heat and it became obvious that the second set of words to its right was a translation; unfortunately much of it had been leached away by the years and the snow in which it had soaked for a few days, and made the going more difficult than it might have been. Still, after several hours they had the bulk of it done, and after many linings out and corrections, Mabel had in front of her a fair copy. When they were finished, and the glow-box had finally darkened, she began to read the whole thing through as Violena took up a Pytchleyesque pose by the fire, her eyes closed.

She looks tired, thought Mabel, knew it was more, recognised that same weary tension as something might have the moment before it snapped. Decided anyway to read on.

'"I have, in the evening, playmates,"' she began, '"darkness and light, most beautiful . . ."'

2

Playmates in the Evening

'IT'S GOLD,' SAID Stroop. It hadn't taken him long to shake himself from awe, and he'd gone to the fireplace, picked up one of the objects from the mantelpiece. 'No doubt about it. It has the right weight and just the look of it, as well.' He kept turning the small golden egg in his hand, felt his own warmth seep into its surface. He could hear Pytchley standing behind him, his cane grinding spasmodically into the compacted earth of the cot floor, the air rasping with each slow breath he took, wondered if perhaps the man had more wrong with him than just his foot. 'Do you remember what I said to you last night, about Bittlestone?'

Pytchley was finding it hard to move, hard to breathe. He leant heavily on his cane, felt it shift with his weight, felt for the first time in years the scars across his back and torso begin to burn as if the grapeshot had not long torn through the pathetic tunic afforded the man on the field. 'Bittlestone?' he echoed. Could not understand where Stroop was going, wasn't sure he wanted anyway to go there.

Stroop replaced the small gold egg in its nest of ash. Thought of the other things that had troubled him, the inability he had had of connecting one thing to another, of the boy who had burnt in the tower, of the things that the young lad had told him down on the bridge.

'When we found Bittlestone,' he continued, 'there was something missing.' He turned, looked at Pytchley, saw the other man stare right through him, his eyes still fixed on the mantelpiece. 'Remember he used to collect butterflies?' Pytchley nodded. 'Remember he had a notebook down on the bridge when he was found?' Pytchley nodded again, Stroop continued, 'He'd a chain around his neck, which had been broken, and he used to keep something on it, which the boy Davy talked about.'

Pytchley didn't want to think of the bridge, didn't want to think of Bittlestone, didn't want to think of any of it. More than anything in the world he wanted to be at home at Astonishment Hall, sitting in the library, maybe watching Violena work on her catalogues at the table, maybe have the frizz-haired maid bring him something special that Ada had made. A pear tart cooked in a custard of eggs and cream, he thought, perhaps a vanilla ice and a slice of quince butter. He didn't want to hear what Stroop had to say, and yet the man Stroop went on.

'I have thought all along there was some subterfuge at work. Something going on below the surface. Bittlestone's greatest possession was a revolving pencil he had earned from one of his collectors, and yet we found no sign of it, despite the fact that his notebook was open and had plainly been written in that very morning.' Stroop recalled the notebook, the sparse strokes and signs, the day's date and the words 'Seraphim – n/t'.

Pytchley moved. Every bone in his body made him feel stiff and old. He took a few steps, sat down in the mildewed chair that seemed to be kept upright by the patchwork of mould and splinters that formed its base, looked into the ebbing fire.

Stroop did otherwise. He had seen something else in the corner, hidden erstwhile by the formidable shadow of the room. The wind had increased its step and stamp, had begun to mask its movements with the flurries and scurries of snow it flung at the remaining windows of Bellpenny's cot. Outside, the horses snuffed and snorted, uncomfortable, only partly shielded from the rising ferocity of the storm that had already laid off the canal workers three miles distant, seen the ever-present curlews hunch themselves down into the heather, the men into their tents to play their games of cards and throw their dice and drink whatever grog and spirit they had, which was plenty. Stroop did not hasten the few steps it took him to cross the room, did not hear the sag of Pytchley as the air went out of him and the world became again too much, too big, too hard to comprehend. Stroop went over to the shrouded desk and pulled away the stain-ridden, mould-rotten sheet.

'"'I have, in the evening, playmates,"' recited Mabel, '"'darkness and light, most beautiful gold."' She checked her notes again, checked Violena, who was standing like a poker against the fireplace, went on with her translation. '"'How long did you sleep? All night long, all my younger days. And now, I rise up. But where did you live? In high mountains and caves, glacial rivers everlasting. You hold me in your hand and we are one again."' Violena moved like a leaf in a hidden wind. Folded herself into the chair that Pytchley had sat in the night before, sat just like him in his obvious despair, put out her hand just as he had done, though there were no ruined chestnuts to pitch into the fire.

'Go on,' she said. And Mabel did.

It had taken them all afternoon to get a working version of the poem and its partially lost translation. They had both read it several times over, and made several versions. But now Violena was asking her to read the whole thing through again and Mabel knew her voice would tremble at those few last words, knew that Violena saw in them something she did not see. It unsettled her, but she put her head to her notes, carried on. '"I live in high mountains, in glaciers everlasting. You hold me in your hand And we are together. And it is time to go into this world, to take or to steal, but rightly to possess, and it will not be finished until we are together. Until we are as one."'

Pytchley turned round in his chair as Stroop lifted the corner of the grimy material and pulled it gently away. A fine layer of dust was disturbed by the updraught of the moving sheet, shielded for a moment its contents. The desk was crude, knocked together of birch-wood planking, must have been old because the wood now shone in elbow-places like mahogany. A crucible was poised above a spirit lamp and small lead and wax moulds had been neatly laid in a newly hewn shallow trough. But what shocked was not the contents on the desk but the objects strewn casually about its feet and legs.

Pytchley had stood up, moved over to Stroop's side, could not have been more distressed had he been again at Mysore, standing amidst the slaughterhouse of battle, the stink of blood and sweat upon his cheeks, in his nose, the screams of horses and men as they fell at every turn. As at those same times, it was the brutality that held him speechless, and it was up to Stroop to describe what they were seeing.

'This would have been a clock, I imagine, and this a salver stripped of its gilt,' he had crouched down to look more closely at the graveyard of what once had been beautiful things.

Pytchley stared over him, hiding Stroop in his shadow, his stick hovering uncertainly in the air. The sweat pricked out on his forehead as he saw the broken carcasses of watches, pitchers, caddies, an ornamental toothpick holder in the shape of a hedgehog now denuded of its quills, the broken spines of ancient books, their large, curly capitals scraped free of illumination, leaving fine ruts and scrapes across the vellum, leaving the letters of vermilion and emerald naked without their tracery; a small rubble-heap of clockwork insides and pieces of miscellaneous metals. He could have cried to see Orcutt's Perspective Box broken open, the tunnels and caves discarded, the lenses smashed, the walls picked apart to remove its foil. The dismemberment of so many beautiful things was too much for him and he turned abruptly, went to stand by the door, heaved it open, stood looking out over the pitiless moor, blank and white with the unconcern of snow, gathering once again in the low growl of cloud that rolled towards him like an army over a sunless plain.

Bellpenny had wasted no time in regretting what he had found and forged and left behind. He knew who it was at the cottage, knew what they would find, had left his life several times over and would lose no sleep over starting it again. His only thought was whether he had the time to finish this part of it off right. Thought about the Dvoshka boy in his pit, the mild surprise he still felt that the boy should have remembered him at all, let alone crossed the sea to find him. The first time he'd seen him, during that tunnel fall, and again when Bellpenny had been drunk and shouting his mouth off the night he had been released from forced labour. He remembered that all right. Most men had been offered to be kept on in some capacity or other, had come to the emerging city with nothing else to lose and nowhere else to go, and there were always jobs, maybe not good ones, but jobs none the less: new cities, not only Odessa, but all along the coast, and they needed all the labour they could get. But not he. He had always been a taciturn man, a man who kept his own quiet; had had that striped on him more than once, but that one night of release he had drunk himself into shouting, remembered his own words: 'Eden, that's where I come from and that's where I'm going back.' He'd slurred his words. He'd lashed out at his supposed friends, fellow convicts who'd chosen a different path, had had to be restrained because he couldn't stop shouting it: 'Eden! Eden! Best place a man can be, if he wants to start again.' And he had known too, after the interminable hangover that had lasted several days, that he had meant it, and that Eden was where he meant to be. Hadn't known the boy had heard him and why should he? But he had. And the boy had come. And the boy had burnt the tower and caught the fever and broken his toes at the canal and pushed Bellpenny's shoulder against the wheel upon which he had been resting. Had put the rest of his life into motion. Too late to stop now, even if he'd wanted. Time to move on, and all that was left to do here was cover his tracks.

'Let's go over it again.' It was Violena. They had just finished collating their notes: the work they had done on the Komensky text, the wallet-poem, the carefully chronologised letters of Uwe Dvoshka to his parents, the bleak timing of theft and murder, the mysterious name of Bellpenny. They had been silent for a few minutes, when only the spitting of the fire and the rising wind could be heard, and then Violena had suddenly come back to life. She had stood up, lit the lamps, asked Mabel to lay everything out side by side the length of the large library table, spent a while longer rearranging this page or that, making a note on a separate leaf of paper and laying it above one or other of the original documents.

Mabel thought, this is just what Stroop would have done if we had a table big enough, had a wild thought of knocking down the kitchen wall and laying out one giant slab of oak all the way from the range through to the next room.

Violena spoke as if reading Mabel's thoughts. 'They'll not be long now. It won't have taken more than two hours to ride there and another two back, assuming they can find the place at all from Ada's instructions. Let's see if we can't find something to surprise them on their return.'

Once beyond the ridge, Bellpenny had lowered his sack, withdrawn a pair of boards, the ends of which had been steamed and pressed into gentle curves, the grain streaked brown with pine pitch. One more thing the Russians had taught him. He quickly strapped them on to his boots, tightened the simple buckles about his ankles, set off quickly down the drovers' path, the snow compacted by the wind, the going downhill and easy, though the wind was against him. He took the ridge and skated the side of Brougham Crags, headed straight down by Ascham, avoided Bedlington, came out a while later on the lip of the hill opposite Astonishment Hall. He stood there a moment, silhouetted against the sky, a black crow on its rock. He looked at that strange building, at the way it crept spreadeagled up the cliff-face like a man hunting for guillemot eggs. Reminded him of Bittlestone, come chasing his butterflies over Bellpenny's personal patch of moor, how he'd seen that butterfly man scouring around his cottage with his nets and jars, arms outspread as if he had leant into the wind and not fallen. How he'd come across Medan the very day he had been burying his aunt, and not in a box, just in the ditch by the sheep byre.

'Dead, is she?' he'd asked, and Medan had only nodded. 'Not want the doctor to see her first? Strange kind of colour, ain't she?' Medan hadn't replied, had just put the flat of his spade to the turned earth, brought it down once or twice hard.

Bittlestone had got the message and moved off with his nets over his shoulder, his jars clinking in his sacking satchel. He'd spread a few rumours through the valley, had Bittlestone, about the boy who was now alone up on the hill. About maybe how his aunt had died a bit quicker than she might've. No one had ever approached him though, and he'd only heard them years later, when he'd come down to the valley for something or other, when people no longer recognised him, talked to him as if he were someone else. But still. He had known it must have all started with Bittlestone. Well, now it had finished with him too.

He thought of the Italian sailor he had stolen from so long ago, another man who could not let things lie, would not rest until he had scraped through every den and rat-hole in Odessa, finally finding the man who was wearing his ring. Called in the guards. Proved his ownership by the thin scrawl of engraving on its rim. *Remis velisque*, he had shouted in triumph, by oar and sail – who else but a sailor would have such things written on a ring? Who indeed, Bellpenny had thought, as the shackles had been clamped about his ankles and the ropes tied to his wrists and he had been led away to those long years of labour in the labyrinths. A harsh sentence, but a cheap workforce, and for Medan it meant breaking stones, making plans, biding his time, working out what it really was he wanted from this pittance allotted him as his life. Wondering even now if the things a man desired were ever really worth their price. All the stealth and stealing he had perfected in the few short months since his return, the simplicity of taking apart a thing another man had spent his lifetime making, the extraction from it of something of the purity that he felt was missing from himself. He thought of those still moments bent over his crucible, watching the gold melt and ease out from where it had been so imperfectly hidden, in watch springs, in ornaments, in boxes that could be broken down, the soft pool of it as he poured it into his moulds, the utter calm that came over him as he sat and waited for them to cool. The peace and satisfaction that pervaded every inch of him when he broke the moulds open, when he rolled his own new world out into the degradation of the old.

Across the river, he saw that lamps had been lit in the library windows of the Hall, though surely the day was hardly past its noon. He licked his lips, felt them crack like oyster-shells, tasted the salt of the Black Sea, thought maybe he might even go back there, watch the new city as it built itself up from its cliff, hollowed out its feet to raise its head. And he thought of that box again, the one he had seen when he had landed from the steam-barge at the back end of autumn, followed the people who went up to the Hall, the big hand with its preposterous exclamation, his old canvas bag upon his back, his feet unshackled, his mind beginning to wander, the old sharkskin wallet in his jacket pocket. He had felt the weight of that wallet multiply a hundredfold as he'd bent down to put his eye to the box's lens, found himself without warning inside that box, imprisoned once again inside its caves and caverns, locked within the catacombs as if he could never escape them, the lie it gave of their beauty when all it had been to him was dark and dust and the ceaseless crack of his bones. And that awful noise, as if the walls were falling in upon him, as if the dust were ready to sweep through the collapsing passages and choke him at last, squeeze out from him what little life he had left.

He remembered how his work-gang had first come across the Dvoshka boy that time when the mine had given way, how he'd felt the air being sucked out of his lungs and his feet being torn from his ankles as every last man of them struggled backwards in the overwhelming darkness to save themselves, seen the eerie green illumination of the cave where the boy had been working at God knew what. Thought of the boy's book, the story it had told of the man who had journeyed across the world to find his happiness and his profession. Just like himself. And just like himself, the traveller had found that no matter where you went and what you did, all a man would ever find was the poverty and delusion he had tried to leave behind. In his book, Dvoshka's traveller had found the city at the centre of the world, and the palace at the centre of the city. Wisdom, they called the palace, but in the end it turned out to be only vanity, and the queen who ruled it a pretender to the throne. Bellpenny stared down through the wind and the wet white snow, which had just begun to fall, had never thought much of religion, had laughed at the seriousness with which the boy read out his book. But he saw it now, his own city of darkness and the palace within it at its centre. He bared his teeth, felt the stretch of his mouth, the ache of his gums; remembered how in that book, the city had been destroyed as had the queen who ruled inside it. Started to slide his boarded feet down the slope towards the river, which wound like a moat between him and the traveller's goal.

Here it comes, he thought, as he looked down on Astonishment, it's the Alltsaman. And here it comes.

Violena and Mabel had taken their time, both walking slowly up and down the table, adding a few more notes, a couple of pages with large arrows linking one thing with another.

'Any first thoughts?' Violena had asked, and Mabel had looked up at her, glad to have been asked, glad to see a soft smile on Violena's lips as she waited.

'Well,' she was a little hesitant, didn't want to be laughed at, knew at the same time that was something Violena would never do, 'we've the common theme of labyrinths and caves.' Violena raised that single eyebrow and Mabel went on. 'There's the initial fact that Komensky calls the world a labyrinth and there's several references in Uwe's letters to some of the caves he's explored, and the one about . . .' Mabel moved slowly down the table, followed her own arrow with an outstretched finger, '. . . yes, this one here, almost the last one, the one that talks about the acoustic dimensions of the catacombs and how they'll help his big project.'

'Good,' said Violena, who had obviously thought of this connection herself, though she didn't say it, added helpfully, 'and let's not forget Mr Orcutt's Box.'

Stupidly, Mabel had. She looked with accusation at the experimental Perspective Box he had built for them, wanted urgently to redeem herself. Went quickly on, 'And we've the tower incident. First the burning of the tower at St Weonard's and then the mention of the tower in Komensky's book.'

'Ah,' said Violena, 'and I wonder if you know where that tower is?'

Mabel was confused, narrowed her eyes, scanned the notes, but Violena put a hand gently on Mabel's shoulder, pointed to a map on the wall. 'There's no reason you should know this, but the tower of St Weonard's marks the eastern boundary of the estate lands. And where was the tower in Komensky's book?'

Mabel still didn't understand what Violena was trying to say, shook her head slowly as she replied, 'On the very edge of the city?'

'Exactly!' Violena's grey eyes had the same gleam Mabel had seen when Stroop came tramping home from one of his expeditions, already opening the mud-spattered satchel around his neck, reaching for the pencil-sharpener so he could write down one more piece of the puzzle that was his Sense Map of London. 'So,' Violena continued, 'we've two towers and two cities, and at the centre of one is the Palace of Wisdom, the embodiment, as it turns out, of all the world's excesses and ills. And on the other we have Astonishment Hall.'

Mabel gaped, and before she had time to stop herself she blurted out the first thing that popped into her head: 'You can't mean that Uwe Dvoshka is going round murdering people because he thinks he's walked into his own book!' There was a second of silence and then Mabel put her hand to her mouth. 'Oh my God, Violena, I'm sorry. I shouldn't have said that.'

Violena stood rigid as a milestone, only her hands twitching slightly, which she had clasped characteristically against her lap. 'And why not?' she said softly. 'Such things have been done for less.' She didn't think of Pytchley and the idiocy of war he so often spoke of with too much brandy in him, nor of Roze Hanka nor the Mrs Bittlestone she had never met. She saw instead the picture in Komensky's *Orbis Pictus*, his little handbook for children depicting all the things of this world, the plate that showed a burial and every object in the picture named and numbered: the bier, the priest, the mourners, the urn, the grave, the stone and the epitaph. And lastly, at number ten, the bell tower. '*Funere produente*,' she murmured. 'As the corpse goes along, the psalms are sung, and the bells are rung.' Mabel looked at her feet. Had nothing to say. Violena saw the ancient book again under its glass casing, remembered Halliday Weeems telling her that every month she should unlock each case and turn a single page in every book so that some day she might know them all. Wondered why the burial in Komensky's *Orbis* was followed by a scene of theatre, and the page after that showed a woman walking on a tightrope and a tiny man flinging himself head-first through a hoop. Saw some of the pictures that had gone before, which named every bird and animal, the description of the planets and the four elements: fire, water, air and earth, and all the things that grew upon them or by them or in them. Saw the very first picture in the very first page of the book, which sought to teach every child the knowledge of the world: the master with his cane, the boy looking up at him, his cap in his hand, the master with his finger almost touching his lips, as if to make the child heed the words he was saying: *Veni, puer, disce sapere* – Come, boy, and learn to be wise, and afterwards we will go into the world and see all there is to be seen. That was what Halliday Weeems had done, she thought, and Pytchley, and the Dvoshkas' son. And then they had returned, just as the master and the boy reappeared in the last plate of the book exactly as they had appeared in the first. Just as Halliday Weeems had made an *Orbis Pictus* of his Hall. They had all arrived back to where they had started. At Astonishment.

Violena didn't know that Bellpenny had skimmed his way down the valley and taken off his boot-slats and stowed them in his sack and crossed the bridge that lay across the mouth of the weir. But maybe if she had done, she wouldn't have been surprised. After all, she might have thought, he is only doing what the rest of us have done, and tried to close the circle.

3

Getting Things into Perspective

IN THE COT on the hill by the ridge of Brougham Crags, Stroop had finished his examinations. He had found what he had thought he would find. The only thing that surprised him was finding it here. He had not left Jack and Thomas idle while they had been at the Hall, had sent them out with instructions to mingle with the estate workers and staff, which he had known they would do anyway. But he had given them, or rather Thomas, specific questions to ask. One had been to enquire about various local thefts. He had felt sure, on first hearing about it, that the theft of the Perspective Box could not have been an isolated incident, and Thomas had proved him right. Had told Stroop a number of things had gone missing hereabouts: the odd clock, several watches, in one case just the hands of a dial from an old grandfather clock whose glass face had long been gone. Small items had been missed from a few of the bigger houses – snuff boxes, several items of jewellery. Some of the women in particular had been vocal, having been accused of theft and 'let go', though nothing had been proved. Also gone from one or two of the churches hereabouts had been the occasional crucifix, a particularly valued prayer book, some piece of eucharistic miscellania. And all since near last autumn as far as Stroop could gather, though in most cases no record had been made nor complaint forwarded and the only person who might have known more was now dead.

He wondered if Finkel Hanka had ever made any connection between these small stealings, if he had even been told. Had also thought of asking Jeremiah Pytchley to make a search of Finkel Hanka's office, assuming he had one, had put it off, seeing the other man's obvious distress. It could be put off no longer. He knew what he had seen, remembered Violena's two-line inventory of what had been stolen that night at the Hall: Maximillian's Perspective Box, which of course was the overriding loss; and the small gilt salver that had been missing from the corridor-table outside, which he knew without doubt to be the one he had seen not two minutes before, its dull pewter pitted where someone had gouged off the gilded facing. He knew the what of it, and now the why. Saw the small ellipses on the mantelpiece, the size of blackbirds' eggs, the moulds on the desk in which they had been made. Understood at last the theft of the Perspective Box, whose octagonal walls had been lined with golden foil, a metal so malleable it could be pressed into every shape and corner, be painted over with oxides and acids but still retain its own simple properties, which could not be tarnished; retained its essential nature. He understood, as he had not done before, that it was some kind of simple greed that lay at the heart of everything that had happened. That the green top of the salsify and solanacae might be different, have different leaves, different flowers, but deep below the soil, the root was the same. And so it was with greed and theft.

'Major Pytchley,' Stroop said as he pushed himself up from his knees, winced as the arthritis bit, wondered if there would ever come a time when the apothecary would give him something more efficacious than ginger to chew on to ease the pain of London damp.

Pytchley still stood at the door of the cottage, didn't stir. Stroop called again and Pytchley turned to him. His face was so grey Stroop thought the man might faint, but he pulled back from the air and the outside and looked at Stroop. Looked at the screw of paper in his left hand.

'I found this,' he said. 'It was down the side of the chair.' He hadn't undone the piece of paper, just handed it as was to Stroop. He exhaled his air much as a chimney might exhale its smoke. It was just something he had to do or he would die. It occurred to Stroop that this was a man who had often thought about dying, and who probably wouldn't much mind when it finally came. Remembered how he himself had wept to think his time had come, had regretted the things he had not done. Had still not done, though his Sense Map of London was going well, as were his other lists, and he would surely regret not having time to finish them. They had always been his need and his passion. But now, there were other things. He wanted to know how Thomas would turn out, if Jack would ever learn how to count to ten, if Mabel would ever go to her garden of dead people without him, and be the better for it, and who it might be with. He had a sudden vision of leaving this valley alone, of having Jack and Thomas and Mabel choose to stay behind him and saw his own dread in Pytchley's face. Could not bear it.

'Let me see,' said Stroop, pushed away those useless thoughts which always came to him with the snow, looked beyond Pytchley through the open door. It was falling now, the snow. He saw it though it made no sound, saw the wet tick of it at the rotting windows, at the hem of the doorjamb, tried to string his thoughts into order, like the wood-bearing barges he had seen on his way here: one leader with its huff and puff of steam, the others tagging on behind, one hand after another, hauling a way up the valley. And Pytchley handed over the screwed-up plan that Medan Skimmington Bellpenny had forgotten to take with him, didn't really care about anyway, and certainly didn't need, had actually hoped that someone would find and act on.

Stroop took the paper; it was thin and damp and might have torn had not Stroop taken the time to eek it out of itself and its many crimps and crinkles, put it on the ancient birch-wood desk and carefully pull it open. He laid it bare. Stared at it, saw its signs, recognised the crude code it had sought to disguise itself with. And now he knew. Saw that it was not Uwe Proctor Dvoshka they needed to worry about, except where he might be, but that someone else had slipped into his skin and meant to use his fingers for his own.

The moon-dog project was going well – Maximillian Orcutt had seen it in the girl's eyes. Had seen she was at least a little enthralled; wanted to get it just right for Violena Sedge. He'd thought a lot about her since he had come here, which admittedly hadn't been all that long. But how often did you meet a woman who talked about tightening spray nozzles? Never, until now, was what he thought, and never again, was what he knew. It had taken five long years since he'd first applied for lodge-space and longer sending papers into the Society, and all that time she had been here waiting, maybe waiting for him. Obviously there was Major Pytchley, but Orcutt had seen nothing between them but mutual respect, couldn't believe there was anything more on either side. There had also been the valley constable, Finkel Hanka. Orcutt didn't like himself for thinking it, hated having been there when they had found what little there was left of him, but there was no remorse in Maximillian Orcutt for a rival who was gone, that whatever there had been, nothing could ever come of it now. That the way was clear for Maximillian Orcutt. He had never wanted much, but what he wanted, he usually got, eventually. He had patience and he would tap, tap, tap and tinker at a thing until he got it right, no matter how long it took, just as he was doing now with the moon-dogs. Just as he would do with Violena. And by God, she was something he wanted, had never met anyone like her, thought possibly she had never met anyone like him. He had hopes. He nursed them. He wanted her.

He heard the soft knock at the lodge door, cursed momentarily the appearance of a another curious lodge-guest interrupting his labours, then had another thought and hoped it might be the young girl come asking for more supplies for the glow-box, of which he had deliberately given them too little, had another vial ready, was waiting to be invited back up to the Hall. Quickly, he pulled himself out from beneath the moon cabinet, thinking it might even be Violena herself who had come.

He was disappointed. He saw a man still chapping hesitantly at the door, sandy-haired, round-faced, looking like he'd been soaked in buttermilk, not looking much like the usual sort of guest, but you could never tell. He gestured the man in, saw straightaway that the man's height was almost equal to his own, almost the exact height of Violena Sedge, thought he might as well put this man to some use.

'Just one moment,' he said with exuberance, guided the man to the spot he had marked out upon the floor in chalk, where the girl had stood a few hours earlier but had been the requisite few inches too short.

'Do you mind?' he asked, and Medan Skimmington Bellpenny had not minded in the least. He'd only come to find the roll of foil the man had used in his Box, the one that Medan had so meticulously taken apart in order to remove the purity within. He had expected a thin layer of gold leaf, as had been implied in the explanatory note beside the Box in its exhibition space up at the Hall. But when he had extracted it, he had found something quite different – an amalgam of some kind, a mixture of metals that had the look of gold but that was lighter and quite malleable, had a thickness about it so that it could be laid out and tailored like a cloth. Medan had been fascinated by it and had come for more, hadn't expected to find the lights of the lodge on or anyone in residence, assumed they would have closed the place down in view of recent events, of his own activities, took it as a bonus when he'd looked in through one of the windows and seen the back of the man within. Even better when the man invited him in, asked him to stand on a particular spot in front of a large glass case, then slid himself beneath the cabinet. Hadn't expected to take his prize with such ease.

Medan Skimmington Bellpenny stood there looking into the deep blue of the case, saw his own face reflected there and, behind him, the work desk scattered with tools. Didn't see the moon begin to rise within the case, saw instead the hammer that lay there unguarded. Leant behind him. Picked it up.

'I forgot something,' said Mabel.

She and Violena were still exploring their themes, everything laid out on the table. It wasn't quite as neat as it had been, the papers having been shuffled a bit here and there, a few more pages added, including a map of the whole area, which Violena had spread out and which practically covered everything else. They had put in pins to mark St Weonard's, the heronry, the canal works, the Hall, the possible place of the Bellpenny property, Brougham Crags, the circle below Black Fell.

Violena was busy marking the tracks that linked all these places, trying to work out the various routes that might have been taken at any one time, the line from the Hall to Brougham and over to the Bellpenny place; another from the Bellpenny place to the canal works and on to the heronry. A third, fourth and fifth route connecting these various places to the Hall.

Mabel had been copying out the wallet poem, her mind moving quicker than her fingers as she struggled with the unfamiliar letters and words. She had re-examined the wallet itself, but discovered nothing more, other than that the shagreen from which it had been made was unusual. She had checked a few books out from the stacks, had found one that listed the sharks of the northern seas, had taken a quick trip to the sea-specimen lodge, and come to the conclusion that most likely the wallet had been made from Greenland shark. Had also discovered in passing that this was the only shark in northern waters that laid eggs, not gave birth to live young – an interesting fact, though insignificant. Nevertheless, she had added it to her notes, just as Stroop would have done, heard him telling her you never knew when an odd fact here and there would come in handy. She completed the laborious task of writing out the original poem word for word so that it was legible without the use of the box, marvelled at the intricacies of a language she didn't know.

Ég á á kvöldin leiksystkin
Myrkur og birta
Fugustur gull

Hvađ lengi sváđ er?
Alla nóttina
Öll minn yngri arum
Nüna ég upp rís

Hvar búiđ Þér
Ađ háfjöll og hellir
En jökullvatn
Eilífur

Mig Þer hafið ì hendinni
Við erum saman
Nú er mál að leggja af stað
I Þennan heimur
Að taka að stela að eiga

Það er ekki allt búið
Þar til erum alveg
Alltsaman

Having done that, she began to write out the translation they had garnered from the strange words, 'I have, in the evening, playmates, darkness and light' and it was when she reached the third verse she suddenly looked up.

'I forgot something,' she said out loud, 'another cave. There's one here in the poem too. "Where do you come from?" It asks, and the answer is, "from high mountains and caves, glacial rivers."' She waited a moment for a response, got none. 'Violena?' she asked, saw Violena, one hand holding up a pin as it hovered over the map, the other bracing herself against the table. Only slowly did she answer, still not taking her eyes from the map.

'I forgot something too,' she said. 'There's a dene hole up on the moor going towards the canal works.' Her hand came down and in went the pin.

'What's a dene hole?' asked Mabel, not surprised that her own discovery had not merited much interest, wondered if she was trying too hard to find patterns that weren't there.

'A dene hole is an ancient structure dug down into chalk.'

Violena wasn't looking at Mabel. She was gazing up at the library domes, at the small crisscrossing of crystals compacted by the snow above. She was remembering the time Finkel Hanka had taken her up there that first summer she was here, when he was still trying to impress her with everything he knew. 'They take the shape of a long-necked, round-bellied bottle. The opening is usually about three feet wide and dug right down to a depth of sometimes twenty or more feet, depending on the thickness of the chalk. Small foot-holes are notched out down the neck to allow access, often in a spiral form, so you can lean across the width of the hole and move down without falling.'

She remembered Finkel Hanka holding her feet as she lay down on the coarse grass and edged her way out over to see what she could see. Just darkness, like the chute to a coal cellar, and a small circle of sunlight far below. It's nearly thirty feet to the bottom, she could hear him saying, I know because I've dropped a rope in. I could take you down there if you like. Violena kept her eyes on the snow-draped domes; didn't want to look down, afraid of what she might see. She went on with her explanation to Mabel, heard her own voice speaking in a monotone, remembered the words she had read in one of Weeems' books, had sought it out the moment she had got back to the Hall that afternoon those many years ago, wanted to show Finkel Hanka she could learn about them too.

'Some of them are thousands of years old, and most have fallen in, left only craters and depressions in the land to show that they were there. But some have been preserved and even used for hundreds of years. Particularly the ones which had been converted into chalk mines. Almost always this means that the original bottleneck access has been considerably widened and the foot-holes obliterated. But the central cavern at the bottom is usually pretty much intact.'

He had taken her down the very next day, tied a rope around her waist and shoulders like a girdle and lowered her all that way down, using an old may tree standing nearby as a fulcrum. The bark had been smoothed and grooved by many generations of this use, the rope being wound about the trunk and hooked over a strong branch. Violena shivered as she recalled the horror and excitement as she had been lowered down like a worm on the end of a fishing line, her throat tight with the fear of what she might find, had only managed to reach the place where the cavern roof began to open out and she felt her feet detach from the relative safety of the access shaft and enter a vast cold space that she couldn't see. And then she hadn't been able to stop herself, had begun to scream at Finkel Hanka to get her out. She had heard him laughing softly up above in the sky and the sun, and how he had let her dangle helpless for a few moments, her fear prickling and sweating at her skin, the urge to draw up her feet so intense she could hardly breathe. And then he had pulled her up, twizzling and shaking into the sunlight, hauled her out on to the grass, which she had clutched at it with such relief her nails were stained green for a week.

She closed her eyes briefly, tried not to see the rest of it, but did. Saw her own self standing as soon as she was able, her face high and bright and haughty, her hand lifting and slapping him so hard across the face he lost his balance and fell and almost went rolling into the pit; how she had grabbed at him to stop him falling, and he had spun round in her hold and hugged her to him, laughing, always laughing, the lines of her fingers still bright on his face. The only man who had ever laughed at her, she thought, the only man who had ever made her scream. She remembered that fear so vividly, that bubbling in her throat, knew there had been an excitement to it also, a kind of delight that he would always be up there to haul her back out. Except of course, that now he wasn't, and never would be.

'Violena?'

She heard Mabel's voice, opened her eyes. Tried to remember what she had been saying. Saw the pin sticking into the small white space marked on the moor.

'The chalk pit.' Violena recovered, carried on talking quickly to cover over the memories she didn't want to have. 'There's only one in this entire area. All the others are down south, mostly Sussex, but we've a tiny strata of chalk up on the moor. Uncle Weeems had several theories as to how it got there. Either way, there was no doubt it started as a proper dene hole, then got widened into a small chalk mine. It's far too small to be of commercial value, but has been used locally for years. When the canal works began, they went down there, hollowed out a few more tunnels, but it wasn't much use to them either and it's mostly been abandoned. Hardly anyone knows it's there any more.'

Mabel had moved round the table and she too was now looking down at the map, the spray of pins across it like the fan of the poplar hedge, the arc that joined Bellpenny's cottage over the moors to the canal and on down through the heronry to St Weonard's. The canal slowly growing out from Eden and over the moors, diverting the waters from one river into another as they went, flooding one valley, closing off another. And the Hall, almost dead centre, and the dene hole above it, a few miles south of the canal. The perfect place to be if you wanted to be at the middle of it all. The perfect place to hide.

'Mabel,' Violena unfolded, braced her hands against her back to ease the strain, 'go and see if Mr Orcutt can join us. I think we need to take a look at that dene hole and to do that, we need some way of getting down, and if anyone can figure a safer way than a rope and tackle, he's the man can do it.'

Stroop didn't waste any time. He opened his notebook, folded the two legs of the thin note about a page, not caring if it tore; had already memorised all he needed to know. His foot knocked against the carcass of the Perspective Box where it lay in bits by the desk floor, didn't care about that either. Just like Finkel Hanka and Bittlestone and the boy in the tower, it was dead and gone and there was nothing he could do about that now. He wondered briefly how long they had been here, in this only just deserted cot. Thought perhaps half an hour, not much longer. Unlike Bellpenny, he did divert to the mantelpiece on his way to the door, pushed the golden objects into his pocket.

Pytchley had moved to one side, had seen Stroop's momentum and removed himself just in time to stop from being shoved to one side. Stroop had his head down, the faint reflection of light on snow making his skin seem to shine for a moment, as if there were no bones beneath.

Pytchley followed behind, saw Stroop pushing impatiently through the snow, moving away towards one of the broken-down sheep byres, trailing alongside the dry-stone wall that led to the left.

Then Stroop was shouting at him, 'What is there this way?' and Pytchley saw his hand pointing off along the length of the wall.

He shrugged his shoulders, shook his head, had no idea, didn't think there was anything down there at all.

Then Stroop was back beside him, hurrying him on, struggling to get his foot back into the stirrup of his horse, had neglected to undo the tether with which Pytchley had tied the horses to the rings in the cot wall. Saw the hurry and the panic in the other man's eyes, asked nothing, said nothing, unstrapped the reins from their holding places, gave the door a quick pull-to, hobbled quickly to his own horse and launched himself on, didn't even notice the creaking of his foot as it parted briefly from the strap that held it to his ankle as he swung himself across the broad grey back, knew this kind of action, understood it, reacted and ran with it just as he had always done. He shouted at Stroop, caught at the horse's reins as he passed, hauled him along a different path.

'A quicker way!' he yelled, wondered if Stroop had heard or understood. The wind up on the ridge was shrieking, shaking the snow from the heather, sending the loose scree flying, creating low-crawling devils from the wet dust. But Stroop must have got his meaning because without another pause, he let Pytchley take the lead and Pytchley banged his heels into his horse's flanks and away they went, flying along the ridge, ignoring the precipitous crags that were falling away from their feet. Pytchley felt the flow of the animal's muscles between his knees, the kick of its head as it tried to lift its way from the wind, the flick of foam from its lips. His blood burnt like war in his veins, tingled beneath his skin, made every part of him pulse with the bravado of the battlefield: that fool's embrasure of fear and recklessness and exhilaration as he raced head on to cut another man down or be cut down. He didn't know which. He didn't care. Heard the sky rumble above him as if to urge him on.

Mabel stepped quick and quiet across the grass, had come out of the door and to the right of the small courtyard garden of gravelled paths, yew hedges, gates, anything that would slow her advance, knew now the shortcut that would take her directly to the old deer lawns and the lodges scattered about them like mushrooms, knew the one she was heading for, saw it sitting tight on its little knoll, the clear view one side to the river, the other back up to the Hall. Dark clouds had rolled over the sky, still rolled as they settled, underbellies heavy and yellow with snow that had yet to fall. She looked up the valley, saw the dark heads and peaks of Brougham Crags, hoped Stroop and Pytchley were on their way back already, recognised a sky that was ready to sweep clean the little chessboard of fields and houses below it, nullify the game. Felt the damp soak through the tips of her shoes on to her toes, the steady uprising of the wind through her shawl, the loosening of the pins that held her hair against her neck, the thin silk of her sleeves begin to lift and billow. She was thankful when she saw the light of Orcutt's lodge flickering in the windows, felt her throat tighten a little at the thought of seeing him again, wondered if she might ask to see the moon display once more, wondered at the adjustments he would have made, knew he had made them for Violena.

She saw the door open and a man standing in her way, caught a slight warm smell on the air and a dreadful recognition seize at her heart like a clamp. She saw the man. And he saw her. Mabel didn't wait, did not shout, did not stop nor pause but turned and ran and ran and ran across the damp grass, both hands clutching her skirts up from her knees, her shawl left behind her where it had slipped from her shoulders, her hair tipped entirely from its pins, the small light flakes of snow soaking into her dress as they began silently to fall and Mabel running, running, across the lawn away from Maximillian Orcutt and his lodge and the man who was just standing there and the smell she already knew and hated, knew what must have happened, her throat hard and tight, her one thought to get back to the Hall and draw every bolt and turn every lock that she could find.

Stroop had thrown himself on to his horse without thinking, went to pull away, found the horse protesting as Pytchley tried to loose its reins from the ring. His head might have been a mulch of worms: the footprints in the snow by the dyke, the big map up in the library, the direction of the canal works, the track of the old drovers' road, which short-circuited the path leading back from Brougham and went direct to Astonishment. Beside him, Pytchley had asked nothing, just mounted his horse, started a fast pace back up the track from which they had come and called something Stroop couldn't hear but felt his horse being pulled away from the track and up along the ridge. He caught a brief glimpse of the valley laid out before them, the dark broil of clouds and the curtain of snow rushing over the moor towards them.

'He's heading for Astonishment,' he'd shouted into the wind but Pytchley hadn't heard, was tearing all out, hell for leather, and all Stroop could do was try to follow, could hardly catch his breath as the cold began to freeze his face and throat, knew they had no time.

Stroop couldn't begin to see the path Pytchley was taking them, but trusted he knew well enough which way to go, saw the hamlets of Ascham and Bedlington away to the right, and the flight of scrub that led along the valley, tipped precipitously down to where the canal pooled its end and the river began to divert its course.

And then he saw something else: saw the valley and the Hall surrounded by its lodges, moated by the woods and the dark rising of the moors. Thought of the note in his pocketbook, already knew what those initials meant. He tried to shout out as he saw Pytchley briefly turn his head to check on him, Stroop almost slipping sideways off his horse and into the snow-softened scree, Pytchley shaking his head, pointing forward with his crop, his eyes glinting in the afternoon light before it slid away behind the clouds, Stroop clinging on, the breath knocked out of him at every jolt, the rub of his bones against the saddle, the bite of his teeth against his tongue, the warm taste of blood in his mouth, the jolt of utter panic that had wiped his mind free of every thought except the urgency of going onwards, onwards towards Astonishment.

Uwe Proctor Dvoshka was still in his hole. Had stopped eating moss, no longer had the strength to find it, could no longer eat it anyway, his throat was too dry. He lay under the circle of damp light that was given him, his mouth open to the few lazy drifts of snowflakes that found their way in. Could not begin to describe the joy it gave him to feel something fall from another world, the yearning he had for more. He lay on his back looking at the opening above, unmoving, watching the shadows of the dimming sun, the spin of birds that sometimes rose above him, the dark mystery of clouds beyond.

The foot within its clog was no longer his own; he watched it with dispassion as it changed colour, became blistered, black, and swollen, felt only a slight pang about his ankle if he ever tried to move it, which he didn't. No longer wanted to move anything ever again. Knew that any history he would write would not be one of glass or bells. That he would never make his parents proud, that this was all he would ever be, that nothing he could do now would make a difference. That maybe this was everyman, and that it never made a difference anyway whatever any man ever did. He moved his hand, managed to give a feeble pat at his breast pocket, felt Paradise and the Labyrinth that surrounded it. Wasn't this just what the book had taught him? That there was nothing in this world worth finding and that any man trying was a fool? He remembered how the pilgrim had finally found his rest, how the broken ladders in his heart had been mended and the windows once shattered had been re-formed, how the pilgrim had climbed the ladder and looked out of the window and seen the world at last for what it was, and seen not the abyss that surrounded it, but the Face of God. Will I ever see that? thought Uwe; hoped he might glimpse it before he died, hoped he would see one more night and one more dawn.

Bellpenny saw the girl when she was twenty yards distant, had just been turning out of the door. He knew who she was, had been watching the Hall for a while, ever since the Dvoshka boy had come crawling into his life. He didn't hurry, just stood there, curious to see what she would do, knew she would do something, waited for the shouting to start. But it didn't. She never made a sound, just turned away from him, started running her way up the lawn. He hung there for a few seconds watching her, the wood of the hammer's handle still warm in his hand. It always happened this way, he thought, without sadness or rancour; this was always how it went. In the end there was never anyone left to stand beside him; in the end, they always turned away.

Mabel got back to the hall and hurtled through the door, dragged closed every bolt she could find. She moved like a whirlwind down the hall to the library, shouted out to Violena to ring every bell she could find and close up every hole there was into the Hall. Violena saw Mabel, her face pale, her throat flushed, her clothes and hair all awry. That the girl was absolutely terrified, Violena had no doubt. She went to catch Mabel by the shoulders but Mabel was too quick and ducked beneath her.

'Oh, please!' Her voice was under siege of nerves and shook with every syllable, 'We have to tell everybody. Please. Just get them here. And, oh my God! Where's Jack and Thomas? Oh, Violena, please, we have to find them. He's here, I'm telling you, I've seen him. Bellpenny's already here!'

Thomas was on his way back from the stables when he saw Mabel whirling like a top across the grass. He'd just washed his boots in the pump-pond and the water had trickled in over his ankles, made the leather stiff, his feet inside their woollen stockings wet and uncomfortable, but not for a moment did it stop him. He tore off over the lawn, skidding and sliding, the barely melted frost already beginning again to freeze in the cold afternoon air. He tried to shout, but his throat constricted, made reed-pipes of his voice and she didn't hear. Fear brittled his bones, prickled at his skin, made mincemeat of his stomach, but still he didn't stop.

He didn't notice the pigeons fly like shrapnel from the blasted oak, nor feel the twist of his ankle as it hit the over-ground roots of the bloodberry tree struggling against a climate not its own. He took a rough tumble as he passed the old chestnut, spiny-jacketed seeds digging at his knees, clambered up from all fours and went on. Would have gone off after Mabel to the Hall but saw where she had run from. Saw the light thrown weakly from the doorjamb of the lodge, saw the spread of darkness within and the body it surrounded. Like St Weonard's-on-the-Water, he might have thought if ever he had been there, and like St Weonard's, the water was still rising.

On top of the ridge stood Pytchley and Stroop, the weak sun sinking behind a grim grey waste of dirty-bellied clouds. Stroop had no more breath to expend, had collapsed over his saddle like a nun to her prayers. His hands gripped hard at the reins, pushed the bloodless scars into leper-white welts. His trousers were pressed into shininess, labouring at the horse's flanks and sweat. He'd not been built for this, he thought, felt a line of knots where his spine should have been, the addled amalgam that passed for conscious thought.

No more time to think on it though, for Pytchley was already hurling himself over the edge of the hill, zigzagging down some unseen path, leaning back against the steepness of the slope, hooves kicking the snow from the heather, sending sharp sprays of stones into hidden gullies. His speed and energy were terrifying to Stroop, who had only ever seen this man tired and broken, had never glimpsed the soldier who'd screamed and raged across the Indian plains with his horse bleeding and failing beneath him, his musket firing at every turn. Stroop could only hope his horse would follow, could feel its dark muscles strain beneath the sweated stubble of its mane, felt his own hands shaking as he gripped the reins. Then it was off, pluffing its gums from long yellow teeth, snorting as it fought to stay on its feet, to keep the leader in view. It understood the call to battle as Stroop had surely never done, dismissed the grit-laden snow as Stroop could never do, took them sure and fast by the billets of dead bracken and gorse, right down to the river valley, the harsh smell of burning, water-sodden ox still redolent in the air as they passed the farmyard.

Pytchley increased his speed, and Stroop had no choice but to follow. They took the tow path at a gallop and thundered along through the village and sharp left across the bridge, the boards shrieking beneath their hooves. Stroop raised his eyes a moment, was horrified to see Pytchley take the shoulder-high hedge that kept them from the grounds of the hall, had no more time for fear as his own mount took it up and over, landed him like a sack of millet hits the quern-stone, and away they went like foxes fleeing from their fur across the lawns that led up to Astonishment and its Hall.

Mabel had already begun to run from the library, down the hall, past the stairwell to the outer door, into the hedged walkway to the stables before Violena caught her up, grabbed her by the shoulders, held her still. Mabel ceased at once at the harshness of the grip, and it frightened Violena more than she could say to have that sudden acquiescence at her fingertips, felt the adult melt into a child. She looked down on the mouse-brown nest of hair, saw the girl's forehead glisten with its worry, the untrammelled tracks running from eyes and nose.

'Oh, Mabel,' was all Violena could say and at once the arms were about her waist and the girl started to cry without control. Violena remembered the story Major Pytchley had told her, of the way Mabel had lost her family, and it almost broke her heart to think that perhaps these things were upon the girl again. She might have held that child for ever, wanted nothing more than to keep her from any other harm, thought a ghastly thought about Finkel Hanka and the children they might have had.

But it was Mabel who suddenly pulled herself apart, drew a quick hand across her face. 'We've no time, Violena,' she said, the tears stopped up, her voice steady, as if she were the parent and Violena the child. 'I apologise. I was worried. Jack and Thomas . . .' She stopped speaking, took Violena's hand and started a quick pace back down the corridor from where they had come, past the stairwell, surged round the corner beneath the stuffed monkeys, her fingernails scrabbling at the door bolts she had only a few minutes before set to. 'We've got to hurry,' said Mabel as she threw open the door, flung herself back into the afternoon she had so recently fled.

Violena saw the way they were going, saw the path beyond the yew hedges that they were taking, knew then, and didn't want to know and couldn't stop herself from screaming somewhere deep inside her stomach. It's Maximillian, she thought, oh God, it's Maximillian, and with Mabel she ran into the shadow of the trees and down beyond the Hall on to the grass and across the open lawn. But before they were a hundred yards distance, they heard a keening sound like a saw going through wet bark, saw Thomas hauling, hauling something from within: a pair of shoulders, a body broken, Maximillian Orcutt's badly shaven face, a pale moon rising oblivious in its glass case just beyond.

Pytchley and Stroop were hammering up the lawns, had no place to go but on, saw the Hall grow from its cliff with every thundering pace. They took no care of where they passed, of the small pocket of deer they unnerved, of the dark-eyed lodges scattered across the grass and any who might be within, looking out. Stroop wondered that Pytchley had found such urgency, could almost see it cascade around him, felt it enter and grow within him with every breath. The light of a sudden dimmed behind them as the clouds took their path across the sun, cast long shadows before them, stretched Stroop's own shadow five hundred yards out from his feet as if he had been pulled from glass. The tip of his shadow pushed furtively at the lodge that lay ahead, at the open door of greasy yellow light, at the small figure crouched upon the jamb. It was Thomas. He was trying to pull something out into the afternoon. He saw Mabel and Violena rush towards him, leant down as they reached him, covered Thomas like a cloak, felt the tremor and trip of his heart, the rabbit scenting the stoat, knowing it was too late and the burrow breeched.

Of the two of them, Pytchley got there first, dismounted with the grace of a Cossack who has never clapped eyes on cork, let alone made a foot of it.

'Violena?' he said, but did not wait for an answer. Saw the situation. Assessed. Decided. Acted. 'We must get this man up to the hall. Sofa in the study's the quickest place.'

He bent down, moved Thomas gently to one side, scooped up Orcutt's shoulders and began to straighten. Already Violena went to take his feet, hugged them to her chest as Thomas came up beside her and took the strain, his strength restored by the calm and order in Pytchley's voice. Stroop arrived at the empty space they had left as they began with their burden across the lawn, Mabel's quick step leading the way, running to reach the window and lift the latch. Stroop struggled with twists of girth and stirrup, collapsed from his mount like a bag of bruised potatoes thrown without care upon the scale, hurried to right himself, rushed forward to help, saw with dismay the dark halo left in the hardening dew by the blood from Orcutt's head.

Together they passed the curtains, which stood like soldiers, the major in Pytchley sweeping the cushions from the sofa with one decisive hand, laying his burden gently down with the other. He turned, started to rip an ancient tapestry from the wall, tore it into strips as it fell from its hanging, flung open the weak-hinged door of a cabinet with such force that the wooden panels shrieked and parted from a hundred years of service. The others stood gasping, standing, uncertain, watching the flow of blood from Orcutt's head-wound seep unstaunched into the rich brocade and embroidery of roses so carefully sewn by some woman's hand long ago. Pytchley didn't flinch or wait. He caught up a rum bottle by the neck, didn't care that it was a treasured memento from his first campaign, the plaque around its breast praising his own part in the capture of Martinique in '62. He grabbed at a nearby bowl, tipped out the exotic plumes of lyrebirds and ostrich, trampled them to the floor as he went about his business, brimmed it full with his makeshift bandages, soaked them through with the alcohol that had been maturing over forty years.

Violena was at his side, took up the basin, put it into Mabel's outstretched arms, began to pull the strips out one by one and tie them tight around the dark red wound and crush of bone that sat at its centre, like stones shining in a deep dark well. Stroop reached the window, the two horses following obediently on their way to the stable yard, Jack arriving from nowhere to take up the reins, lead them on.

They none of them saw the form that slipped along by the yew hedges after them, halted a moment by the gate, put out a hand to touch its metal just as he had done those several weeks before. Bellpenny stood for a moment. Another man might have been admiring his own cunning in having double-backed upon his tracks and giving his pursuers the slip, might have surmised the girl who had seen him would have raised the alarm and sent a hundred estate men scarpering off behind the lodge and over to St Weonard's to beat him out from the woods and the moor like a grouse who had escaped the hunt. But not Bellpenny. He never wasted his time trying to understand why he had done what he had done, nor what had driven him to it. That it might be a deep upwelling need to fulfil the only thing he knew of a mother he couldn't remember, a last grasping at her words, the lullaby she had sung him, would never have occurred. He would have spat at any man who posited such specious lies, had already flung her and her nonsense poem as far from himself as he could. He couldn't know it had been unfolded to the eyes of others only a few hundred yards away. Thought less of the list he had drawn up to catalogue his infamy, to cast the blame, to allow him to carry on as he had done without discovery. Was as blind to his own inner mechanisms as was the mole that needs to dig, or the worm that needs to crawl. He did understand survival, knew he would not be safe to return to his cottage, retrieve the things he had worked so hard to obtain. Had always been a man to leave things behind, just as his father had done before him. The lack of care was its own liberation and he saw only the things that lay before him, was fascinated by the figures that moved within the window beyond, felt the pride of a puppeteer who has made a modest success of his show.

And then came that girl again, the one who had seen him just a few moments after he had hammered home his last nail, taken up the roll of gold he would take with him to his new life, wherever that would be. He thought of her, of the lines that had worked their way across her face in her concern. Wondered briefly what it would be like to have such a girl care so much for him. But not for long.

Oddly, as he turned to go from the gate, he thought of the Dvoshka boy's book and its everyman pilgrim, remembered how he had been so far and seen so much. Just as Bellpenny had done. The pilgrim had finally found the Face of God within his own heart, but Bellpenny knew that if he looked inside his own, there would be nothing there. And it pleased him. There was no Palace of Wisdom within himself to be found and destroyed, brick by brick, by some moralising trickster. There was only the world on one side, himself on the other, the dark yawn of the abyss between them.

And there was that girl again. She was standing at the window, looked out a moment and turned her face a little to the left as if she could see him standing there, watching. But she couldn't, and she didn't, and she drew the curtains against him and cut him off from the kind of life he had never known. He went his own way, past the bloodberry and the chestnut and the oak and the stables.

Ten minutes later found him on the incline to the moor, his hands scrabbling at the heather to give him purchase, the wind coming in from the north and the west, forcing the tears from his eyes as he brought his face to meet it, knew how precious was his time and his purpose and his life. Knew where he was going, and what he must do.

4

Possession

IN THE STUDY, Pytchley had ordered everything like a military campaign. Thomas had been sent to the stables for medical supplies, had returned with proper bandages and Jack, who came in like an undertaker, tall and stiff, his gangly arms crooked like cricket-legs to his sides. Thomas had told him everything, and the moment he came in he went to Mabel, kissed her cheek, took her hand briefly in his and rubbed it with his own. She had been so thankful to see him she almost cried, but one look at Violena's face as she leant down over Orcutt, the pallid skin over his cheekbones like canvas pulled across a frame, kept her from calling out and pulling the boy to her. Mabel understood grief. She understood shock. She set Jack on the footstool by the fire and bid him stay, went back to Violena and her basin, started soaking the new bandages Thomas had brought and handed them over.

She glanced at Pytchley. He stood, as was usual, by the fireplace, but was so straight and taut he might have been a spindle-staff and his green eyes had a flash about them no one in this room had ever before seen. He had made them pull up Maximillian Orcutt until he was almost sitting, until Violena had to take his head in her arms to stop it from tipping forward to his chest. He had seen this kind of thing before, said Pytchley, knew the best way was to keep the blood from pooling in the brain; made them take his boots off, raise his feet, keep the blood around the centre of his body, around his liver and his heart.

Mabel had also looked at Stroop. He was dishevelled, had rips in his clothes, hair caught up in some kind of weird maelstrom that made it stand up from his head. But his face was calm, had regained his familiar look of earnest thought that Mabel trusted without question. He'll get us out of this, she thought. He'll know what to do.

And as amazing as it was to Stroop himself, he found he did. He spent a moment surveying the room, saw Violena kneeling by Orcutt's side, replacing the crude tapestry strips with surgical bandages. Saw Thomas and Jack huddled by the fireplace, Mabel near by, had such a feeling of thankfulness to have them all alive and with him that for a moment he could think of nothing else. And then his eyes drifted to Pytchley, to this man who had been a solider in a former life, who had come here to Astonishment to resurrect the legacy of an explorer who wanted nothing other than to understand the world around him, and to allow other people to understand it as he had done himself. He felt shame. Shame that he had not done enough to prevent this last assault, which might yet prove murderous, more shame that all he really wanted at that moment was to be transported miraculously back to Eggmonde Street and his own library, and have Jack and Thomas bickering at his feet about where they were going tomorrow and Mabel calling in easy from the kitchen that such and such was cooked and could they please stop everything and get here now.

Stroop also saw Maximillian Orcutt lying there bleeding, thought about his own mortality, wondered if anyone would take his library on when he was gone. Mabel, he thought, Mabel would do it. He looked at her, a smaller version of Violena, trying to lend her any strength she had left, thought again the things he didn't want to think, that perhaps she might be better off here. His morbid introspection was interrupted by Mabel smiling up at him, that look of absolute and impeccable trust shaking him back to the here and now and the things that needed to be sorted and done.

'Major Pytchley,' he said, his soft voice sounding loud and tall in the hushed room.

Pytchley took his hand from the mantelpiece, turned to face him. Stroop could have sworn he saw the man's hand twitch as if he had been about to salute. Thomas and Jack stood up as one. Mabel placed the basin on the floor, touched Violena's shoulder as she rose, saw the slight lift of her chin, the pallor of Orcutt below her fingers. Left them to their sad pietà, and went to join Stroop. She had known he wouldn't let them down. She had always known it, was pleased and proud to play her part, and knew that the end, whatever it would be, was near.

The chill of the afternoon had drawn a sketch of mist over the moor, the wind making it rise and fall in ever-changing phantoms, slipping through the heather with soft shingle-whispers as calm and cold as a winter sea. Uwe Dvoshka watched the fog close off his own small world from the sky above, saw the ephemeral tendrils drift down upon his walls, feel their way into the nooks and niches of his prison. It reminded him of the communal ice house in a village outside Orava whose name he couldn't recall, only the tall wooden tower of the church and the bell with the prayer engraved around its rim, and the ice house. The six steps leading down to the tunnel, the long corridor and its four dividing doors, which separated the heat of summer from the vault where the ice was stored. Several chambers were built into the corridor walls, one for grain, another for wine and beer, a smaller one packed with snow from floor to ceiling, embedded with stacks of meat, mostly boar and venison, and strings of unfilleted fish.

As he'd been led down the corridor and shown the village wealth, the darkness had seemed to shimmer and sigh as each door parted company from its heavy oaken frame, broke the airtight seal made by sheepskins soaked with tar, the cold air rising up from the scraped rock floor to greet them, forming wispy columns about their warmth, become wraiths in the flickering light of their lamps, made the walls of stone appear to breath and move. The air was thin, the straw used to insulate the walls and roof had begun to rot, release noxious gases into the air, gave a wobble and dizziness to his steps. And then that great chamber of ice, fifteen feet in circumference, dipped in the centre like a goblet filled with wine, the edges pulled away from the stone, packed with barley straw, and where a man had once fallen, three years since, trying to hack a block from the ice, and how he had slipped like a wedge between the two cold surfaces and within minutes was dead. When they'd hauled him back out with ice-hooks, he was stiff as a board, his eyes frozen into his head like painted marbles, his lips a love-in-the-mist blue.

Uwe Proctor shivered a little as a curl of mist sank into his hole, touched his forehead, wound itself about his own exuded breath. He didn't mind, felt an almost euphoric relief at its touch, knew now it wouldn't be long. That at last he could pay for the things he had done so wrong in this world: for the farmers he had ruined, their savings and families destroyed, for the boy in the tower. Mostly the boy in the tower. He grimaced to see himself in the mirror image of that boy's death. Here was depth where there had once been height, cold where there had been heat. Thought it unutterably sad that of the two of them, he doubtless would have the better death, had calmness and quiet instead of fear and confusion and the awful pain and crackle of flame. The tears slid down his cheeks to think of it, knew he had no right to the contentment he had found down here in his hole, the things he had done, which that boy could never now do.

Remembered the joy of taking his first step in his familial land, the sense he had of returning, of belonging, of being where he had always been meant to be. The nail in its hole, the hand within its glove, the bell at last in its right tower. As he was now. He hoped this would be the final night to see him through, that his account could be settled and things done.

He thought he heard the soft growl of a wolf, knew it couldn't be so, looked up anyway at the sift and swirl of mist that formed his sky. The very last thing he expected to see was the rope coiling through the boil of clouds above, saw it straighten and dangle, straighten and dangle, like a pendulum loosed of its weight.

Against all the odds, half an hour later saw Maximillian Orcutt still alive. Stroop had difficulty believing a man could still function with more than half his blood gone into the upholstery on which he lay, saw the wisdom of Pytchley's creating of it a reservoir in Orcutt's chest, draining the extremities to supply the vital organs, drying out the marshes to feed the fish pond.

Now it was time to put his own skills to use. He'd recovered from the bone-shaking, brain-breaking trip that had brought them from Bellpenny's cottage to the Hall. He'd had a few spare moments to try to write things down in his head, compare the lists, join up the salient dots. He'd gathered Pytchley, Mabel, Jack and Thomas around the desk, laid out the small piece of paper from his pocket, taken out his pencil.

'We found this up at what we assume to be Bellpenny's cottage.' He glanced at Pytchley, who stared straight down at the paper. 'I wondered about it when I first saw it, the strange columnar codes, the ticks.'

He pointed his pencil over the paper, drew everyone's eyes with his own.

CF/QW	AH/VS	
KM	JP	
GC	C	√
CH	?	
LdC	MO	
LgC	B	√
F/M	B	√

'Look at the initials,' he prompted, 'and the ticks.'

Pytchley was looking more like a major by the minute and Stroop detected a flash of impatience in his eyes, as he strove to understand and could not.

'Imagine,' said Stroop, 'what we know of the book Uwe Dvoshka carries around.'

Violena was still kneeling by Orcutt, but her hand had ceased its movement and her head was slightly to one side as she listened and Stroop illuminated.

'Komensky divides the world into six classes: firstly, family and matrimony, then the professions a man might take, vilifying each one in turn: the labourer, the learned, the cleric, the governors, and worst, the top strata of the military and the knights.' Stroop paused, tapped at the paper. 'Komensky's pilgrim's search for worthiness in the world brought him to the Palace which ruled the land, and the Queen of Wisdom who ruled the Palace. It doesn't take him long to discover that their wisdom is vanity, and watches as the palace, and everyone in it, is destroyed.' Stroop waited. No one said anything. Stroop began reading out the letters, 'CF/QW, AH/VS, the Castle of Fortune, the Queen of Wisdom . . .'

But it was Violena who finished the sentence, supplied the words they all should have guessed at. 'Astonishment Hall,' she said without any intonation in her voice, 'Violena Sedge.'

'Correct,' said Stroop, followed by a moment of silence, 'and the two Bs would be Bittlestone and the boy. The C would be the constable. Finkel Hanka.'

Pytchley swore under his breath, felt his heart-rate quicken, the old familiar surge in him as the stratagem of the enemy was finally comprehended. Stroop moved his hand lightly across the paper, 'The boy represents family, Bittlestone the labouring classes, the constable, the law of the land, the governors. And here,' his pencil rested by the MO, although by now everyone, except Jack, had seen the pattern.

'The learned classes,' growled Pytchley with such an edge to his voice, it might have sliced an ox in two if had stood before him and got in his way. All eyes had moved to the form on the sofa, to Maximillian Orcutt, and Pytchley strode across the room and stood for a moment by Orcutt's side, one hand outstretched across Violena's head, though he didn't touch her. Then he carried on, took a brass key from a hidden hook behind her and unlocked a long cabinet recessed into the wall, covered by an old oil of Masada, the last of the besieged on the brink of the declivity, making ready to throw themselves down the sharp sides of the cliff, Pytchley's own personal reminder of the futility of war. He opened the cabinet, extracted several long-barrelled rifles, tucked two pistols into his belt, another in his pocket. He turned to the alarmed faces that looked up at him, for he had indeed appeared to have grown several inches that afternoon.

'This must not be allowed to continue,' his voice sounded so loud and low it made the windows vibrate slightly in their frames. 'That any man should think and do such things is monstrous.'

Stroop's voice was calm where he stood facing Pytchley by his desk. 'He doesn't think such things, Major, he doesn't think them for a moment. It is a ruse, a convenient excuse, a way to cast confusion over what he is really about.' And Stroop's hand came out from under his jacket, released the objects from his fingertips, watched them roll and glint, and finally stop. Here were two of the golden eggs swept up from Medan Bellpenny's mantelpiece; the others having been scattered from his pockets as they fled across the moor, flung back to the mountains and the rivers in which they had been born, and to which they truly belonged.

Medan had fought a blind war across the moor, stumbling along sheep tracks he could hardly see, searching for the bearings that usually made it so easy for him to steal his way here and there, from boulder to boulder, tarn to tarn, tramping across the orange spindles of last year's bog asphodel, the bedraggled tufts of cotton grass, the splintered old skins of vipers betraying the hollows where they had battened and fattened below the scattered dolmens of stones. He knew this moor so well, could fix his direction by the ridges of Brougham and Black Fell, the flow of the river going on down to Eden, the ponds of brack and marsh and bulrush, the seahorse-swamps of bracken that unfurled their bright green banners in the spring. Thought of Bittlestone pinned to that bridge like one of his butterflies; was pleased to know that though he might not be here this spring to tend to his cottage, neither would Bittlestone be either. No constant wondering if the man were creeping over his land with his nets, no need to worry he would come back yet again for his blasted chalk-hill blue, destroying Medan's peace and calm, leading tramples of other feet over to his pit. Saying those other things he had said so long ago about Medan killing off his aunt.

The mist cleared a moment, showed him the strangled

outline of a small tree, the brief rear and scaffold of the canal works behind, thanked the feet and habits that had brought him right after all. Speeded his pace, adjusted the rope coils slung about his shoulder, sharpened his plans, arrived at the chalk pit, called out the boy's name and let down the rope into darkness.

'We've got to find Dvoshka.' Stroop was decisive, had laid his arm on Pytchley's, stopped the older man's precipitate march to scrape up every man and boy he could find and go in search of Bellpenny, scouring the land around from hedge to harrowed field. 'Find the boy and you'll find Bellpenny.' Pytchley had fixed him with a look like the pin through a Bittlestone butterfly, but had stopped. 'I am sure of it,' Stroop stressed every word, 'I believe I know the beginning of all this, and it leads to only one end.'

They had all stopped then, Violena at her bandages, Jack and Thomas rolling the gold across the carpet, through their fingers, holding it up to catch the light, watching the reflections make goblins of their faces. Stroop felt Mabel close beside him, felt her trust in him, told them to come on, and led the way down the hall, speaking as he went.

'Uwe Dvoshka fled his disaster and came to Eden to start again. He was feverish, but he found work at the canals, tried to locate his old friend Bellpenny. At some point in his search he came upon St Weonard's, who incidentally is a patron saint not only in England and Wales but also in Bohemia. The coincidence must have been striking.' They had passed the monkeys and the stairwell, Stroop flinging open the library door as he went on. 'Here he was on the brink of his new world, and then, just as in the book, the pilgrim at the outskirts of the city finds the tower and its bell, and the old Bohemian name. And although we don't know the precise nature of what happened to him in Russia, it must have involved bellfounding, as such was his trade.'

Stroop had moved around the table, for once not focusing on the herringbones of books, but looking about the walls, seeking something he could not find, turning instead to the table, carried on with his theory as the others came in about him, circled Stroop like a parliament of ravens.

'So here he is in his new world, his new Eden, and all he finds is a replica of the old one he has tried to leave behind. As his own book says, human toil resembles water being poured from one glass into another, and the futility of it became too much for him. And he tried to destroy it. He burnt down the tower, which represented his past, returned to the canal works in such a state of fit and fever that almost immediately he had an accident and broke his toes. Once in the Surgeon's Hole he started babbling out Bellpenny's name. The man is found and he takes his old friend home to his cottage on the moor.'

Pytchley began to expound that if such were the case, why had they not found him there that afternoon? But Stroop held up his finger as if testing the direction of the wind, closed his eyes for a brief moment.

'Ah,' he said, without opening his eyes, 'and this is where the two stories begin to twist and twine together like spring-winding snakes. There had already been a number of petty pilferings and mislayings hereabouts,' he opened his eyes, smiled at Jack and Thomas, acknowledged their contribution, 'and of course there was the theft of the Perspective Box and after that, the labyrinth really began to roar.'

He took up a sheet of paper, pointed with his finger down the list. 'Missing clocks, watches, gilt salvers, ornaments, snuff boxes, perspective boxes, revolving pencils. Open your hand, Jack.' Jack did. The golden ellipse shone within his grubby hand as if he held a small sunset in his palm. 'All taken to be stripped and broken down to their bare essentials, to the little scrips and scraps of metal that might contain a trace of gold. Remember the poem? "I have, in the evening, playmates, darkness and light, most beautiful gold"? Why the man was so obsessed with the poem and his quest, we may never know, but obsessed he was. And skilled. And these small things were his prize.'

Stroop picked up the egg-shaped ingot of gold, held it aloft between his fingers, wondered why it promised so much to every man it had ever possessed, wondered why they could not see that in essence it was the same, if less useful, as Komensky's pilgrim had observed, than lead or tin or brass or iron. That a pigeon's egg could be of more intrinsic worth than gold could ever be. He heard the creak of Pytchley's foot, saw him look briefly at the gold and turn his face away as if he had seen such things before, thought the exact same thoughts that Stroop had just entertained. Abruptly Stroop released the golden egg, watched it bounce upon the paper-matted table, then roll from the surface on to the floor. Not one of them made a move to retrieve it.

'The Dvoshkas' son –' said Stroop – 'Bellpenny means to blame him for all this. He probably left that note deliberately for us to find, knowing what we would make of it. He has hidden that boy somewhere, and if we don't get to him first . . .' He didn't finish.

Mabel trod on his foot as she pushed in front of him, brushed off several sheets from the map Stroop had earlier spied, hanging on the library wall.

'We know where he is.' She looked excitedly from Stroop to Violena, who had raised a single eyebrow and almost smiled. 'We worked it out earlier, before you came. It's got to be the dene hole,' she said, stabbing the map with her finger, indicating the dark furling of moors that enclosed the small circle of Astonishment Hall and all who stood within it, and the pin stabbing a hole right through the pit of chalk.

Uwe saw the rope, put out a weak hand towards the slip-knotted end.

'Put it round yer oxters, lad, and I'll pull you out.'

It must be Bellpenny, he thought, wondered why he had come back for him, had been so sure he would never come, that no one would ever come, felt the small surge of life still within him and did as he was bid. It was painful even to move, had to haul himself the few feet to where the rope urged him on, tried not to tug at it with his fingers, to be too eager to be brought back into the world above. Only minutes before, he had been hoping the next few hours would be his last, but now that salvation had come, he grabbed at it with both his hands, thrust his head and shoulders through the noose, felt the knot tighten against his chest, heard his own voice weakly calling, reverberating from the stones, up into the mist. He could still see nothing above but felt at once the rope begin to take the strain, heard its threads creak and tighten, found his body lifted from off the cold stone. He tried to aid his rescuer, put out his hands and feet but found his efforts only made him twist and add to the encumbrance of the load.

'Keep yerseln still,' growled Medan Skimmington Bellpenny through gritted teeth, his voice a disembodied fox-bark through the mist, his strong, stone-breakers' shoulders grinding as his hands hauled at the rope, gained each marking knot as it came, felt the burn of each one on the curl of his fingers, scraping the lifelines from his palms, eating out their own canals, their own labyrinths into his flesh.

Pytchley almost ripped the map from Mabel's fingers, looked hard at the spot she had marked, had already begun to roll it and thrust it underneath his arm.

'Wait! Wait!' cried Violena. 'I must come with you! You'll never find it.' He glanced involuntarily at the roof domes, knew without having to check a clock that it was after four and the sun had only thirty more minutes in the sky before being swallowed by the maw that waited behind the fells of Brougham.

'I know it,' he said. 'The tree is marked on the map.' And Violena knew he was right. She herself had sketched it in. The only tree for miles around that had survived the grasp of the lime-hating heather at its roots, found a tap-line down to the water hidden deep within the chalk.

'But how will you find it?' she asked, almost plucking at his sleeve as he passed her by, heading for the library door.

'I know it,' he said again. 'I have ridden these moors, I've followed the surveys traced out for the canal. I've seen where it lies.'

'But the time,' persisted Violena. 'It's a forty-minute walk.'

'Fifteen on horseback if I take it hard.' Already he was calculating the animals in the stables. The two they had ridden that day were of no use. Already worn out, they would not be able to take the pace. The hunter was off at stud, one of the carriage horses was lame, the other needed shoeing. That left the old cob and its older sire. They would have to do. They would do. 'Stroop, you're with me. The rest of you, stay here.'

'But, Jeremiah . . .' Violena was almost weeping, and the sound of her voice brought Pytchley round upon his heels. The old Pytchley. The gentle Pytchley.

'Stay here, Violena. Send one of the maids for Dr Thacker. Look after Orcutt. There's nothing else you can do.'

He took her two hands in his own and kissed them, then he nodded at Stroop over her bowed head and strode on.

And Stroop followed. The last thing in the world he wanted to do was get back on a horse, but he understood the man's reasoning, knew that time was against them with every minute gone, whispered quickly to Mabel, 'Stay here. Look after Violena.' And then he too took the door and was marching to the major's quickstep towards the covered walkway and the stables.

Bellpenny fought with every breath he had to haul that boy up from the depths. He cursed and praised each blow his arms had ever made, every pickaxe shaft he had ever lifted and let fall, every rock, every stone he had hacked from the walls of mines and canal steepings, every strong bull-sheep he had ever wrestled to get it tied and sheared. He brought that boy up inch by inch from his abyss, felt the mist pervade his throat, dampen his lungs, thicken his every breath. And then he saw the boy's spindly hands appear at the edge of the pit, start to clutch convulsively at the grass, and still Bellpenny kept at it, even when his boots began to slip upon the heather and the stones he'd braced himself upon began to move, when he felt his back and heart would break with the strain. And then the boy's face appeared like a grey shadow within the mist, and he gave one last haul, one final effort, saw the boy drape his waist across the lip and hoped he could hold on, because he, Medan Bellpenny, could give no more.

They rode out like Lucifer from heaven with thunderbolts on their heels, left the stableboys wide-eyed and panting from the orders and the saddling and surprise. Stroop had Thomas hoisted up behind him, Pytchley had Jack. He might have commanded soldiers and Astonishment and even Violena, but was no match for boys who would go where they would go. Stroop tried to ignore the bruises and sores, felt Thomas's wiry arms about his waist, saw only Pytchley's advancing pace and swore he would not be left behind.

They took the hill behind the stables and Astonishment as if it were no more than a paltry slope that children like to think a mountain when they skim down it on toboggans, galloped through the heather as if it were not there, ignored the mist that tried to have them blinkered, Pytchley leading like a devil hiding for home.

At the dene hole, breath and life came hard. Bellpenny lay back upon the trampled heather, could hardly draw in air, felt every muscle cramp, felt the warmth of blood seeping from his hands. He could see that Uwe was too weak to do anything other than roll a little on to his side, and Bellpenny knew that time was against him. Thought of the old tale he had been told about the hour-glass, how the more sand falls, the wider becomes the hole, and the older gets the man, the quicker goes his time. Started to ease himself up, managed to crawl on his knees to Uwe Proctor's side.

'Hold fast,' he gasped, and Uwe felt the strong fingers about his waist and chest, feeling for the knot that had moved upon his back like a stone. He couldn't begin to wonder what had passed to make this man return and give him back the life he had been so willing to surrender. Felt Bellpenny's short warm breath in his ear, felt him straddle his legs about him from behind, despised himself for being so overjoyed to have his life offered back to him, for having so quickly forgotten all that he had learnt down there in his hole, in his self-made prison.

'Thank you,' he rasped as he complied to Bellpenny's fingers on his elbows, made his arms fold and slip through the rope that had held him fast in his ascent, breathed deeply and with overwhelming gratitude as the other brought the rope up over his shoulders.

Stroop had no idea where he was going, what was behind him, if he could ever find his way back; could feel Thomas's small hard body against his back, and was absurdly grateful for it, for the warmth it gave him in this land of blindness and mist.

Since they had gained the hill, they had lost sight of

Pytchley but could still hear the sound of his horse's flight. Thomas's hands had crept around to the reins and taken them in his own, steered the cob in the right direction. Stroop began to feel his enthusiasm for the plot waning, wondered if he had been wrong, if Mabel had been wrong, and this was nothing but a wild-goose chase over these ghastly moors and through this ghastly mist, from which – who knew? – he might never return.

But then there was Thomas behind him, and with him, his hands on Stroop's, expertly guiding the horse Stroop felt so apart from, as if Thomas too had read the map and knew where they needed to go. Stroop took a breath, held it in, tried not to close his eyes, closed them anyway. Felt the moor and mist close about him like he was a scallop within its shell being bartered at a quayside stall. Felt panic. Then comfort. Knew that Thomas was behind and Pytchley was before, and felt the lists in his head start to rumble and compute, knew that whatever they would find, they would find.

The noose tightened so slowly about Uwe Proctor's neck that he hardly questioned it. He had been about to thank again his benefactor, had started to stretch his arms, take deep breaths from the mist and moor, thank God he had been given another chance, sworn to himself he would seek out his parents' house. Go home. His proper home. Whichever one that proved to be. And then he felt the boots against his shoulders, the pressure against his spine, the awful heave that was taking him back towards the edge of the pit. He took a breath, knew it would be his very last, felt himself tumble from the ledge and out into the abyss. Thought one brief thought, that the stiff boy would at least be waiting to pull down on his boots, that the tower had, after all, taken its retribution as its own. That Uwe Proctor Dvoshka, and all the bad things he had done, would finally be gone.

Pytchley didn't see the moor, the mist, the heather. He saw the men that had once ridden before him in some other war, their legs still slit in half beneath their knees by enemy swords, the horses that had fallen, the men they served crushed beneath their panic-driven hooves. He saw again the blood of Maximillian Orcutt and all the men he himself had pushed into a graveyard pit and buried; the stink of them, the half-covered stench of their flesh, which had liquidised beneath the unforgiving sun. He cursed his lack of sight, his own fool sense of misdirection, the map he had curled like a whip at his side. He saw the mist, saw it dance as if it were the seven veils, felt Jack's grip as he clasped his hands about his sides. And then he saw. For just a moment only, as the mist lifted and fell back as in a breath, but he had seen it. That old may tree, broken-backed by the constant wind, bare-branched and winter-withered, but there it was. And he hauled his reins to the right and the west, and within five minutes they were on it and Stroop was dismounting behind him and they had seen the rope that tightened from the tree and led down over the ledge, and Pytchley had taken out his pistol and made his shot.

Across the moors, below Black Fell, in the circle of snow that covered the burning ground where Finkel Hanka had met his end, the buzzards looked up from the rip of gizzards and gut that had made their meal, heard the rip of the bullet breaking through the silence that had drawn the afternoon to evening. The sound echoed in the slat-shaped, mist-filled caves of the crags, disembogued small shivers of scree, sent them scurrying down the rain-worn stone into gravel rivers, or on out over the edge into nothing.

'NO!' Stroop shouted as he saw Pytchley raise his gun, had run to the lip of the pit and gazed down on the small dark head he could see hanging below him, the twitch of white fingers at its side, knew what Pytchley meant to do and could not bear to think how far the feeble figure below him might fall. But then the shot cracked out and filled the air about his head, seemed to ring on for ever, as if the mist had acted like an echo-chamber or a bell and caught the sound, expanded it, sent it back out in ever-expanding circles. Oh God, he thought as he looked out over the abyss, saw the fading hoop of light at its base, the crumple of the boy as he moved from blue to black, the severed rope curl down upon him like the snake of Eden.

He found he had pressed his hands to his ears when he finally raised his head, saw the sun choose that very moment to begin to slip below the crags, saw Pytchley silhouetted against a blue-rose sky, standing solid in a sudden lift of mist, his outline shaking slightly as he braced himself and replaced his gun; saw worse: saw Jack still on the major's horse, throwing his feet into the stirrups, shouting 'Hie and hie!' and thundering off over the darkening tussocks towards the canal works and the stiff-necked pulleys, which stood like demons against the evening sky.

* * *

Bellpenny had heard the horses coming over the moor, had kicked the boy over the edge, heard the creaking of the rope against the trunk of the tree and was confident it would already be tightening its grip on the boy's throat, if it had not already broken his neck. He could hear the clink of stirrup and saddle, the snorts of horses being pushed hard, the slight turn of direction they took towards the pit. He could almost smell the sweat of them and their human cargo as he tried to calm his breathing, get enough air within his lungs to enable him to move. His heart was going like a hammer to the anvil. He could feel the prickle of his blood running through his veins like a hare exploding over the meadows with the hounds upon its heels. He was exhilarated. He could feel the turning of the earth beneath his feet, knew the mist would move about him, hide him and protect him, that his pursuers would not find him, would find what they were meant to find. Would find the boy and his weak ways and the self-tied noose about his neck, the confession of his book still in his pocket, the sickness of his body, the blackness of his heart. The girl had seen him, that he knew, but who would tie these things together when they found the boy already dangling from his rope and Bellpenny long gone? Why would they look, and what would they find anyway if they did? Only the mist on the moor and the night drawing about them, holding them fast and secure, like coins trapped within a purse.

Jack had enjoyed the headlong gallop up away from the Hall and on into the outstretched arms of the moor. He felt wild and alive, almost laughed as he pitched from one side to the other, clutching at Pytchley like a mooring rope, slipping wildly as his knees lost their grip when they slowed suddenly, slewed away to the west. He might have been a rainstorm riding through clouds, the misty droplets dampening his skin and hair and clothes, the wind at once against his face and neck, pushing him on. He almost fell when Pytchley, with no warning, suddenly pulled the mount to stop and standing, slipped with no word from his saddle.

Jack looked. Saw the dark outline of the pit, which sank away into the earth, a line of white about its lip, a thinner towrope tethering it to the bent-over tree, the faint twang it made as it still moved and the wind ran over it, under it, like a humming violin. He heard Stroop's horse panting up behind him, saw Stroop stumble clumsily to the ground, Thomas after him, running for the edge of the pit, the flinch of Pytchley's hand as it moved to his belt, pulled out the pistol, set it to his arm to keep it steady, and pulled the trigger.

The noise almost blew his ears right off his head, but in the flash of light that accompanied the blast, Jack saw a shadow slinking low across the heather. Something like a fox, he thought, and drew his brows together, tried to see the thing again, made of it a picture in its frame, hung it against a blank white wall and knew what he had seen. He hadn't even thought about it, just lifted his body light and quick into the still-warm saddle, slipped his feet within the circles of the stirrups and hied up the horse, headed off past Pytchley and his gun, past the bent-backed tree and the rope, which was thrice-times tied about it like a noose, its severed end loosely trailing in the heather.

★ ★ ★

Pytchley tucked the smoking pistol back into his belt, stood for a moment, felt the hairs on the nape of his neck rise up at the sound of the gun and all it had once meant. He found himself shaking briefly within his skin, then a whoosh of breeze behind him, a dark shape pass him by, thought the horse was bolting, put out his hand, but saw the straight black back of Jack and heard his cries to urge the horse go onwards, couldn't begin to wonder what the boy was doing or why or where he was going, could only hope he wouldn't go far and that he would find his way back.

He started to run instead towards the tree that Violena had marked so precisely on her map, had tried to calculate the length of rope that might be left, had seen that it had been several times tied about the trunk to give it purchase, make sure it wouldn't give below its burden. He heard Stroop call to him, saw him standing like a pale streak at the mouth of the abyss, hoped to God the man wasn't going to fall as he had a sway about him and his hands still welded to his ears. No point in trying to call to him. Just needed to get on with the job. Went to the tree, started to haul up the slack, push it back through its knots, which were hard and tight as ash-buds before the green has broken through, felt someone come up behind him, was surprised to see Thomas at his side, his nimble fingers working at the knots as if he understood the urgency and had come to him instead of the instinct he must have had to go to Stroop or follow Jack to who knew where.

Stroop struggled on the brink, couldn't move, had feet of stone, skin of sweat, saw the body slip below him into darkness as the sun's grey light leached away from the sky. Then he felt a hand on his arm, saw Thomas looking up at him, pulling him away from the edge, felt the life return to him, his heart begin to beat again, forced his hands away from his ears.

'Take this,' ordered Pytchley, and thrust a knotted end of rope at him. 'Thomas, come here.' And Thomas went, and Pytchley began to tie the rope about Thomas's chest, below his arms.

He shook his head at Stroop, who was about to protest, and Thomas said quietly, 'It's all right, Mr Stroop, really it is.'

Pytchley gave Thomas a quick pat on the head. 'He's the lightest of us, and the smallest, he'll go further on what rope we've got. With any luck he'll be able to climb the last few feet if the rope won't take him all the way.'

Stroop took a deep breath, felt his mind slot its pieces back into place, tried to give Thomas a reassuring smile.

'And when you get down there,' Pytchley gave Thomas his last instructions, 'try to get the rope off him, loosen it at least. Put your fingers on his neck and see if you can find a pulse; get him into a sitting position.'

He shivered, heard his own voice steady and calm, couldn't bear to think of being lowered into the darkness of that hole, of having to share it with the corpse that most probably lay beneath. Thomas himself didn't seem bothered. He'd been in worse places, spent worse nights under bridges, curled in a pitch-dark crate or cellar, had learnt to live with fear forever tugging at his collar, whispering in his ear, growling at his back like a great black dog. He grinned up quickly as he positioned himself over the edge of the chalk pit, began to lower himself down, found holes in which to perch his feet, waited patiently for Stroop and Pytchley to begin to pay out the rope, take his weight, lower him down. Closed his ears to the growling of the dog.

Between Brougham Crags and the Black Fell ridge, the valley stretched flat as floorboards where peat and moorland reached its height and the river meandered through its soggy plateau as if it had no place to go and was in no hurry to get there. The valley caught the wind from the north and the west, and when it blew hard, it scraped the land clear and clean like a currycomb, leaving only the long lines and furrows where the peat had been worked or some cotter had scraped out a field for winter fodder. Now though, the long strip of the canal had been blasted through it and the wind laid low, had allowed the snow to creep and drift and accumulate in holes, and hide the heaps the spalders had made as they had pickaxed their way through the bedrock left after the explosives men had done and moved on.

Medan saw the canal works in the distance, the high humped shoulders of the slag mounds, the skinny necks of the pulleys, the shadow of the hill at the other end, half-blown through. He had his bearings now, knew that his cottage had been left far behind him over beyond the Black Fell ridge, that Astonishment lay to his left, Eden to his right, and his way must be straight across the valley and over the crags, and down and down towards the sea and the nearest ship that would take him on and get him away. The mist still aided him, would confound any followers, but the snow had deepened to the leeside of every clump of heather, made the going hard, the way ahead difficult to see as he was always having to look down to watch his feet.

He glanced behind him, but could no longer see the little tree and the pit it guarded and marked. He stopped and cocked his head, heard the strange low hum he knew so well, knew the setting sun had released the wind from the high hills, knew it would be on him soon and would disperse the mist, make him easier to spot than a coot on a frost-covered pond.

He drew his coat about him, set off across the plain, glad to see the strip and cut of reeds poke their way above the snow, knew the marshy ground beneath his feet was solid with the cold, would take his weight, knew also the river was behind him and would cause no obstacle, that he would hear the several burns that ran their way beneath the snow and could be easily taken at a stride.

The noise behind him was so unexpected it squeezed his heart to a painful knot within him, released it just as quickly, sent a surge of blood thudding to his neck and head and hands and feet. He stopped one second only, but knew what he had heard. Was as certain of it as night follows day. He'd heard a horse. And it was coming this way. He began to run and stumble amongst the reeds, breath raucous and rancid in his throat, tried to think clearly in his panic, knew he had to find a place he could bundle up, stay out of sight. Maybe the man was just on the way to the canal works. It happened. Not usually so late, when the light was on its way to dying, but it happened. He told himself this, but wasn't fool enough to be convinced. There was no one going to the canal. There was only him. And whoever was following behind.

* * *

Jack moved the old stallion by instinct, placed his hands softly either side of the mane, the reins loose in his hands, his knees nudging the animal to the left or the right. He wasn't going fast now, had slackened his pace, was trying to listen. Heard the gentle wrinkle of river pass through ice-jingled banks, the crump of hooves through clean, dry snow, a strange sort of sighing that might have been wind on the hills. He heard other things: a snipe frightened up from its sleeping, *nik-nakking* low across the heather, another bird, a curlew maybe, whirring its feathers for warmth in its nest. And something else. The arrhythmic sound of a man trying to move slow and quiet, and Jack knew he was on his mark. Still he did not speed, knew he had no need of it, had crept up on many a chicken in its yard, many a rabbit by its burrow, many a calf in its shed. Jack didn't know the meaning of alarm, except when he read it in other people's faces. He didn't really know why he had done what he had done, only that there was no one else to do it. So he leant down low over the old stallion's neck, made himself small and quiet, whispered to the horse to be small and quiet just like him, and together they moved over the frozen marshes without urgency, without hurry, just one foot after the other, one step waiting to see what the next would bring.

The rope paid out and Thomas went down. An inch, a foot, a yard, ten yards. He saw the circle of light above him fade, the darkness at his feet begin to grow. No longer could he see Stroop's silhouette on the brink of the pit, knew though that he was there, that Pytchley was behind, both holding the rope tight in their hands, felt no tremor of fear, only a dim excitement that made him want to cry out to them to hurry it on and get him down fast to whatever he might find. Found it difficult just to dangle and do nothing with his hands and feet, was almost glad when they shouted down that there was very little slack and was he almost there, and he shouted back a yes, that he could see the bottom and could do the rest, take the weight off the two who were so far above him. Swung himself agin the rock to find a purchase for his hands and feet, which he did without difficulty. Climbed down the last bit that was left him, faintly annoyed to find that there was only a couple of yards left anyway and he could have jumped.

'A-hie!' he shouted, on getting his feet upon the ground and swiftly untying the rope from about him. Just as swiftly he moved to the fallen figure a brief distance to his right. Only now did he feel the fast prick of panic; remembered running to the lodge, finding Maximillian Orcutt almost swallowed up by his own blood, his need to try and drag him out and away from it. But there was no blood here. It was dark and he couldn't see very well, but he knew what blood smelt like and there was none of it here. Just a pile of spent fire to one side of him and the unmoving figure to the other. He wriggled fast as silverfish from the rest of the rope and rid himself of its last ties, took the two strides to the fallen man's side. His face was so grey and bloated, it stood out like a tick on a dog's ear, and Thomas quickly did as he had been told: forced his fingers under the rope to free the man's neck, tore his nails from the quick to get the knots loosed, so tight were they, caught up the inert body till it was sitting, spread his hand against the man's heart and neck and waited. Waited another moment. And another. Felt the slightest pulse of movement against his palm and started shouting, shouting, 'He's all right! He's alive! He's alive!'

And then he waited. Again. And for just a few seconds there was no answer and Thomas had the awful thought that there was no one else in the world but him and he would be left down here as the other man must too have been, and the tears pressed so hard against his throat he couldn't speak.

Nothing such for Jack. He had never been alone. There had been his mother and then there had been Stroop. And then there had been Stroop and Mabel and Thomas. And from that day on he knew that wherever he went, whatever he did, there would always be someone with him, no matter what. And so he didn't stop. He saw that the mist was lifting, dispersing, heard a faint noise, as if the moon had sighed as it came up off the crags, or the last glimpse of the sun as it slipped below the ridge. Thought nothing of it, except that things were as they should be, and went on.

Medan Skimmington Bellpenny never saw that old rim of sun disappear behind the fell. Had his face turned to another side, had waited for the wind he knew was coming, wasn't prepared for its ability to disguise and deceive him. He went on, but blindly, was distracted by the coming of the night and the wind that he thought he had understood, was running because he knew someone was behind, took the collar of the cutting without seeing it, thought it was a blank bridge of snow between two banks, hadn't even seen the slight slip from the sides. Fell, because the snow, as he had known it, had been scoured from the edge last time he'd seen, last time he'd passed from his cot to Astonishment. But this snow: it was new snow, and this wind: it was new wind. It hadn't done what he had expected. It hadn't hidden him, but exposed him. His old convict mates from Siberia had told him that, had told him never to trust what wasn't already within his skin. Don't trust them, they'd said, but he had not really listened, had always thought he knew. Don't trust them, they'd said, because they will always trick you. There is the wind and the snow, and you think you know them, but you don't. And he hadn't. So here he was, tumbling at last from the sure grip of his life. Bottom of a long, hard five-yard ditch. Stunned into dizziness. Terrible, awful pain. Legs most likely broken as he'd tumbled down the cutting into his own despair. No one will ever find you, that's what the Siberians had told him. Not in the snow. Not in the wind. Never in both. Live with it, they'd said, but he knew he never would. And he wondered about his creations, wondered who would find them now he was gone. Wondered if they would understand why he had made them.

His mind was chilled and he didn't think of the ring he had once stolen, that had set him to this way of being, nor of Finkel Hanka, nor Bittlestone, nor the fellow at the Hall. He did think briefly of the girl who had seen his face. Wondered if she would remember him. Thought lastly of the roll of gold he had so often felt beneath his fingers, of his mother's words, her soft singing. Of Alltsaman. And if he'd done enough to reach it. Looked up into the paleness of the newly forming night. Saw the moon, saw the last wreaths of mist dispersing, saw a small arc of greyish green.

Closed his eyes. Waited for the cold and the night to steal from him, as he, so many times, had stolen.

Pytchley and Stroop worked fast, caught up the rope that Thomas had loosed from about him, worked the pay-out knots free, gave them extra length, brought the old cob mare to the side of the pit, tied one end to her saddle, threw the other back down into darkness. Thomas too worked swift and deft, dragged Uwe over to the rope and looped the few spare inches through his belt, tied a sheepshank as Pytchley had showed him, called to the upstairs world and watched as Uwe, slow but sure, began to rise.

Jack heard the wind begin to sigh down from the hills, watched as the mist began to rise and wreathe and then disperse, saw a few fingers of it cling to the surface of the snow, sink down into the cuttings, rest upon the surface water of the hidden burns. He could see the scuff of snow where the man had been, where he had kicked it free from the scrub of bilberry and heather, the bare scrawl and scruff of reeds pointing the way. He followed it forward, towards where the moon was rising from the crags that lay opposed to Brougham, the ice around it shining in soft and pale circles, pallid pillars and bows forming momentarily as the mist dispersed or crept along the ground, sought the sough of water, the depth of the cuttings, settled like sleep upon and in them, cleared the land free for the snow that was beginning again to fall.

He saw the man inert, fifteen feet below him. No longer could he see the carcasses of sheep and hare and deer, nor the rolled-up pincushions of hedgehogs. Just a man, lying on his back in the snow. His two legs crooked outwards, his arms by his sides, his two eyes closed. Jack saw all this: the crags, the night, the moon and the bows that formed about it, the gentle, halting fall of snow, which soon would cover all that he could see, the absolute perfect silence of it all.

He knew then that what had started was now finished, and he whispered the words into the old stallion's ear and stroked his neck. Then he turned him back upon the path, went to find Thomas and Stroop and Mabel, thought, for the first time since they had been at Astonishment, of London and Eggmonde Street, and home.

5

Nightfall and Astonishment

14 March

THEY BROUGHT OUT Medan Skimmington Bellpenny's body the next morning and took him to the canal workings and the Surgeon's Hole. Uwe Dvoshka went with them, confirmed the man as Bellpenny, told his tale of Russia and the Black Sea and the locusts and the tower. Wept for the stiff boy he had killed, asked his name. No one knew. Oldmixon, who had come to see the show like everybody else pressing around the Surgeon's Hole, listening inside the tent and out, took off his hat, held it between his burly hands, pushed his way through the crowd.

'George,' he said. 'He was called George, as I mind it.' He looked at Stroop with a shyness so strange to him it made his face go red and hot. 'Said as I know's everyone hereabouts. I even mind 'im, now I sees 'im.' He nodded down at Bellpenny, who was pale and rigid with death and his last night's cold.

And then Uwe Proctor cried, really cried, until his eyes

closed with the swellings of remorse, and the doctor got out his special cure liqueur and forced an ample pint of it down Uwe's throat before taking up his saw and separating him from the clog and the foot that was black with gangrene. Offered to put it in a pickle jar to remind him of what he had done. And Uwe took it. He would not be prosecuted, would not see the inside of a gallows' noose, would live out the rest of his twenty-seventh year and go on into his twenty-eighth and his twenty-ninth and the rest of his life, if he chose to live it. Go back to Bohemia and his bells. Start over his little *History of Glass*. Make his parents proud.

Maximillian Orcutt was not so lucky. He survived the egg-shell cracking of his skull, but came out broken. Like a clock that has lost its workings, his face was blank, and though the hands still moved, they moved at random, and no longer told the time. No longer knew what time was. Spent most of it sitting in front of his moon-bow case, watching it rise and fall and rise and fall, watching it with a wonder that did not have the faintest understanding of what made it work. No longer knew how anything worked again.

He clung to Violena and she to him. He was a child to her now, and to Pytchley, and often of an evening they would drink a little too much wine and wind up the Labyrinth that was left them and see a little of the old Orcutt and weep over the genius and the intellect that had been for ever lost.

It was a sad Stroop who took his last goodbyes of Astonishment and took the steamer down the canal to Darlington, went on to the mouth of the Tees and set sail on a boat back to London. He was not alone. Jack and Thomas were with him, and Pytchley, who was taking the Perspective Box blueprints down to London, would set an award for the first man in the Weeems Society to reconstruct it as once it had been.

There was also Uwe Proctor Dvoshka. Pytchley would take him to his own foot-fitter, get him made a new one of cork, just like his own. And then they would go to his parents' house and see the son embrace them so stiffly he might not have been their own. And then they would drink sherry, like the English do, and Uwe Proctor would sit in his chair and weep and tell to them all the things he had done. And they would love him still, and all his life he would feel he never deserved it.

And that left Mabel.

She stayed behind with Violena and Astonishment, took a crowbar to the four unopened crates of books and sought solace and accomplishment with every new page she turned, wrote catalogue cards and cross-referenced one unto the other. She gained the keys to the locked cabinet room of the library, and every month that passed she went into that perfect, quiet, ship-like room with its boarded, portholed walls and mirrors, watched herself recede into infinity, as she had once watched Violena do. And in the evenings, she and Violena tried to teach Orcutt fox-and-geese, small games of cards, backgammon. But they were all too complicated, and in the end, they brought the moon-bow cabinet into the library and he would sit and watch and sit and watch, while they burrowed at their books.

She knew she wouldn't stay for ever, only until the first

leaves of autumn began to fall and the swallows went and the geese began their long journey from Scandinavia and Siberia, and maybe even from the Black Sea shores to here. And then she too would return to the place and the people she knew best and loved. She would always have Astonishment, and would often return. Would know that Jeremiah Pytchley and Violena would always be there for one another and for her. And long nights would pass and long years would go before she stopped weeping for Maximillian Orcutt and all he might have been and never now would be.

Ipsing Sansibar still ferried his goats over to St Weonard's-on-the-Water. He would sit there as he had always done and smoke his pipe, wait for the easing in his back. He would lean against the old stone wall of the churchyard, watch the waters lap and rise at his feet, knew that every year saw the water take a little more, another inch of beach and shingle breached, another little piece of land lost and gone. He would look over at the other shore, saw the steps disappear beneath the water one by one, saw the tower rise again on its little hill and the water rise towards it.

The villagers rebuilt that tower stone by stone, sawed the wood and set it right, made a new carapace from the old. The bell was saved, had not been truly harmed by fire or fall, would one day be rehung as it had always been. Would still toll out the peals of weddings and of funerals and of the coming storms, gather the workers in from the fields. Would one day maybe ring out in remembrance of the stiff boy Ipsing found he missed more than he could have known.

'George,' he said to himself as he relit the pipe that had

gone out, his old mind wandering over what had passed, as his goats wandered over the grass between the toppled gravestones. 'His name was George.'

And was glad beyond reckoning that at least the boy's name would be remembered, if only by himself.